Hallmark
PUBLISHING

DEAD-END
DETECTIVE

A Piper & Porter Mystery
from Hallmark Publishing

USA TODAY BESTSELLING AUTHOR
AMANDA FLOWER

DEDICATION

for Nicole Resciniti
superagent, rock star, dear friend

ACKNOWLEDGEMENTS

Special thanks to everyone at Hallmark Publishing for supporting this book. I am so very excited to be working with all of you, and looking forward to seeing where this new adventure will lead.

Very special thanks to superagent Nicole Resciniti, who fought for this title, and to editor Stacey Donovan, who helped me make the story so much better and who was so kind during the process.

I also would like to thank David Seymour, Mariellyn Grace, and Delia Haidautu for their support while writing this mystery, with special thanks to David, who helped with some key twists in the plot.

Love and thanks to my family: Andy, Nicole, Isabella, Andrew, and two sweet boys.

Finally, thanks to God in heaven for every amazing opportunity. My expectations were passed years ago.

"There is nothing more stimulating than a
case where everything goes against you."

—Sir Arthur Conan Doyle,
The Hound of the Baskervilles

CHAPTER ONE

H OW DID THIS BECOME MY life?
That was the question I asked myself when I was halfway up Mrs. Berger's oak tree and staring into the angry green eyes of her orange Maine Coon cat, Romy.

Romy didn't like being in the tree any more than I did, but he was the one who'd gotten us into this mess.

"Hi Romy," I said in my sweetest, I-love-animals voice.

Romy bared his teeth.

"Be careful, Darby!" Mrs. Berger called from below. "I don't want Romy getting hurt."

I tried not to dwell on the fact that she had no concern over whether or not *I* got hurt.

I'd been drafted to save the cat on my daily lakeside run this morning when Mrs. Berger had flagged me down on the sidewalk in front of her home.

The gray waters of Seneca Lake were in view directly behind Romy. It was early morning, and a handful of small fishing boats rocked on the thirty-five-mile-long lake's gentle waves. Now on the cusp of autumn, it was a postcard scene with the red and ocher leaves reflecting off its blue-gray waters. Ducks and geese bobbed on the water's surface as they made their way from Canada to points farther south.

"Is Romy all right?" Mrs. Berger's voice wavered.

I looked to the ground, and for a moment, the world spun. I was only twenty feet high, but on my precarious perch—literally out on a limb—it felt like a hundred feet up. I gripped the tree's trunk for support. "Romy's fine. A little grumpy, but otherwise completely fine." I brushed a lock of my shoulder-length brown hair that had escaped from my ponytail out of my face.

"Oh, poor thing. Tell him if he comes down, I'll give him a whole can of tuna instead of his typical half. I know he must be peckish from his wild adventure."

I was peckish, too. I should've grabbed a snack before I went out the door. There was always a twenty percent chance of cat rescue on my run.

I glanced at the cat. "You get that?"

He narrowed his green eyes. I narrowed my brown ones back. I found it was best with Romy to present myself as an equal, even if Mrs. Berger might not think that was true.

She stood below the tree in a mint-green pantsuit with matching bowler hat and perfectly set hair. She propped herself up on a mahogany cane—which could be used as a poker or pointer, depending on what the situation required. She wore her hair in pin curls and got it set every Tuesday morning at Mary Bee's Beehives in downtown Herrington, and she loved her cat.

Ornery Romy, the disgruntled Maine Coon, was showered with love and affection that he both relished and detested.

At ninety, Mrs. Berger was the oldest resident of Herrington, and she'd lived in her home on the shores of Seneca Lake for the last sixty years. She owned forty acres of prime lakefront property, and she let all of it remain wild except for the land immediately around her little ranch house. To the south was the imposing Lake Waters Retreat, a luxury resort where the rich and richer went "to get some work done," as my father said. They came from all over the country for special skin treatments, face-lifts, and other services. To protect the well-to-do clientele's privacy, the retreat was locked up like Fort Knox.

Lake Waters Retreat and builders throughout the Finger Lakes would've loved to buy Mrs. Berger's little house, flatten it to the ground and turn it into something profitable, but Mrs. Berger wasn't selling. Mr. Berger had been gone for over a decade now, and developers had given up trying to convince her.

She would tell people, eyes sparkling, "They're waiting for me to die, but what they don't know is I might outlive them all. Won't they be surprised when that happens?"

It was very possible. Mrs. Berger wasn't showing any signs of slowing down. The only thing she couldn't do was climb a tree to save her cat. Then again, she had me for that.

"Be careful getting him down. He's very upset. He might hurt himself," Mrs. Berger warned.

If I reached out and tried to grab Romy, I'd surely be scratched within an inch of my life—which was why I had a bath towel slung over my shoulder. It was a new strategy I wanted to try. I'd asked Mrs. Berger to lend me one, and she'd gone straight to her linen closet and pulled one out, no questions asked. I appreciated the vote of confidence and hoped it wasn't premature.

"Romy," I cooed. "Don't you want to come down from that tree? It can't be any fun being up there all day, can it?"

I took a breath and looped the towel over Romy's back. Before he could figure out what was happening, I climbed up to the next branch and grabbed him around the middle with the towel between us. I wrapped him up burrito-style, making sure his head was free and I was out of the way of his biting teeth. It worked! I couldn't believe it.

The climb down was much more cumbersome because I was going backward and one-handed, my left arm wrapped around the very upset Romy. I was six feet from the ground when my foot missed a branch.

I fell and landed flat on my back, hard. Air whooshed out of me and onto Romy, who was still in his towel. He lay on my chest and stared me in the face. I pushed him off before he could bite my nose. He hissed and flopped to the side, still trapped in the towel cocoon.

Mrs. Berger poked me with the end of her cane. "You all right, Darby?"

That was a more difficult question for me to answer than she could possibly know.

She leaned a little farther over me and met my gaze. "Your eyes look normal, so I don't think you have a concussion." She waved her hand. "How many of me do you see?"

"One."

"Good. You're fine. Mr. Berger was a neuroscientist and always told me how to look for signs of head trauma, but I can call the EMTs if you want to be sure."

"No!"

I struggled to my feet. If she called the ambulance, the police would most likely come, because there wasn't much other policing to do in Herrington. If the police came, there was a high chance my ex-boyfriend would be the one they'd send out, and this was the last way I wanted him to see me: flat on my back in running clothes covered in orange cat hair with a ninety-year-old woman poking me in the ribs with her antique cane.

That didn't really say, "Hey, I got my life together without you."

Even so, I was pretty sure Police Officer Austin Caster knew I didn't have my life together—even without the visual evidence.

Romy struggled, his body writhing under the terry cloth fabric. I quickly unwrapped him and jumped back with the same trepidation park rangers use when releasing a bobcat in the wild. Mrs. Berger scooped up the cat and held him to her chest.

"You're the best detective I know. You always seem to know where to find Romy when he wanders off."

I wished I could say she was right, that I was the

best detective, but I was certain I wasn't. Had I been better, I wouldn't be about to lose the business I'd spent the last decade of my life building.

CHAPTER TWO

Mrs. Berger and Romy were safely back in their ranch house when the soles of my running shoes hit the pavement of Lakeshore Avenue. I was certain Romy was being told what a brave cat he was for surviving his self-inflicted ordeal and lapping up that can of tuna. To have the life of a cat—wouldn't that be great?

My pace was slower now and my rhythm was off because of my fall from the tree, but I kept running because I was stubborn that way. I didn't think I'd ever be one of those natural athletes who loved to exercise, but I did so out of pure will and necessity—I never met a cookie I didn't like.

My turnaround was the highest point of Lakeshore Avenue.

The curve at the top of the hill held a beautiful view of the lake below and two other lakes in the distance, nestled in the foothills. On a crisp September day like today, the leaves were beginning to change colors. The cool breeze off the lake chilled my sweaty body, but after a hard run it was welcome relief.

Even so, it was stupid to run there. Cars and vans, driven by distracted leaf-peeping tourists, careened around the corner as the driver and passengers focused on the vista instead of what might be right in front of them—like me. A five-foot-one runner decked out in bright yellow-and-black spandex.

The village reminded me of tiers of a cake. The first tier was at street level, where most of the businesses and offices were. All of them—including Two Girls Detective Agency, our private investigation firm—were in old converted houses. The second and third tiers gave glimpses of private homes and trees.

Two Girls was on Lakeshore Avenue to my left. I sprinted the last blocks and doubled over, catching my breath in the small front yard.

I hit my stopwatch to check my time. It wasn't bad, considering my episode in the tree with Romy. I braced my hands on my upper thighs, gulping air.

There was a black, expensive-looking car in the driveway. It certainly hadn't been there when I'd left. This could be good news or very bad news. I'd put my money on the latter.

The detective agency was inside a large brick colonial with a wide front porch and swing. There were brightly potted mums on the porch. That was our office manager's handiwork, not mine. I stretched my sore muscles outside, then walked into the building, knowing that both Nat and Samantha would already be in the office.

It worked out well that I lived above the agency, because we had a surprising number of clients who came to the office after hours. It wasn't a bad thing to have someone here twenty-four seven. Samantha, on the other hand, lived in a large Victorian home not far from Mrs. Berger, in a gorgeous spot with its own boat dock. The house had been in her family for over five generations. The Porters were one of the oldest families in the village.

The front door of the agency opened into what used to be the dining room of the house, but was now the waiting room and Nat's workspace.

Nat was in her early fifties, with silver-streaked blond hair and blue eyes. She scrutinized me over her tortoiseshell eyeglasses. On her desk, there were three jars of pennies. Two were full, and one was a third of the way there. Nat collected pennies like other people collected postcards. She was always on the lookout for the rarest and most valuable penny. But even if a penny didn't have value, she kept it and put in a jar. I could only guess how many jars were at her house.

"Darby Piper, don't you even think of dripping sweat on my office floor."

I put my hands on my hips. "I'm not dripping sweat. Goodness sakes, Nat. I don't sweat, I glow. That's what Grammy always said. Ladies glow; men sweat." It was an old argument. We both knew the script by heart.

She snorted. "You look like you went through a car-wash strapped to the roof of the car." Before I could think of a smart retort, she continued. "I filled your water bottle. It's in the fridge, and I put a bottle of chocolate milk in there for you too." She pointed at the small, glass-doored fridge we stocked with water for clients and other guests.

I crossed to the fridge and scooped out the water bottle and the chocolate milk. "See, Nat, that's how I know you love me. You always anticipate my needs." I took a slug of the water and then set the bottle on top of the fridge before cracking open the chocolate milk. "I don't know how we'd get along without you." I took a smaller, more ladylike sip from the milk bottle.

She shook her head before she turned back to her laptop. "I don't know how the two of you would get along without me, either. That's for sure and certain. I couldn't leave the care of the two of you to Gumshoe."

I laughed and glanced at the ten-foot-long couch that ran the length of the room in front of the window, where my Ragdoll cat, Gumshoe, was stretched out like a fur rug. Like most Ragdolls, Gumshoe was docile and languid and always appeared to be on the verge of falling asleep, unless he was hungry. Samantha had bought the couch to give waiting clients somewhere to sit. I'd had no idea she'd bought something so huge. It had taken three delivery people to move it into the house, and to my dismay, they'd removed the door-frame to fit it inside. But Samantha had been determined. Nine times out of ten, she got her way.

Why she'd wanted such a long couch was a mystery. She'd severely overestimated how many clients we'd have sitting in the waiting room at any one time.

To date, the couch had never been filled, and it was the favorite spot for Gumshoe. At the moment, he lay in his sphinx pose. He narrowed his eyes at me as if he knew I was thinking about him. I wouldn't have been the least bit surprised if he did. He seemed to know all and turn up in the oddest places in the agency. He also sensed when clients were allergic to cats, and chose those moments to rub his lithe body around their legs, so that they could have a sniffle to remember him by.

Still drinking my milk, I walked over to Gumshoe. He lifted his head, granting permission for a chin scratch. He allowed this for two point two seconds, and then lowered his head, my signal to stop. He was a very particular feline in every respect.

"I see the prince has decided to let you pet him. He never lets me do that," Nat groused.

"I think it's only because I live here. I'm the one who feeds him, aren't I? This is his thanks for the food, and even that is tempered." I smiled at him. Being a bit of an introvert myself, I could understand his singular ways.

Nat snorted.

"Where's Samantha?" I asked, looking around. "That was quite a car in the driveway. Maybe she'll get a big new case and stay."

Nat shook her head. "Matt Billows' offer is hard to pass up." The local resort owner wanted Samantha to come on as the head of security at Lake Waters Retreat.

I frowned. "What about what we've built? How can she walk away from a decade of work? How can she put both of us out of a job?"

Nat shrugged. "I don't think there's anything we can do now."

I bit my lip, knowing she was right. Samantha owned sixty percent of the agency. I only owned forty percent. When we started the business, she was older and had more money. It made sense for her to own more, but now I was sorry I'd agreed to that. Holding most of the company, she could cash in the entire place. When she did, I'd lose the office, my home, and maybe a good portion of my reputation, because people would wonder why Samantha Porter had left.

Nat sighed, but before she could answer, I heard a deep voice coming from Samantha's office in the next room.

"We'll chat more tomorrow, but I'm excited about this opportunity for us both. Trust me, Sam," a man said.

My stomach dropped as I recognized Matt Billows' resonant tenor. He was the source of all my problems. I frowned at Nat. She looked down at her desk.

"This will be a successful partnership for all involved," Billows added. "With your knowledge of how these fools operate, you'll be just the person to keep them out of Lake Waters." A door closed somewhere down the hallway. "I'm very excited you're on board. I'll have my lawyer write up your contract today."

I bristled, and the fur on Gumshoe's back stood on end. He hissed. At least the cat and I were in agreement on this.

CHAPTER THREE

G UMSHOE JUMPED OFF THE BACK of the couch and dashed out of the room as Matt Billows and Samantha walked into the main office. I half-wished I could run away from this situation, too, but I needed to stand my ground, spandex and all.

Matt Billows was cool and calm. Perfectly dressed, perfectly straight teeth, and dark hair that would be a great addition to any male hair loss commercial. It waved slightly when he moved, but it never fell out of place. It was magical in that way.

Samantha Porter had just turned forty last week and was a beautiful woman, sturdily built with snapping green eyes and lustrous dark curls. She stood tall, close to six feet. When Samantha came into a room, she had a presence.

At five one, I didn't have much of a presence at all. But what I lacked in stature, I made up for in gumption—or so my grammy had always told me. People tended to underestimate me, which was an advantage as a private eye. Samantha's superior height was a bit of sore spot with me, because when we were at odds, she used her height to her advantage. She did at this moment as well. I could tell by her expression she wasn't happy to see me.

I lifted my chin and stood there flushed, breathing heavy, chocolate milk dripping from my chin, but I refused to break eye contact with her until she looked away. She finally did.

I wiped at my mouth with the back of my hand and stared at Billows. "What are you doing here?" It wasn't the politest greeting, but it was as much as he deserved.

"Oh, Darby, it's so nice to see you too," Billows said smoothly. "I'm sorry you weren't able to make it to our meeting, but Samantha gave me your apologies." He looked me up and down. "I can see you were otherwise occupied."

I didn't know how it was possible since I'd just run three miles, but I could feel my face become even redder.

He smiled as he walked past me, and then he turned and said to Samantha, "I'll be in touch."

I waited until the front door closed before I said anything. "I can't believe you."

"Darby, don't start," Samantha said.

"Don't start? Don't start? How can you even say that when you went behind my back to talk to Billows? We're partners, Sam, and that's not how partners work."

"I needed the details about the offer he was making me so we could make an informed decision. You're too emotional about the whole thing to even hear him out. He said he'd have a spot in Lake Waters for you too." She handed a file to Nat.

Nat took it without a word and turned back to her computer. She'd heard our argument so many times before that she had the ability to tune us out. I wished I could do that, but it was my dream on the line.

I stared at Samantha. I'd thought it was *our* dream—our shared dream. I was sorry to learn I was wrong.

"You were talking about me to him? That's a dirty trick to take a meeting without me. You might have sixty percent of the agency, but I still have forty percent. I should be informed when you're making decisions that impact our business."

"You were on your run," Samantha said without looking at me. "I know how much that means to you. I didn't want to interrupt."

I took a breath. "I don't believe you. I wouldn't be the least bit surprised if you planned this meeting during my run so I wouldn't be here."

"Don't be ridiculous. Honestly, Darb, at times you're so overdramatic."

"Overdramatic? Am I overdramatic about losing everything we've built over the last ten years?"

"We aren't losing anything. Matt has positions for both of us in the company. That's stability. Isn't that something you want? It's what I want. I need to start thinking about my future. I don't want to be working until I'm in my eighties."

"Come on," I shot back. "You turned forty and act

like you're on the brink of retirement. I *know* there's something else going on here. The Samantha I know and love wouldn't do this. You like having your own company. You like being your own boss."

"Maybe you don't know me as well as you thought," she said without looking at me.

I stepped back like she'd punched me in the stomach. "Maybe I don't," I said quietly.

She turned around. "Matt said—"

"Matt, huh? Now you're on a first-name basis?"

"Darby," she chastised. "You're behaving like a child. This is a smart business move, and you'd realize that if you'd set your emotions aside for one second and look at the situation critically."

"I have looked at it critically, and we're fine."

"But we aren't getting anywhere. We've flatlined in the last three years. We're making enough to pay our bills and our meager salaries, but we aren't growing. Don't you want to grow and make something more out of your life?"

"Not if it makes me a sellout," I said, knowing I sounded exactly like the teenager Samantha had accused me of being. "I don't even know why he'd want you to work for him. He already has a security team. What's he going to do? Fire them all and bring you in to save the day?"

She wrinkled her nose. "Lake Waters plans to make a lot of changes to increase its business."

I laughed. "So you'll be shooing away paparazzi all day. That sounds like a really exciting job."

"It doesn't matter if it's exciting. It's stable, and

Matt's right. With my surveillance experience as a private eye, I know how the paparazzi think when they're trying to get the money shot. I'm the perfect person for the job. I asked him to bring you on too, and he agreed."

I frowned.

Samantha sighed. "It's stable and easy work. It's something I need right now."

"I told you things we can do to drum up more business, but you ignored all my suggestions."

"I'm tired of shaking trees for business, Darby. Don't you ever get tired of chasing after small-time criminals and finding lost dogs? I want an easier life. There's nothing wrong with that."

I rubbed the back of my neck. "We're helping people."

"Sometimes I'm not so certain of that. We also hurt a lot of people with the information we find."

"I can't believe you're saying that. When we started this place, the idea was to create an affordable option for people who needed help. You're betraying that ideal."

She shook her head as if I couldn't possibly understand.

"What does Logan say about this?"

Her head snapped in my direction, and I immediately regretted asking. Logan Montgomery was a town council member and Samantha's long-time boyfriend. They'd been together since before we opened Two Girls.

"Logan and I aren't together any longer."

I blinked. That was the last thing I'd expected to

hear. Well, the second; the first would've been that she wanted to leave Two Girls. If Samantha was closing the business she loved and breaking up with her boyfriend, something more was definitely going on.

"I wish you'd tell me what the real problem is," I said. "I can help."

She stared at me for a long moment. "You can't. This is bigger than you or me, Darby. This is bigger than Billows. You couldn't possibly understand."

I threw up my hands. "Help me understand, because I really don't. You told me when we opened this agency that you became a private eye for your dad. Now you're walking away from it?"

She glared at me. "It's not fair to bring up my father."

I bit my lip. Maybe she was right. It was a low blow. When Samantha was ten, her father had come home from work, interrupting an apparent burglary in their home, and had been killed. The culprit or culprits were never caught. Her life goal was to find out who killed him. She didn't believe it was a random act. She'd chased many leads over her adult life trying to find the truth, but had never gotten anywhere with it. I knew how much that frustrated her.

She shook her head. "I have to go." She started for the front door. "I need to follow up on the Multigrain Market case."

"You can't close the agency without me," I called after her.

She turned around and frowned at me. "That's where you we're wrong, Darb. I own the majority of the company. I met with Patrick last night. I can dissolve the company without your consent." She took a breath. "And I will. I'm going to sign the papers tomorrow."

The breath was sucked out of my chest. Patrick Hartwell was our attorney. We kept him on retainer. Many angry people we'd caught doing wrong had threatened to sue us over the years. Pat was worth his weight in gold.

She looked me in the eye. "Don't make me choose between what I have to do and our friendship. Because my duty comes first."

"Your duty? What on earth are you talking about? You don't have to do this," I said.

"I do. You can't possibly understand, but I do." With that, she walked out of the house. The front door gave a soft click when she pulled it closed.

In my damp running clothes, I shivered.

CHAPTER FOUR

B ANG, BANG, BANG. THERE WAS a vigorous and unrelenting knock on my front door. As soon as I heard it, I knew it was the police. This wasn't the first the first time I'd received a late-night visit from the cops. It wasn't a common occurrence, but in my line of work, it wasn't unheard-of, either.

Gumshoe, who'd been sleeping by my feet, hissed and jumped to the floor before disappearing underneath the bed. Ragdolls weren't known for their bravery, and he was a perfect example of the breed.

I glanced at the clock as the banging continued. Four a.m. Really? I rolled out of bed, grabbed a hoodie from the back of a chair, and slipped it on. As I padded down the stairs, my foggy brain went through all my open cases. I couldn't think of a single one that might have a reason to involve the police. They were all small-time crimes, the dirty work that apparently was now beneath Samantha. The work she wanted to escape.

At the front door, I peered through the peephole and saw Austin Caster. My ex.

I closed my eyes for a moment and steadied myself. Of course it would be him. My hair was a rat's nest, and I wished I'd taken the time to brush it or at least throw it back in a messy bun.

Bang, bang, bang. There was no time to worry about my hair now. I knew better than to keep the police waiting.

I took a breath and opened the door, chagrined that Austin looked wide awake and as handsome as ever under the soft glow of my porch light. His uniform was pressed and crisp. He had blond hair and blue eyes and looked like a cover model for a beach magazine. Very fine lines raced from the corners of his eyes from squinting in the sun on his sailboat. When Austin wasn't at work, he was out on the lake. If anything, the lines made him even more attractive. They gave his face character. I wished my crow's feet gave me character.

"Austin," I blurted. "What's going on?"

He was a seasoned cop who had entered the police academy the day after high school graduation. He was also my on-again, off-again high school sweetheart and boyfriend for the past decade-plus. It was exhausting. I'd heard he was dating someone new, a sweeter-than-sweet kindergarten teacher. Apparently, after all that time with me, he was looking for something completely different. I knew this because my best friend Maelynn had made a point of telling me as soon as she'd heard, and Maelynn, who owned the coffee shop in Herrington, heard everything first. I wouldn't be surprised, even at four in the morning, if she already knew why Austin was on my doorstep.

I tamped down the old feelings that seemed to come up whenever I saw him. I put the kindergarten teacher out of my mind. He wasn't on my doorstep in his uniform for a social call. Beyond him, I could see his partner, Zack Louter, leaning against their cruiser. Louter, a bodybuilder type, had a perpetual scowl on his face. He wasn't happy to be there, either. I wouldn't have been the least bit surprised if he'd set Austin up with the kindergarten teacher. He hadn't been a huge fan of mine since I'd proven he'd arrested the wrong man on an assault and battery charge five years ago. Louter could milk a grudge.

Being a P.I., I knew all the police in Herrington well. I had to; it was important to keep a good relationship with the cops, even Louter, as much as I could, because there were times I needed their help and information. And even though they'd deny it, there were times they needed mine, too. I wasn't above taking a box of cupcakes to the department when I needed to bribe them into helping me with a case. Maelynn's husband was a world-class baker and made the very best cupcakes I'd ever eaten, and I'd eaten my share of cupcakes and cookies. If something had sugar in it, I was a buyer.

Austin's favorite cupcake was salted caramel crunch from Maelynn's coffee shop. I'd always had one in the box for him.

"Darby." Austin smiled at me, but it didn't reach his eyes.

I wrapped the hoodie a little more closely around my body as if to protect myself from whatever he was about to tell me. "Why are you here, Austin? It's the middle of the night." I wanted him to cut to the chase. Now, that I knew about his girlfriend, there really wasn't anything else for us to talk about.

"They sent me because the chief thought it'd be easier for you to hear from me, since we..." He paused. "Since we go way back."

I made a face and made no attempt to cover it. Why would anyone think it'd be easier for me to hear bad news from Austin? In fact, getting bad news from just about anyone else would've been preferable—even from Louter.

Suddenly fear gripped my chest. "Is it my dad?" If it was, why hadn't my mother or my sister called me? Maybe they hadn't had time because he'd taken a bad turn. I grabbed Austin's strong forearm. "Did he have a seizure?"

He shook his head. "No, it's not your dad or anyone in your family. It's about Samantha Porter."

I blinked. That was the last thing I'd expected him to say. "Samantha? Is she all right? Is anything wrong?"

"According to her doctor, you're her emergency contact."

I was? I hadn't known that. I shook my head. It didn't matter. None of it mattered until he told me why it mattered.

"What's wrong with Samantha?"

"There's been an accident," he said with a deep frown. His blue eyes were almost white in the porch light.

"Oh my God. Is she in the hospital? How badly is she hurt?" I started to back up. "Let me grab my keys and phone, and we can go right now."

"We don't need to rush to the hospital." He shook his head. "I'm sorry. She's dead, Darby."

I blinked at him for a moment. I stood on my doorstep barefoot and in my pajamas, staring at my ex-boyfriend, trying to process his words. Samantha? Dead? How was that even possible?

I didn't cry. Why didn't I cry? Because my brain wouldn't accept what Austin was telling me. What did he know? The first time he'd dumped me had been right after senior prom. He wasn't right about everything.

Austin studied me. There had to be a whole host of emotions racing across my face, but not one of them reflected acceptance, because this simply wasn't possible. And I made sure Austin knew that.

"You have to be wrong. Samantha is fine. One hundred percent fine. I saw her today—well, yesterday now—and she was in perfect health."

"It was a car accident. She might've been in perfect health during the day, but now she's gone."

I narrowed my eyes. "Is this some kind of sick joke?"

"I wouldn't do that, Darby," Austin said, and

for just a moment there was a glimpse of the boy I'd adored since school.

For all his faults, I knew that was true, and that was when the truth hit me full force. I pressed the back of my hand on my forehead, and a wave of dizziness and nausea washed over me.

"I think I need to sit." Without saying another word, I plopped down right there in the middle of the entryway.

Austin stared at me as if he was at a complete loss as to what to do.

A tear rolled down my cheek. Samantha had been my mentor, my friend, and my partner. I couldn't believe she was dead.

"Are you all right?"

It was such a mundane question. One of those questions everyone asked when someone was profoundly upset; one I would've asked if I'd been in Austin's position. But now, being on the receiving end of such a mundane and maddeningly kind question, — my friend had died, so no, I wasn't all right—I knew I'd never make such a careless comment to another person again. Was I all right? Did I look all right? Despite the wave of grief and anger and confusion that washed over me, I held back all the sharp retorts that came to mind. It wasn't Austin's fault.

He crouched beside me, and I had this strange flashback to when we were teenagers and he was on the football team and would run over to me sitting on the bleachers after practice. I was so small he'd crouch down to give me a quick kiss on the lips before he ran off to the showers. He did that every time I was there, until one day, he stopped and waved at me from the field before hitting the locker room. That was the beginning of the end for us. But it hadn't been, not really. That scene would play out in one way or another over the next ten years. It was as much my fault as his for letting it happen.

"But I saw her today. She was fine. She was fine." The words came out slowly. like they were on a delay of some sort.

"When was the last time you saw her?" Austin asked.

"This afternoon. Here at the office." I swallowed and didn't add that we hadn't spoken after our argument over Matt Billows' visit.

"Is there someone I can call for you?"

I thought about this. My parents or Maelynn would run to my side at a moment's notice. They'd make me eat soup, drink tea, and watch a romantic comedy on television. I didn't want any of that. I wanted to be alone to process this new reality. I shook my head.

"Not even Maelynn?" he asked. Of course, Austin knew Maelynn was my best friend. After he'd dumped me the first time in high school, she'd egged his car.

I shook my head. "No, thank you." My responses were more measured now.

He held out his hand to help me up. I stared at it like it was a lizard on a vine, but then I realized, even in my confusion and grief, how stupid I was being. I grabbed it, and he tugged me to my feet.

"How was Samantha when you last saw her? Was

anything bothering her?" Austin asked. As he did, he beckoned Louter to come in the house.

Several thoughts occurred to me. One, Samantha was really gone. And my life from this point forward would be altered irrevocably. Two, Austin's body language had shifted. He was in full-on officer mode now. His hands were on his belt, near his gun but not on it. His legs were shoulder-width apart. And the questions were strange. They were questions he wouldn't have asked if this had been a by-the-book automobile accident.

Oh heavens, did they suspect suicide? Samantha had been many things—stubborn, opinionated, funny, commanding. But she'd never shown any signs of depression, not in all the years I'd known her. If she had been struggling with something, she would've sought treatment and dealt with it. She'd been pragmatic about *everything* in her life.

"Did she seem stressed when you last saw her?" Austin pressed again. The same question, phrased a little differently.

I didn't like what he was implying.

Austin and I stepped from the door. He inclined his head to signal the other officer to come inside. Officer Louter's presence set off a second alarm in my head. What had been a routine courtesy visit to share the news of a loved one's passing seemed to be taking a different twist. When Austin continued, "Darb, you don't mind if we ask you a few questions,"

I knew what would happen next.

This was the start of the good cop/bad cop routine,

not the way it played out in movies where one officer was badgering and the other sympathetic. No, this was the stealthy version. Austin kept his focus on me, his expression appropriately sympathetic, while Louter was scanning every inch of my home and cataloguing every detail. Something definitely wasn't right here. You didn't work around police officers and with criminals for the better part of a decade and not pick up on "cop mode."

It's a trap.

I licked my lips. "She was always stressed to some extent. We're in a demanding business."

"Did she say anything to you about that recently?"

"We...spoke about the business." I didn't want to tell him we'd had an argument. Something felt off about his line of inquiry. If it was really a car accident, the questions should've been different.

He examined my face. "What about the business?"

I cleared my throat, not the least bit surprised that Austin recognized my hesitation. There was a reason he was so high-ranking in the department at such a young age. No one would fault him when it came to crime. His stupidity only applied to relationships, which I knew from personal experience.

I countered with a question of my own. One I should've asked from the start. "Was anyone else hurt? Were there any other cars involved?"

He paused as if carefully considering his words. "That's what we'd like to know. The evidence shows she lost control and went over the side at the top of

Lakeshore Avenue. We want to find out what happened to cause her to do that."

I stared at him. She died on the same curve I ran to every day.

"Do you think another car was involved?" I asked again.

"Possibly. Why don't we all sit down and talk?" Austin suggested, but it wasn't really a suggestion. "We want to ask you a few questions."

I chalked it up to shock, maybe disbelief, because rather than come straight out and ask Austin, "Why *are* you asking these questions?" I only nodded. "We can go into the waiting room." I turned, stepped into the waiting room, and turned on the light. I sat in the middle of the giant couch. Both Austin and Louter stood. If possible, that made me feel even smaller. "Can you sit?"

Austin grabbed the chair from Nat's desk, but Louter took a couple of steps back and remained standing. He folded his arms over his broad chest, which caused the muscles in his arms to press hard again the fabric of his jacket. His stance was wide as if he was bracing himself to chase someone down at a moment's notice. I guessed he would've loved to tackle me to the ground.

When Austin moved the chair, Nat came to my mind.

"Nat should know," I said. "Someone should tell her."

Nat was going to be heartbroken, too. I cringed at the idea of telling her. Grief swallowed me up all over again. I wasn't sure I'd be able to speak to answer the questions I knew were coming.

"We'll tell Nat," Austin said. "Is there anyone else who should know? Did Samantha have any family?"

"Just her nephew, Tate. You might remember him from high school. He was a few years ahead of us."

He nodded. "I remember. Do you know where I can find him?"

I shook my head. "I'm not sure Samantha would've known. He bounces around. The last she told me, he was somewhere in Asia."

"For the Army? Didn't he join up after high school?"

"He did, but he's not in the Army any longer. He left years ago." I didn't add anything more to that. I didn't know why he'd left the service, and it wasn't something Samantha liked talking about.

Austin nodded. "We might be able to track him down. Anyone else?"

I hesitated. "Logan Montgomery should know."

"The town councilman. She's been dating him a long time, right?"

I didn't say anything.

"Is there something you're not telling me?"

The thing was, I liked Logan, but when bad things happened, the significant other was always a suspect. "Samantha mentioned yesterday that they broke up."

"Did she say why?"

I shook my head.

"And when did they break up?"

"I don't know that, either."

"Did Samantha have a drinking problem?"

I blinked at his quick change of subject. "No. She never drank more than a glass of wine here or there, and she'd never drink and drive, if that's what you're trying to imply."

He went on to ask more about the cases we were working on and why Samantha would be out so late. I didn't know the answer to that last question. We were working any number of cases that might warrant late-night surveillance.

I didn't know how long I sat there answering questions, but it felt like seconds and an eternity all at the same time. Most of the questions were about our clients, but I told him over and over again that I couldn't think of a single client who'd be angry enough at Samantha to harm her.

Austin finished getting my statement, then nodded to his partner and stood up.

I got to my feet too. "Austin, what's going on? Some of those questions you asked me had nothing to do with a car accident."

He looked at me for a long moment.

"Tell me," I said. "I deserve to know if this is more."

He glanced over his shoulder at Louter, who was expressionless.

"Where are your car keys, Darb?"

What did my car have to do with anything? I pointed to the credenza by the wall. "I usually leave them there."

Louter strode over, checked the tray, and even opened the drawer for good measure. He turned back to Austin and shook his head.

"What about your spare key?"

I frowned. "At my parents' house." Now I really didn't like where this was going. "Austin?"

"We won't know for sure, but it looks like Samantha drove off the road."

"But she didn't drink," I said. "I told you that."

"Then it could be something else. The toxicology report will clear it up."

I stared at him. "Was she murdered?" I didn't want to ask the question, but I had to know.

"If the toxicology comes back and she hadn't been drinking, it's possible. We aren't ruling it out."

It was all I had to hear. I knew who'd have the greatest motive for killing Samantha Porter, and it was me.

CHAPTER FIVE

A FTER THE POLICE LEFT, I texted Nat. *You up?*
Yes, was the immediate response.

I wasn't surprised. Nat was an early riser like me. I woke early so I could squeeze in a run before a full day on the job, but she woke early because she said that was how she was wired. She told me once that she woke up at five every morning of her entire adult life. I thought I was crazy for waking up at six every—well, most—mornings for my run. She woke up to read the paper and sip coffee. That didn't make any sense to me.

I wasn't sure what to text next. I didn't know if she knew, and text message didn't seem like the best way to tell Nat her boss and friend was dead.

As if she could sense my anxiety over the message, she texted next: *I know. The police were here.*

I gave a sigh of relief. *They were here too. They just left.*

What do we do?

That was a big question with so many implications.

What did we do in a life without Samantha? What did we do with the agency? The house I was living in that was also sixty percent Samantha's? Heck, I didn't know what would come of our future. What did we do with our day?

I swallowed. Nat didn't text anymore. I could almost read her mind, and from having worked together for so long, I could intuit what she was thinking—*It's your call. You're the boss now.*

I'd never seen myself as a boss. A leader? Sure. But a boss, that was a whole other thing. A boss had to make decisions. This was the first one.

Let's stay closed today, I texted. *I'll check the open cases to make sure nothing pressing has come up. Please put an out-of-office message on all the outlets.*

I can do that last part from here.

When Nat said she'd do something, she did. Samantha and I never had to worry about her following through.

Okay, that'll help.

We were both acting too businesslike, numbed by the loss. It was hard to even imagine a world without Samantha in it. She was such a loud and vibrant person. It was like three people had been snuffed out, not just one.

Darby? Nat texted.

Yeah? My thoughts were on a million things. It was damage control time. I'd learn to grieve and absorb this terrible news soon, very soon, but first, there were things that needed to be done.

We'll get through this in Samantha's honor.

I was glad we were texting and not speaking because I knew she was crying, and if I heard her cry, I'd
break down. I couldn't do that right now. I had to stay
focused, because if my suspicion was right, Samantha
had been murdered, and life for everyone at Two Girls
Detective Agency was going to get a lot worse before it
got better. Two Girls...down to one girl.

*I know. Nat, I have to go. Stay home today, okay? I
can handle everything here.*

Okay, was her last text.

I went over to Nat's computer and logged on under my username. We had a few pending cases at the
moment. There was a woman who wanted us to find
her birth mother. The odds weren't good for success.
She'd been born in the 1970s and, from all accounts,
her birth mother had completely dropped off the map.
I thought she was most likely dead or had changed her
identity. People seemed surprised that identity changes were so common, but people changed their names
and backstories all the time. Most even did this legally.

In another case, Samantha had been working with
a man who believed that his partner was embezzling
money from their health food store right here on Lakeshore Avenue. The shop was called Multigrain Market
and was next door to Mrs. Berger's favorite hair salon,
Mary B's Beehives. I'd been in the market a few times,
but did most of my shopping at the local supercenter
outside of town. The organic foods and other whole-
some items sold at Multigrain were a little out of my
price range.

The third case involved a local stable whose owner

suspected an employee was taking money under the table.

At that moment, the birth mom and the Multigrain Market cases were at the computer research stage. It was frightening the amount of information you could find out about an individual through a casual search on the Internet, and with the right skills and databases, you could find out even more. It wasn't uncommon for us to solve a case without ever leaving the office.

I was happy that none of the cases were pressing, and all had several days left before the deadlines we'd set to respond to the clients. Usually we'd pad those estimated due dates in case something came up. I could never have foreseen that we'd need those padded days to deal with Samantha's death.

Could it be murder? Or was Austin keeping all the options open this early in the investigation? He wasn't one to jump to conclusions.

But I didn't know who or why anyone would hurt Samantha. In our line of business, it could've been any of hundreds of people we'd found guilty or had dug up dirt on. It wasn't a stretch to say that both Samantha and I had made some enemies over the years. But the very notion that someone might go so far as to take her life? It was too much to conceive.

I closed the laptop and felt better that the business end of things was well in hand. It was strange to click through reports and notes like I did every morning, like it was just another day. It wasn't another day. It was the first day without Samantha steering the ship.

It was the first day I was in charge. Tears gathered and threatened to spill from my eyes.

It also wasn't "just another day" because I hadn't gone on my run. I bit my lip. If I went on a run, I'd pass the very spot where my friend had died.

That was when I knew I had to go. I needed to see the crime scene while it was still fresh. When the tire marks were still on the road and plastic from the car still scattered on the berm.

I stood and hurried upstairs to change.

Ten minutes later, I hit the pavement. My rhythm was off again. This time it wasn't because I'd fallen from a tree rescuing a cat. This time it was because I was grieving Samantha.

Tears rolled down my face as I tried to concentrate on putting one foot in front of another. Slowly, I fell into the well-honed habit of running. Even so, the tears kept coming and dripped from my chin to the pavement below.

Twelve years of competitive ballet could train you for anything, I was sure. I'd hoped to be a professional dancer, but after an injury when I was eighteen, those dreams had been dashed. I was lucky to able to run. I'd come to terms with losing my childhood ambition and achieving a more attainable one as an adult: the detective agency.

When I was a senior in high school, I'd shattered my femur after a fellow dancer had dropped me during a lift; I thought I'd never dance again. I was right. I never did dance again, but I also feared I'd never *walk* again. That part wasn't true. I'd spent my first two years of college dealing with surgeries, casts, and pain. At some point during that time, my father, no stranger to hospitals, had challenged me to run a half marathon.

"I can't even walk straight, and you're daring me to run?" I'd cried.

"I bet you can do it." He'd winked. "Why don't you prove me right?"

And I had. In fact, I'd run a half marathon every year since. My dad understood me. He knew I'd needed a goal to keep me going. I needed the same thing now. Today, my goal was to find out what had happened to Samantha.

It was before eight, but traffic was already starting to pick up as commuters made their way to work. I kept to the side of the road. As I ran out of town, toward Mrs. Berger's home and ultimately the top of the hill, I went over in my mind everything Samantha had said to me over the past several days. Most of it had been about the deal with Billows, and most of it had been heated.

I squeezed my eyes and wiped the tears from my face. I hated knowing that the last words I'd said to Samantha had been in frustration and anger. That was something I'd have to live with. As I came to Mrs. Berger's house, she was sitting on the front porch. Romy was in her lap, fortunately. This was not a day to stage a cat rescue.

"Looking good," she called and waved.

I slowed my pace. Other than the resort, Mrs.

Berger's house was the closest building to that deadly curve at the top of the hill. I jogged over to her.

"Darby, you tire me out just watching you. You're out and about a little earlier than usual."

I held my tongue to stop myself from telling her why. I didn't know if Austin and the other police wanted the news out about the accident just yet. "How'd you sleep last night, Mrs. Berger?"

If she was surprised by the question I'd never asked her before, she didn't show it. She furrowed her brow. "Come to mention it, not well. I was startled awake about two in the morning and couldn't get back to sleep. I finally gave up, and Romy and I had a nice pot of tea in the living room."

"What woke you up?"

"A set of cars, flying down the street." She wrinkled her nose. "I'd guess it was those rich folks staying at Lake Waters. They always think they're so entitled. They can gallivant around the Finger Lakes disrupting everyone else's lives just because they have money." She snorted.

Speeding cars at two in the morning? The police had come to my home at four. I knew they would've been on the scene for a while before waking me, clearing the road, removing the debris and the body. I swallowed hard as I thought that.

"Are you sure there was more than one car?" I asked. I'd gotten the impression from Austin that more than one car had been involved, and Mrs. Berger's account seemed to agree.

"'Course I'm sure," she said, slightly miffed that

I'd question her on the details. "I heard two engines. There's nothing wrong with my hearing, miss."

"I would never say there was," I assured her and swallowed again. I could feel bile rising in the back of my mouth. I needed to get to the crime scene and see everything for myself. "I'm sorry you didn't sleep well. I hope tonight is better. I'd better finish my run."

"Won't you stay for a spot of tea? Romy would love to thank you for fetching him from the tree yesterday morning."

Romy hissed at me without lifting his head from his mistress's lap.

I glanced at the cat. Even if I hadn't been in a hurry, his less-than-warm welcome would've convinced me to keep moving. "I'd love to. But I have a busy day ahead of me and need to return to the office." That was the understatement of the century. "Another time, though, please."

"Of course." She nodded. "I understand. You run along and go catch those bad guys."

I was on a quest to find more than just a bad guy, because it seemed more and more likely that someone had run Samantha off the road. I was looking for a killer.

Now, this might've sounded premature. The police hadn't confirmed anything yet. But I *knew* Samantha. She didn't drink and drive. She didn't speed. And she'd lived each day with such passion...her death hadn't been accidental. If there was another car there, pushing her into an accident, that made more sense to me.

I waved goodbye and ran back to the road, wanting to see the crime scene. A few minutes later, I was at the top of the hill. I put my hands on my hips as I caught my breath and stared at the two sets of tire skids on the road. I stopped and shivered as if all the blood in my body had drained into my feet, which felt impossibly heavy. I closed my eyes and then opened them again, forcing myself to look. The skid marks pointed to the ravine, in the direction of Seneca Lake. One set of marks careened away from the ravine, and the other, surely Samantha's, continued into the grass. I couldn't see more of her tire tracks because I was distracted by the tow truck using its winch to pull her car up from the ravine.

I shivered, either from the cold or dismay. I thought the scene would've been clear by now.

I licked my lips and walked around the skid marks to where the tires had dug into the grass, about a hundred feet from the tow truck. The driver didn't notice me. He was concentrating too hard on the task at hand.

Shards of plastic and metal from Samantha's car still lay on the road.

I stood near the edge of the ravine. The trail of crumpled brush and broken saplings showed the route the car had taken. There was a giant scar in a large oak tree about five yards down the ravine from the tow truck. I knew that was where the car had come to rest. If my judgment of the tire tracks was right, Samantha had hit that tree dead on.

My stomach rolled and I had to suck in air to keep from passing out. There was little chance she would've survived, especially if she'd been going as fast as Mrs. Berger had described.

Behind me, I heard a car on the road come to a stop. I pivoted and groaned when I saw the police car. I felt even worse when Austin Caster stepped out of the vehicle.

CHAPTER SIX

I SHOULD'VE KNOWN AUSTIN WOULD HAVE had the same idea as I had to come and check out the scene in the daylight, and he would've wanted to supervise Samantha's car being removed from the ravine. I was surprised he wasn't there before me.

Austin looked as happy to see me as I was to see him. He removed his sunglasses and tucked them into the breast pocket of his uniform. "What are you doing here?"

"Isn't it obvious? I'm doing the same thing you are. Visiting the scene and trying to find out what happened."

He nodded. "What's your take?"

I cocked my head.

"No, really. I want to know."

I walked closer to the edge where Samantha's car went over. I could almost hear her screams. Had she been screaming? For a second, I put my hands over my ears as if that could block the sound in my head.

I took a breath. "Mrs. Berger was woken up at two

o'clock at the sound of cars careening down Lakeshore Avenue."

"You spoke with Mrs. Berger? You're already knocking on doors, talking to witnesses?"

"I wasn't knocking on doors. She and her cat were outside when I ran by."

"Oh, right. Romy, your best friend." The corners of his mouth curled up into a smile. Austin knew all about my tree-climbing adventures with the orange Maine Coon.

"Mrs. Berger thought it was some rich joyriders from Lake Waters, but I don't think so. It was very likely Samantha's car and another vehicle."

He nodded. "It fits the timeline. Someone called the accident in around two-thirty a.m."

"Who called it in?"

Austin kept his mouth closed, and I suppressed a sigh. I'd have to find out that little detail another way.

I went on to explain my take on what might have happened. "This is a sharp curve, and Samantha has lived in Herrington her entire life. She's driven this road a million times. Taking into account the two sets of skid marks, with one leaving the scene, I'd say that Samantha was run off of the road." I gave him a look. I walked back to where the marks began on the pavement. "See?"

"That's what I was thinking too, and it gels with the coroner's assessment."

"The coroner?"

"The preliminary toxicology report came back." He shifted from foot to foot.

I blinked. "That was fast." Like television crime-show fast. In real life, those tests could take weeks.

"Like I said, the report is just preliminary at this point. It won't be officially filed for a few more days. But the police chief asked the lab to put a rush on it since Samantha was such a prominent member of the community."

I nodded. In addition to her job, Samantha had been on countless charitable boards and volunteered away all her free time. "What did the report say?"

"You were right. She had nothing in her system. She wasn't drinking." He took a breath. "We're still accumulating evidence, Darby. But...given the evidence thus far, I'm inclined to think this case cannot be relegated to simply an automobile accident. There are definitely two sets of tires here. The crime scene techs looked at the skid marks. One was from Samantha's car, a Chevrolet sedan. The other is from a compact car with almost new tires."

I froze.

"Didn't you get new tires on your car during the summer, Darby?"

He already knew the answer to that. I'd driven to Syracuse in July and got a flat tire on the highway. Austin and I had still been together then, and I'd called him to come get me. Because the tires on my compact car had been old and the tread all but gone, the tire shop had recommended I get four new tires, which I had. It had pained me to do it because of the cost, and because I rarely drove. Everywhere I went in town, I could run or walk to. I didn't like what Austin was implying with his questions.

Out of the corner of my eye, I caught movement to the right of where the tow truck was pulling out Samantha's car out of the ravine. It could've been a deer or a really big squirrel, but the reflection of light from the bushes told me it was something—or someone— else entirely. I took off at a run.

"Darby!" Austin called after me.

I reached into the bush and grabbed the long lens of the camera, and pulled. Hard.

"Hey!" a frantic voice shouted.

I hauled out the camera and the person attached to it. The man, who was only an inch or two taller than me, wore a black tracksuit and a backward ball cap. His glasses slipped down his narrow nose and he pushed them up and found his footing on the pavement. "Hey, hey! Watch the threads!"

Austin was on the other side of the photographer.

"Who are you?" I asked.

He reached into the pocket of his shiny jacket, pulled out a business card, and handed it to me.

"Benny B, celebrity photographer." I handed the card to Austin and turned back to the stranger. "You're a paparazzo."

"I prefer celebrity photographer, thanks."

Austin tucked the card into the breast pocket of his uniform. "What are you doing here?"

Benny B slung the strap of his camera over his arm. "Word on the street is the woman killed here today is somehow involved with Lake Waters Retreat.

I'm on assignment to find out about Lake Waters, so I thought I'd check it out. The tragedy angle is great to sell glossies."

I glared at him.

"What magazine are you working for?" Austin asked.

"I'm not going to tell you that."

"I want to see the photographs you've taken."

"I think you need a warrant to take my camera, don't you..." He leaned forward to read the nametag on Austin's shirt. "Officer Caster?"

Austin glared at him. "Get out of here."

Benny B grinned, seeing that he'd won. "You got it." He turned to walk down the hill and then his spun on his heel to look back at us. "You hear about anything strange happening at Lake Waters, you let me know, okay?"

"Get lost," Austin said.

Benny B laughed and trotted down the hill.

Austin and I shared a look.

"Could Benny B or a photographer like him have been the one to force Samantha off the road?"

"You mean, like a Princess Diana scenario?" he asked.

I shrugged.

The tow truck stopped as it pulled Samantha's car up onto the pavement. The driver got out and walked over to the side of the Chevy. "Officer, you definitely have paint from another vehicle on this car."

Austin walked over to the other man. "What color?"

"It's white, which makes it easy to see against this

dark blue car," the driver observed, as if he was talking about the weather.

My car was white. I dug my fingernails into the palms of my hands.

Austin's head snapped back in my direction. He knew the color of my car, too.

He turned back to the drive. "Thanks. Can you tow this back to the lab?"

The drive nodded. "Sure thing."

Austin walked back to me as the truck with Samantha's crumpled car drove down the hill.

"There's something else," he said to me.

"Something other than my business partner and friend being murdered?"

He nodded. "There's a rumor floating around Herrington that Two Girls Detective Agency was going to close so Samantha could work at Lake Waters."

I dug my nails in a little harder. Then I released my hands and stretched them out at my sides.

His eyebrows drooped as if in concern. "Darb, I'm trying to help you. You and I both know it appears your car was involved in this crime."

"My car is back in my garage."

"Are you sure? When was the last time you drove it?"

"Three weeks ago, maybe? I don't use it a lot."

"So you can't know it's still in the garage." At that, I wanted to protest, but he went on to say, "The rumor also says you were against her leaving the agency."

"There are a lot of rumors in Herrington," I said, wishing my voice wasn't shaking so much. "People like

Benny B are exactly why Matt Billows wanted to hire Samantha as the head of security at Lake Waters."

"Was she really leaving?"

"Nothing was for sure. Matt thought her expertise would be the best defense against the paparazzi trying to get photographs of his high-end clients."

He nodded. "Celebrities and the rich don't usually want the public to know when they've had some work done."

"Exactly." I nodded.

"What happens to the agency if you or Samantha passed away?"

A wave of wooziness came over me. I knew what he was getting at. He didn't know the exact numbers, but he knew Samantha was the majority partner in our detective agency.

"I—I don't know." But I did. Samantha and I had agreed when we'd opened the business that if something unforeseen happened, the departed partner would leave her portion of the business to the other in her will. It sure looked like I had the biggest motive for this murder. By dying, Samantha had given me the agency and my home free and clear.

"Won't you get the agency now as her partner?" he asked in a casual way I knew had nothing casual about it.

Motives didn't get much better than that. As my ex-boyfriend, Austin knew too much about my life. I was at a terrible disadvantage. I didn't answer the question and was relieved when he didn't press the point.

"Why did she want to work for Billows?" Austin

asked. "I know I haven't spent much time with the two of you recently, but she always seemed very passionate about her cases."

"She wanted more stability. A nine-to-five life. The head of security there would be a cushy job. I think she wanted a break from the grind of being a P.I." I didn't see any harm in telling him this fact.

"And you?"

"I didn't want things to change," I said quietly. I folded my arms. "Things were fine the way they were."

"But why work for Billows? There are other jobs she could've gotten," Austin said.

I wasn't surprised by his obvious distaste for Billows. Lake Waters didn't let the police patrol their resort, which covered several hundred acres. It was a sore spot with the local authorities.

"Darb?" Austin asked.

I met his gaze.

"If it turns out the white paint on Samantha's car is from yours, you're going to want to talk to your lawyer."

And there it was. The single most condemning comment he could've made.

I took several steps back from him as if he had smacked me. He had, in a way—with his words. I stared at him for a moment. "Do you really think I could kill someone?"

"I want to believe you couldn't, I really do, but I have to follow the evidence."

"You know me," I said, unable to keep the hurt from my voice.

"I do," he said and broke eye contact.

A raw feeling settled over me when he looked away.

"Can I give you a ride back into town?" Austin asked.

"No, I'll run home. Thanks." My voice was hollow. I started back down the hill toward town.

CHAPTER SEVEN

W HEN I PASSED MRS. BERGER'S house, she and Romy were no longer on the porch. It was just as well. My brain was crowded with too many dark thoughts to make small talk; plus, I wouldn't have the reaction time needed to avoid a scratch from Romy.

On a normal day, by this time, both Samantha and Nat would be in the office, but this was nothing like a normal day, and no one was there when I made it back from my run—and what a revealing run it had been.

Samantha had been murdered, and I was prime suspect number one. Not that Austin had come right out and said that, but that was the point he'd been trying to get across. He'd told me to contact my attorney, for goodness' sake. He might as well have said, "Contact your attorney, because I'll be arresting you later."

I had to see my car. When I found it safely parked in the garage behind the agency, I'd feel better. It'd be proof, indisputable proof, that the white paint on Samantha's broken and battered sedan hadn't come from my vehicle.

I sprinted down the short driveway when I reached the brick colonial. Without stopping to take a breath, I punched the garage code into the keypad screwed on the side of the garage door frame. The door went up slowly, inch by inch. I saw the lawnmower, rakes, garden tools, and my old ten-speed bike.

My car wasn't there. The feeling of faintness I'd had at the top of the hill came over me again, but twice as bad this time. I held onto the door frame for support.

I stepped inside the garage, as if I needed to move into the spot where the car should've been to prove to myself that it was missing.

The car was gone. Someone had stolen it to run Samantha off the road.

I closed my eyes and rubbed my eyelids with my fingers. When I opened my eyes again, the car was still missing.

Who could've taken it?

The answer was...anyone. I kept my car keys on the credenza in the main office of the agency. Anyone who came into the office could've picked them up at any time in the three weeks since I'd last driven the car. I kept them there because I constantly lost them, which was why I hadn't been concerned that they'd been missing when Austin was there the night before. I hadn't been concerned because they were always missing. There was a reason I kept the second set of keys at my parents': because that way, they were safe from me. My librarian mother didn't lose anything. Ever.

It wouldn't be long until Austin was here asking to see my car. He might even be on his way to the agency at this very moment. It made me sick that my car could've killed Samantha. It wouldn't be certain until my car was found and the paint was matched, but I knew without a shadow of a doubt that it would.

I was being framed...for murder.

I needed to report the car stolen. Under the circumstances, it would be better if I did that rather than the police finding it on their own.

I called the emergency number, and the dispatcher answered on the first ring.

"Darby Piper, is that you?" The dispatcher was SueAnne Clock, a pleasant older lady who'd been eligible to retire a good decade ago, but had stayed on because she loved her job.

"It is. Can you patch me through to Austin?"

"Awww, are the two of you getting back together again? I miss hearing you call for him. You were such a sweet couple. I've been rooting for the two of you."

"No, SueAnne," I said, knowing it was better to squash any rumors that Austin and I were ever getting back together. "I'm calling to report my car stolen, and I think it has bearing on a case Austin is investigating."

"Bless your heart. You poor thing. I'll patch you through right now."

A second later, Austin was on the line. "Caster."

"Austin, it's Darby," I said in a rush. "I came home after seeing you at the accident scene and went to look for my car in the garage, and it's gone. It's been stolen!"

"Are you sure?"

"What kind of question is that? Yes, I'm sure. It's gone. I'm standing of the middle of my empty garage right now." I glared at the lawnmower as if it were in some way responsible for my circumstances. It couldn't be, though. It hadn't worked for years.

"Okay, I'm in the middle of something. I'll send Louter over now to get your statement."

I paced in the driveway until Louter arrived a few minutes later.

He climbed out of his police car and walked to the open garage door. "No car."

I folded my arms. "I'm aware. It's been stolen."

"When was the last time you saw it?"

"Three weeks ago," I said.

"Uh-huh."

My heart sank. He didn't believe me.

Louter finished taking my statement and left. My stomach turned as I watched his cruiser drive away. I was in serious trouble. I didn't know if it would get better or worse when they found my car.

I hurried to my second-floor apartment and took a lightning-fast shower. I needed to get on the case, and quick.

Twenty minutes later, I was dressed in my jeans, a sweater, calf-high boots, and a leather jacket. It was my private investigator uniform of choice. My hair was mostly dry—I knew if I let it dry naturally, I'd have a ball of fluff on top of my head reminiscent of Gumshoe's coif. I grabbed my New York State ball cap from my office and planted it on my head. That would solve my problem, even if I had a serious case of hat hair later. Gumshoe followed me from room to room as I moved through the house. Even after I fed him, he stuck with me. When we went into the office, I peered down at him.

"Are you trying to tell me something?"

He yowled in reply. Not helpful.

I went from the waiting room to Samantha's office. When I opened the door, I was hit by the scent of gardenia. Her favorite shampoo. Tears pricked at the back of my eyes, but I blinked them away. Samantha wouldn't want me to wallow. She would want me to find out the truth.

Her desk was pristine. There was nary a paper clip out of place. As business partners, it might've made more sense if Samantha and I had shared one combined office, because we worked so closely together and spent most of our office time in the same room. But her lack of clutter was the reason we couldn't. I wasn't messy, per se, but my office certainly had a more lived-in look than Samantha's. She'd constantly complained any time she'd needed something from my office that she couldn't find it because of the mess, but I never had any trouble finding anything. I thought she should've understood my system after all these years.

On the flipside, any time I went into Samantha's office, I found exactly what I was looking for. I hoped that would be the case today as well. There had to be a reason why she was out driving so late last night, and her office was the most likely place to find the answer. Perhaps she'd opened a new case without telling me. That wouldn't be typical. Many times, we'd talked about cases with each other even before we'd taken the client on. Then again, she hadn't been typical these past few months. She'd been nervous and critical, and determined to leave our agency for a new job at Lake Waters.

I opened the center drawer in her desk first. It contained the normal office paraphernalia like pens, pencils, and note cards. There was nothing personal there, and certainly no files. I closed it and moved on to the side drawers. Same thing. No personality. I moved over to the filing cabinet. The files were all in place, but nothing struck me as odd. Each case was expertly labeled and color-coded. My chest tightened as I came across Samantha's distinctive, slanted handwriting again and again.

As I continued to scour her office, I noted that her laptop computer was gone. She must've taken it with her last night. That wasn't unusual. Anything of importance would be on the laptop, and I realized it would've most likely been in the car when she crashed, which meant Austin and the police had taken it. Maybe I could ask if I could access the computer. He would probably say no, but there might be important information on it that I needed for the business.

How could my friend be dead? And why would anyone frame me as her killer? Austin was right. I needed to talk to my attorney.

CHAPTER EIGHT

P ATRICK HARTWELL, ESQ. HAD AN office two blocks away from Two Girls Detective Agency in the courtyard district of town. This little pocket of Herrington lay around the city park and was about a half mile from Seneca Lake. There was a giant playground in the middle of the park, a basketball court, and plenty of benches.

Patrick's office was in an old Colonial home, similar in shape and size to Two Girls Detective Agency. As I came within sight of the park, I spotted Patrick shuffling down the sidewalk. His bald head reflected the late morning sunlight. He carried a briefcase, a travel coffee mug, an umbrella, and a winter parka.

I looked up; there wasn't a cloud in the sky. I wasn't surprised Patrick held the parka and the umbrella, though. The man was obsessed with the weather and refused to drive if there was even a possibility of rain. He was quirky to the extreme, but he was a good lawyer, organized and efficient. He was always honest with Samantha and me about what we needed legally to make our business run and how to avoid a lawsuit while doing it.

"Darby!" he called when I was still a half block away. "I have been expecting your call. I didn't think you would show up in person."

I hurried up to him and took the parka and umbrella from his arms. "I thought it'd be better to have this conversation face to face."

He nodded. "Everyone in town is in shock over Samantha's death, but of course, it has the greatest impact on you. There are many things we need to discuss."

I grimaced, but wasn't surprised to hear there were already rumors going around town about Samantha's death.

I fell in step beside him. "I need to talk to you about the future of the agency now that Samantha is gone. I hope that doesn't come off crass. Normally, I wouldn't have come to you this soon about it, but..." I took a breath, knowing I could be frank with Patrick. "The police suspect me of murder, and her will is my motive."

He stopped in the middle of the sidewalk and pushed his glasses up his nose with his free hand. "Murder?"

"It's not certain yet, but it's what the police suspect." I bit my lip. "And since I'll inherit her part of the agency, I'm the prime suspect."

He blinked at me and held his briefcase and coffee to his chest. "Darby, you're not in Samantha's will. She didn't leave you her portion of Two Girls Detective Agency."

"What do you mean? That's what we agreed on from the beginning." I staggered back.

"It's what you've had in your will from the beginning, but it's not what Samantha had. She changed her will three years ago."

My stomach dropped. "What? Then who inherits her portion of the agency?"

He sighed. "We'd better go into my office and sort this out." He started down the sidewalk again.

The knot in my stomach tightened as we walked to the front door of the old Colonial home. Patrick rented the second floor to a local artist, who lived and worked there. In all the time Two Girls had been his client, I'd never seen his upstairs tenant. Samantha and I used to joke that the tenant must've been a vampire.

I frowned. It hurt to remember the jokes she and I had shared, especially knowing something was wrong with the agency.

"You can set those there." He nodded at the coat rack beside the front door.

I hung up his parka and leaned his umbrella against the wall. As I pulled my hand away, I noticed it was shaking. I opened and closed my fingers and willed myself to calm down. Samantha wouldn't do anything to hurt the agency. She cared too much about it. Then, I remembered she'd been planning to sell it to Billows. Maybe I had been wrong about how much she cared about the agency...and about me.

Okay, the agency was one thing, but she cared about me as her friend. She wouldn't do anything that would hurt me. I didn't believe that. It wasn't possible.

He smiled at me. "We'll go right into my office and talk this over. Please excuse any banging you might hear. The artist is going through a more physical stage in his work, or at least that's what he tells me when it sounds like he's throwing barbells against the wall up there." He sighed. "I should really find a new tenant, but he pays on time and always in full. A renter like that can be hard to come by." He shook his head. "In any case, I think you're here early enough that we won't be disturbed. I've never heard him throw anything before noon."

That was a relief. I wasn't sure my nerves could take loud noises at the moment.

"Have a seat. Have a seat." He gestured to the armchair across from his desk. "Louisa is on vacation this week. I hate to see her go, but she works hard, and she's been putting up with our upstairs neighbor for months. She more than deserved a cruise with her husband. Would you like some coffee? I'm at a bit of a loss without her here, but I think I can sort it out."

I was only half listening to what he was saying. I could only focus on the fact that he'd said I wasn't in Samantha's will. I must've heard him wrong. That was what Samantha and I had agreed to when we'd started the business. I'd been there when she'd signed the papers. I'd signed them too. We might not be solving violent crimes, but our jobs still had their dangers: we went to unfamiliar places and questioned people we didn't know.

"Patrick, can you tell me what's going on? I don't

need coffee. I need to know what you meant when you said I wasn't in Samantha's will."

"I meant exactly that," he said sadly. "She came in about three years ago and said she wanted to change her deed and shares in the business. Instead of leaving it to you, she wanted to put it in a trust."

I felt myself relax a little. Trusts were expensive. One of the reasons we'd decided not to go that route was because of the cost. But it didn't matter; if Samantha had left me the business in a trust, that would work fine. Nothing would have to go through probate, which had been our concern from the get-go. That was her choice and I couldn't question her now about it.

I swallowed. "Okay, I wasn't expecting a trust, but I still have control over the business."

Patrick pulled on his collar. "The trust isn't for you, Darby. She left everything to her nephew, Tate Porter."

"Tate?" I blinked.

I knew him, of course, but I hadn't seen him in well over ten years. He was in his early thirties, I guessed; less than a decade younger than Samantha. She'd raised him for over twenty years after his parents had died in a boating accident on the lake.

When I'd been a freshman at Herrington High School, Tate had been a senior. Even so, I'd known him because it was a tiny school. I couldn't remember having any long conversations with him. I'd been consumed with ballet at the time, so determined to make it into a ballet company when I graduated from high school. I hadn't had much time for friends or anything else. It wasn't until the next year that I'd begun noticing Austin's attention, then had started dating him, and thus had begun the seemingly endless on-again, off-again hamster wheel of our relationship.

Since Two Girls had opened, Samantha would mention Tate from time to time and the country he was wandering through at the moment, but she hadn't heard from him as often as she would've liked.

"What does this mean?" I was still processing what he was telling me. "Why would she leave it to Tate? He's not a P.I. It makes no sense."

"Well, whether it makes sense to you or not, that's what happened." He swallowed. "It means Tate owns sixty percent of the business and sixty percent of the agency building."

"My home? But I live there. Am I going to be out on the street?"

He shook his head. "No, of course not. I'm sure you and Tate will be able to come to some sort of agreement when we track him down."

"You didn't tell me."

"She asked me not to. I respected her wishes." He fumbled with a ballpoint pen on the top of his desk.

"I can't believe this. We were partners. We were supposed to be in this business together."

I folded my hands in my lap, clasping them together until the knuckles turned white. Again, I felt betrayed by Samantha, and then the guilt of feeling betrayed when she was dead washed over me. I released my hands and pressed them flat against my thighs.

"Do you have any idea where I can find Tate?" Patrick asked.

The last few months, she'd been acting so strangely. I'd thought it was because I'd been so against her leaving the agency, and she'd wanted to do it so badly. But in Patrick's office, I now wondered if it was something much bigger than that—perhaps the reason someone wanted her dead.

I swallowed. "I'll look to see where he might be. Maybe there's a clue in Samantha's house. From what she said when she did speak of him, he's sort of a nomad. If you hear from Tate first, will you let me know?"

He nodded. "You do the same." He paused. "I'm sure we can track him down. Until we do, you can continue to live in the agency. I'm not sure you should take on any new cases, though. We don't know what Tate will want to do with his portion of the business. You might get in trouble if you have to suddenly break contract with a client because he wants to sell."

Sell? This was feeling worse and worse by the second.

"But what about the open cases?" I asked.

He thought about this for a moment. "I think you can handle those, but I wouldn't take anything else on until you talk to him. If we can't find him, of course, we can petition to keep the business open."

"So, I'm supposed to do nothing until Tate returns. I have to pay the bills for the agency and for myself. I don't think the utility and credit card companies will care all that much that I can't find Samantha's heir. They'll want their money."

He nodded. "I don't think it'll be much longer before we track him down. The police are looking too. He can't fall off the side of the planet. Everyone leaves a trail. We'll find him."

I took a breath. "What about the funeral? Do I need to wait until we find Tate for that?"

He opened a drawer in his desk. "The funeral is all planned, and Samantha wanted you to handle it."

He held out a large manila envelope to me. "I took the liberty of alerting the funeral home she chose. They'll transport the body as soon as the police release it. According to Officer Austin Caster, that should be in a few days."

Darby was written on the envelope.

Anger and confusion rushed through me. Samantha had pulled my business out from under me, yet she'd left me the task of making sure everything went well with her funeral. What kind of gift was that? Even with the confused emotions running through my head, I took the envelope. She was still my friend, my partner, and my mentor. She deserved her last wishes to be fulfilled.

I knew Samantha. There would be very little for me to do. She would've had it all perfectly planned. Just as she'd had the trust for Tate perfectly planned. She wouldn't have done that on a whim. She'd done nothing on a whim, which made it even odder that she'd wanted to sell the agency.

"Have you looked at it?" I asked.

He nodded. "There's a note in there for you. I haven't read it. It's sealed, but I did look at the general plans."

I sighed. "Thank you for contacting the funeral

home. I'm dealing with so much right now that it helps to have one thing off my plate."

"That's what I thought."

"We need to find Tate, and when we do, things will become easier."

I wasn't so sure about that. "I want this agency to continue for myself and for Samantha's legacy." There was only one problem with my wish: "But I can't afford to buy Tate's half of the business."

"Maybe Tate would be willing to let you work as a detective and just take the profits."

I frowned and wished Samantha had at least told me of her plans. Of course, I would've been upset that she had gone behind my back like this, but at least I would've been prepared. Who knows? Maybe I would've encouraged her to sell, just so I could start fresh and have the finances to at least salvage my home and the business. I could speculate for hours how differently things might have been, had I known. But one thing was for certain: I never would've done this to her.

I stood, holding the envelope to my chest.

"Darby, I don't know if this makes you feel any better, but Samantha cared about you a lot. She saw you as a younger sister, in her way."

I swallowed. I couldn't think of anything to say to that.

CHAPTER NINE

I LEFT PATRICK'S OFFICE WITH THE envelope in hand. Instead of going straight back to the agency, I walked to the lakeshore. There was a small boardwalk with a pavilion at the end. In the middle of the weekday, the boardwalk was almost completely empty, except for a grizzled elderly man sleeping on a park bench while holding a fishing rod.

I walked to the end of the pavilion and stood looking out at the water for a long while. I had to gather my strength to open that envelope.

Finally, I sat on a bench and lifted the tab. At the very top of the pile of papers inside, there was a white envelope with my name on it in Samantha's script. I opened that, too.

Dear Darby,

If you're reading this, I'm no longer with you. You've been a good friend and business partner to me. I couldn't have started Two Girls Detective Agency without you.

I'm sorry to leave this task of handling my funeral in your lap, but I trust you and know you will do everything as I asked. It won't be easy because by now, you will know that I changed my will and what is to become of my portion of the agency now that I am gone. I know this will come as a shock to you, and I know you are most likely angry at me but are feeling guilty about feeling angry, and angry with yourself for being angry. See? Don't I know you well?

I realize I should have told you my plan, and I hoped to do that someday. Well, actually, I'd hoped we'd both be retired and living luxuriously, with no need for this letter to see the light of day. But if you are reading this letter, I never worked up the nerve to do so sooner, and I'm sorry. I should have been braver. I'm sorry I wasn't.

I decided to give Tate my portion of the business. It has nothing to do with you. After he left the Army, Tate has bounced around the world with no anchor. I will let him tell you his story if he chooses. It's not my place to tell, and truthfully, I don't know it all—only what I have gleaned through brief phone calls and text messages over the years.

What I do know is Tate needs direction. He needs to be grounded. I worry about him. It's my hope that you and he can make something new after I'm gone. I have full faith in both of you that the agency will continue and be even better than when I was there.

Thank you for your friendship, Darby. It meant the world to me.

You're the sister I never had, and I love you.

Samantha

I stared at the letter. Why she'd had full faith in us that the agency would live on when she'd planned to dissolve it and work for Billows was a mystery. The letter was dated three years ago, so it was written at or around the time she'd changed her will. What had changed between then and now to make her not want the agency to continue?

I reread the last line, and tears fell from my eyes. I let them. The sleeping fisherman wouldn't care if he woke up and caught me crying, and there was no one else around.

I looked through the other items in the stack of papers. Besides the letter to me, the envelope included an itinerary of what she wanted to happen at her funeral. It was to be a simple graveside service. The on-call minister for the funeral home, whoever that happened to be at the time, would preside over it. She didn't ask for a wake or any celebration. There was no music planned or time for personalized speeches from the mourners.

But how was that fair to those grieving whom she left behind? She may have believed she was making this easier by making it so small and simple, but I was cheated out of celebrating her life.

I decided I would have the funeral as she wanted it, but there was nothing stopping me from having a wake to celebrate her life. I wouldn't even view it as a wake. It would be a party to celebrate Samantha. Hers was a life worth celebrating.

I'd talk to Maelynn about it. There was nothing my best friend loved better than planning a party. She'd been a room mom every year since her son had started school, and his class always had the most ridiculously elaborate parties.

Maelynn would handle that and I would handle the funeral and do my best to run the agency until the police or the attorney found Tate. Then, I would have to make a new game plan. Until then, this was what it had to be.

I got up from the bench, and old fisherman opened one eye as I walked by. "Blessed are those who mourn. That's what it says in the Good Book. You should count yourself lucky." He closed his eyes and seemed to go back to sleep with the sun's rays hitting his face.

I didn't feel lucky at all.

I could go back to the office to search for more clues about Samantha's death, or go to the coffee shop Maelynn owned to discuss the funeral with her. Instead of doing either, I walked in the direction of Samantha's Victorian home. It was a half mile from the agency. Anxious to get there, I started running when I was a quarter mile away. It wasn't the best idea I'd ever had in a leather jacket and boots.

I bent at the waist on her front lawn and caught my breath. When I stood up again, I examined the house. It seemed perfectly normal. The lawn was mowed, the bushes trimmed, and all the leaves were raked. Samantha had left everything just so. One might think she'd done that because she'd known she wouldn't be back to the house, but that was just Samantha. She was particular.

The wooden front steps to the porch creaked as I walked up them, each sound like a wail in the quiet of the morning.

I slipped my copy of her house key into the lock, and it turned with no problem. The door opened into the living room. I could see past a set of leather armchairs and a side table into the dining room. The stairs to the second floor were on my right. The light was dim, so I had only to guess which lump was the couch and which was a pile of blankets on the couch. That struck me as odd. Samantha wasn't the sort to leave piles of blankets lying about. They would all be neatly folded or, even more likely, neatly tucked into the linen closet and organized by color.

I turned on the light, and the lump moved.

"Ahhhh!" I screamed.

"Ahhhh!" the man tangled in blankets on the couch screamed back.

I grabbed the nearest thing I could find for a weapon. It was a hardcover book lying on an end table.

"Don't throw that at me!" The man protested, holding up his hands. "I know your mom is the head librarian, so I bet you could do some damage with that."

I lowered the book. "Tate?"

He smiled. "It's nice to see you too, Piper."

A flush came to my cheeks when I remembered. In

high school, Tate had called me Piper. I didn't know how I'd forgotten that.

In high school, he'd always had a trail of cheerleaders in his wake. He'd had an air of danger too, like he was up to no good. But that had been over a decade ago. I hadn't seen him since he'd graduated and gone into the service.

Tate looked much the same as he had in high school, but he was more muscular. I attributed that to the Army. His dark hair was longer and curled around his ears. Perhaps he'd rejected the short buzz-cut hairstyle after leaving the military. His beard was long and scruffy, and he had a deep tan. I wondered if we'd pulled him away from a Caribbean island. He wore jeans and a button-down shirt that could use a trip to the laundry, or maybe a one-way trip to the trash. His dark eyes bored into mine.

"How did you get in here?" I asked.

He stretched. "Samantha always kept a key hidden under a potted plant in the back yard for me, since I kept losing my keys."

"That's a dumb place to keep it. Someone could have broken in her house at any time."

"Well, it's been there for over fifteen years, so I would say it's okay. Are you going to put that book down now? I feel like the temptation to throw it at me will become too much and you'll hurl it at my head."

I dropped the book back on the table where I had found it. "You know about Samantha."

He broke eye contact with me and stared into the

unlit fireplace. "Yes, I do. The police notified me about my aunt dying."

"Where were you when you heard from them?"

"Why does that matter? I'm here, aren't I?"

I didn't say anything, but it mattered because if he was nearby at the time of the murder, he was a suspect. His inheritance certainly gave him a big enough motive.

He seemed to read something in my face, because he said, "I don't really have a set place to be. I float around and build my life as I go."

"Not all of us can walk away from responsibility so easily."

An irritated look crossed his face, but it was only there for a moment and then it was gone. "There's something to be said for giving responsibilities a break."

"I wouldn't know," I replied.

He smiled. "No wonder my aunt loved you so much. You were cut from the same cloth."

"Does Patrick Hartwell, her attorney, know you're here?"

"Not as far as I know." He cocked his head. "By the way, what are you doing here? How did you get in? I should be asking you these questions, since it's my aunt's house."

"I have a key."

He nodded. "Aunt Samantha always spoke highly of you."

My chest tightened.

"Samantha spoke about you often, too. She missed you."

He winced, and I wished I could grab the words out of the air and shove them back into my mouth. This was no way to start a new working relationship, even if Tate didn't know about the working relationship as of yet.

He squinted as if he was trying to avoid the sun. There was no sunlight on his face. More likely he was trying not to cry. I bit my lip. He had lost his aunt, the woman who had raised him to adulthood.

"It's the truth," he said. "I should've been around more."

I had regrets I had to live with, too, in relation to Samantha, but I knew better than to say that aloud.

He sat up straighter. "The police say she was murdered." He shook his head. "I know she was a P.I. but I never once thought that her life was in danger. She always seemed to be working on small-time crimes. They won't tell me if they have any suspects in the case."

I pressed my lips together. I wasn't going to tell him that he was looking at one right now—and so was I, for that matter.

He stood. "I imagine they're looking at you."

I gasped.

He chuckled. "Come on. You know as well as I do the people closest to a murder victim are the primary suspects."

He was right, but it didn't feel any better hearing it. "I can assure you I didn't do it. I'm not capable of murder, and I would never hurt Samantha."

"Anyone is capable of murder with the right motives." His brow furrowed as if he was remembering some dark moment from his time in the service.

He'd been stationed in Afghanistan during some of the fiercest fighting of the war. I imagined that he, of all people, would know what it felt like to take another person's life. Most likely more than just one. Was that why he'd left the service? He couldn't live with the shame of doing that? I wanted to ask but knew that now, when I'd just met him again after a decade, was not the time.

He rubbed his forehead. "Maybe if my aunt had been knocked over the head with a book, I would be more likely to believe you could have killed her, but you're not dumb enough to run her off the road with your own car."

"The police told you that too?"

He nodded.

"Stop acting like I'm going to hit you with a book," I said.

"You almost knocked me out cold. I can be a little salty about it." There was laughter in his eyes.

"Don't be ridiculous. If I hit you with the book, it wouldn't have done more than give you a bad bruise. If I really wanted to do damage, I would have hit you with a dictionary."

He laughed. "Duly noted. I will stay away from all dictionaries if you are in the room. Do people even have those anymore when everything is online?"

"My mother has a giant one at the library."

"I'm sure she does." He smiled. As he stood up from

the couch and stretched, I caught a peek of his flat midsection. I turned away.

He smiled as if he knew what I'd done. "Yeah, well, tell that to my cardiologist. I think you just about stopped my heart when you came in here."

"You were in the Army. I don't know how something I did could stop your heart."

A strange look crossed his handsome face. I wished I hadn't noticed how attractive he was. "Give me some time to freshen up. We have a lot to talk about. I'll change and we can talk."

I watched him go. While he was gone, I looked around the room. Just like her office, Samantha's house was pristine. The only signs of mess were clearly from Tate. There was the blanket on the floor where he'd tossed it when I held him at bookpoint, and an Army-issued knapsack by the door that looked like it had rolled down the side of a mountain. Maybe it had, considering Tate's wandering lifestyle. There were multiple rips in the bag's fabric that had been crudely sewn together with red, yellow, blue, and even pink thread. The threads in the knapsack told a lifetime's worth of stories, maybe two.

I glanced in the direction of the kitchen, where Tate had gone. A moment later, he came back into the living room. He was wearing the same clothes he'd had on before, but his face was damp, as if he had splashed water on it, and his hair was combed. "We should probably talk about what we want to do."

I frowned. "What do you mean?"

"Actually, what I really want to know is what happened to my Aunt Samantha and which one of your crazy clients killed her." He balled his fist, and I caught a glimpse of how angry he could be, as his brow furrowed and his eyes narrowed into slits. Could he become angry enough with Samantha that he'd run her off the road?

"I want to know that too," I said in a quieter voice.

"Tell me what you know." He sat on the couch and leaned forward, signaling he was ready to listen.

I fidgeted on the seat in the middle of the room as if I were on trial and he was the judge on the bench. In my work as a private detective, I had been asked to testify more than once, but I had never been on trial and wanted to keep it that way.

I moved to the armchair closest to the front door. "The police believe she was murdered by being forced off the road into the ravine."

"The car that ran her off the road had white paint. The officer told me that much."

"Who was the officer you spoke to?"

"He said his name was Caster."

"Austin Caster," I said. I didn't elaborate as to how well I knew Austin.

"His name is familiar. I think he was behind me in school." Tate shook his head. "If the police want to solve this case, they need to find that car. The owner of the car is most likely the killer."

My heart sank into my shoes.

"You know something about the car." He narrowed his eyes.

I didn't say anything. If I said the car was white and

my missing car was white, he'd come to the obvious conclusion that I was the prime suspect.

He narrowed his eyes more. "If you know something about that car, you need to tell me. Samantha was the only family I had in the world. I don't have anyone else now."

I hadn't known that. Samantha had told me once that her much-older brother and his wife had passed away when Tate had been a small boy, and even though she hadn't been much more than a child herself, she'd raised him on her own. She'd been so disappointed when he ran away and joined the Army. She'd wanted him to go into the agency with her and I knew I was a poor substitute. When he left the Army, she'd talked about him coming to New York to work with us. She had been upset when he'd decided not to, but I had been relieved. The agency was working well with the two of us, and of course Nat.

Tate stood up a little straighter. "I don't know what you're going to do, but I'm going to find the person who killed my aunt."

He stared me square in the eye. "I will discover who this person is. Even if it's you."

CHAPTER TEN

I LEFT SAMANTHA'S HOUSE WITH A feeling of dread. Not only did I have to contend with my friend and business partner's death, now I had to deal with both the police and her nephew thinking I killed her. And oh, did I mention that the nephew who thought I was a murderer was, in a way, my new boss? He might not know it yet, but it was only a matter of time.

My stomach growled. I needed food, but more than that, I needed information. I might get both at the local coffee shop. I also needed the friendly ear of my best friend. I walked back in the direction of Lakeshore Avenue. When I reached the agency, I continued down the street to Maelynn's coffee shop, Floured Grounds.

Leaves fell on my head and got stuck in my hair as I strolled past the historic homes—now businesses— that lined Lakeshore Avenue. Most of the businesses had autumn and even early Halloween decorations out on their front porches. In front of the local dog groomer's, a dog-shaped ghost windsock danced in the breeze, and the scent of fallen leaves in the air mingled with the fishy smell of the lake. There was a bite on the wind, but there was still a promise of blue-sky days, pumpkin pie, and apple picking. Everyone I passed on the sidewalk said hello and smiled at me. They were all friends and neighbors, but one of them had framed me for murder. I was unable to return the greetings.

It would have been the perfect early fall day if not for the black cloud hanging over me. Every time I thought of Samantha, tears threatened to fall again. I couldn't have that. I had to keep it together. It was what she would have wanted me to do.

Suddenly I questioned the wisdom of going to Floured Grounds. I knew that the moment I walked into the shop, Maelynn would take one look at my face and know something was wrong, and that was if she hadn't already heard through the rumor mill. She probably had by now.

Straw bales stood on either side of the coffee shop's front door, lined with white and more traditional orange pumpkins. Maelynn had what I called a pumpkin obsession, and she'd started selling pumpkin-flavored everything at the coffee shop the day after Labor Day and would continue it through the end of the year. She also decorated aggressively with the gourds. There was no question what her favorite member of the squash family was.

The pumpkin-shaped bell on the door rang as I entered. The shop was half full. It was early afternoon, so there was a smattering of young moms there with strollers, and a few businessmen and women who used Floured Grounds as their personal office space.

A group of knitters sat in one corner and chattered as their needles dipped in and out of their spools of yarn.

"Oh my God, you're alive!" Maelynn cried, and put a hand on her flawless brown cheek. My friend had a gorgeous complexion; as a teenager, I'd envied it. Who was I kidding? I envied her now. She was the most beautiful person I had ever seen in real life, but the funny thing was, she had no idea. She didn't know her curly black hair and piercing dark eyes were so striking.

Her husband Justin did, though, and I knew it, because if he was in the same room with Maelynn, she was his focus. She had married her high school sweetheart and, as a result, lived vicariously through my troublesome dating life. Maelynn loved a project, and I made a perfect one.

She blamed Austin for everything that went wrong in our relationship. Maybe that wasn't fair, but it was girl code. The guy was always wrong in girl code.

She hurried over to me and covered her mouth. "I'm sorry; that was a poor choice of words. I can't believe you're here! I mean, I'm glad you're here." She pulled me in for a quick, hard hug. "I've been calling and texting ever since I heard the news." She lowered her voice. "About Samantha. I'm so, so sorry."

I swallowed. There were those tears again, threatening to spill over. "Thank you."

"I even stopped by the agency and you weren't there," she said and enveloped me in another embrace. She smelled like coconut and coffee. "I wanted to go back again and sit on your porch until you came home, but Justin said I should give you some time. It must have been a terrible shock."

"It was," I admitted.

She glanced at the people in the coffee shop, and they were all staring at me with open mouths. Did they think, as the police did, that I'd killed Samantha? Was that what everyone was saying in the town? Had it already gone that far?

"Here." She tugged on my arm. "Have a seat at the counter and let me make you a latte." She examined me. "I know you're on a health food kick, but you are getting a dulce de leche, extra cream."

It had been so long since I had let myself have a sugary drink from Maelynn's shop, and at the moment, it sounded like just what the doctor ordered. "Okay." I took a breath. "It's bad, Mae. So bad."

"You cared about Samantha a lot, and you must be worried about the future of the business too."

I folded my hands on top of the table and clenched them together until the knuckles turned white. "It's not just that I'm sad. It's more complicated than that."

"The business, of course, but you will get it sorted. You always do." She put four pumps of caramel into the drink for me. It was going to be way too sweet. "But you lost a friend. We all lost a friend in Herrington last night. It's so awful. I always said something should be done about that turn."

I bit my tongue and wondered if I should tell Maelynn it was more than an accident: it was murder, and *I* was the main suspect. I wasn't sure I could deal with her shock, when I was still recovering from mine.

I'd never told Maelynn about Samantha's plan to dissolve the agency. I hadn't told anyone. I'd been hoping it would fall through and go away. Yeah, it had gone away now, but not in the way I'd wished.

"It's so much worse than I imagined," I said. "Much worse than anyone could have imagined."

She glanced around. There was no one else at the counter. "Tell me. I can help you."

I thought about this for a moment. I needed an ally, and Maelynn was my best friend. Even though there was no one around who might hear us, I was afraid to even utter the words in the lightest of whispers. I swallowed. "The police said she was murdered." I paused. "And I'm the number-one suspect."

"What?" Maelynn yelled.

Now everyone in the coffee shop was staring at us. Half of them were tourists. The other half were locals. I was more worried about the local reaction.

I waved at everyone. "I told her that her favorite ice cream was being discontinued. Nothing to see here."

"I can't believe this," Maelynn said, not registering my made-up story about the ice cream at all. "Are you sure it was murder?" She asked this in her normal speaking voice, which was admittedly louder than the average person's.

"Shh, do you want everyone in town to hear you? Because I sure don't."

"How do you know this?" she whispered.

"It's the direction the evidence is going, and it's what the police believe happened." I swallowed.

"Which police officer? They all come to the café

for their daily coffee, and I want to know which one of them will be getting decaf because he or she thinks you could kill someone."

I made a face.

"It was Austin, wasn't it? That toad. No, he's lower than a toad. He's a fly a toad eats. No, lower. He's—"

I held up my hand. "I get the idea."

She slapped her hand on the counter and got more strange looks from people in the coffee shop. "I'm really upset about that ice cream. It was my favorite flavor!" she said as loudly as she could without shouting. Then, more quietly, she said to me, "Austin said this to you, and to think I believed the two of you should get back together. Next time I see him, I will give him a piece of my mind, and he's never getting full caf here again."

"Please don't. The evidence is very clear. That's not Austin's fault. He's doing his job, and I think he needs the caffeine to keep at it." I pressed my hands on the counter.

"I can blame him if I want to, and I do."

I suppressed a smile. Despite the horrible day it'd been, it was nice to know my best friend had my back. Even so, I had to temper her enthusiasm for making Austin's life miserable.

"He was doing his job," I said again, a little less forcefully this time.

She reached across the counter and squeezed my hand. "I know this will get sorted out. Who better to find out what happened than you? You're the crack detective in this town."

I wished it were true, but finding lost pets and exposing sleazy business partners was a lot different than finding a killer. I didn't share this doubt with Maelynn, though. One of us needed to be confident in my abilities.

"You're right," I said. "If the police think it's me, I'm going to do my job and find out what really happened. It's all I can do. I'm a detective."

"Darn straight." She pumped her fist and then dropped her arm. "Do you know how to solve a murder?"

"The principles of deduction are the same, and I can't sit back and wait for Austin and the police to come to the right conclusion. I knew Samantha better than anyone. I spent more time with her than anyone else did. If anyone might be able to sort out what happened that night, it will be me."

A customer came up to the counter, and Maelynn held up a finger to me. "Hold that thought."

She rang up the customer and made his drink. All the while, I made a mental list of the people I needed to talk to and the places I needed to visit to follow Samantha's last movements. I had a greater sense of urgency, too. I didn't know when Tate would learn about his inheritance. When he did, that could change everything for me at the agency.

Maelynn thanked the customer for coming in and returned to me at the end of the counter. "What are you going to tell your parents?"

My parents had not been on the list of people to talk to.

"Why do I need to tell them anything?"

She cocked her head. "Girl, your mother is at the library right now probably hearing about Samantha's accident from five different patrons. I'm surprised she hasn't called you yet."

"I don't think—"

I was interrupted by my cell phone ringing. I pulled it out of my pocket and saw it was my mom's private line at the library. I showed Maelynn the screen.

She folded her arms across her chest. "Told you."

"I'm not sure I can deal with talking to her about this just yet. You know how she can be." I loved my mother, but she definitely was nosy with a capital N. She wanted to know everything about everything. I suspected that was why she'd chosen to be a librarian. She spent her days looking for information. She also wanted to know the most about her two daughters. She wouldn't rest until she had all the facts about what would happen.

In truth, I was the apple that didn't fall far from the tree. I was a private eye, after all. My career centered on finding the facts, too.

The call went to voicemail. My phone immediately began to ring again.

"If you don't pick up, she will keep calling until she drives you insane." She scooped the phone from my fingers. "Hello, Mrs. Piper," Maelynn said into the phone. "No... No... Darby is fine. She is...umm...dealing with the police right now, but..."

I groaned. I didn't think Maelynn telling my mom

that I was "dealing with the police" would be much comfort.

"Right...Right... I'll be sure to tell her to call you when she's free... You bet... I know, it's so sad... Okay...bye."

Maelynn ended the call and handed the phone back to me. "You owe me one."

I wrapped my hands around my mug. "I know. Thank you. You're the best friend any girl could have."

She nodded. "Don't you forget it, but I won't be able to put your mother off forever."

I nodded. "I know. I'm going to talk to my parents about it. I just need a little more time before I'm inundated with questions."

"Understandable. Is there anything I can do for you? I mean, other than feed you sugar and coffee all day?"

"Actually, there is." I went on to tell her about Samantha's funeral. "She didn't ask for it in her plans, but I would really like to have a wake, or more a celebration-of-life party for her. I feel like I need to do more."

She held up her hand. "Say no more. I'm on it. We will have the party right here after the funeral. I'll take care of it. You don't have to think about a single thing. Just let me know when the funeral will be."

I stood up. "Thank you, Maelynn. I don't know what I'd do without you. I have to get going on this case. It's the biggest of my life."

"You barely touched your latte," she said in dismay. "Let me put it in a to-go cup for you, and you need to eat something. Justin made a fresh batch of your favorite orange scones as soon as we heard the news. He felt so bad for you. He went to the market to pick up a few things. I know he'll be sad to have missed you."

She removed a scone from the display case and tucked it in a small brown paper bag. "If you need anything, you know where to find me."

I took the bag from her hand, and she leaned over the counter and kissed me on the cheek. "We'll get through this."

I nodded and tears sprang to my eyes, making speech impossible. I exited, taking my latte and scone with me.

CHAPTER ELEVEN

I HAD MADE IT TO THE sidewalk outside of Floured Grounds when I heard brisk footsteps behind me.

"Darby Piper, I need to talk to you."

I turned around to find a very angry Logan Montgomery standing just four feet from me.

Logan was a self made man who owned a small chain of local gyms in western New York, and he was also on Herrington's town council. In his fifties, with silver hair and the physique of a man who worked out every day of his life, which he did, Logan was handsome. I'd thought that he and Samantha had worked because they were both small business owners and because neither one of them had ever talked about the need or desire to get married. Even so, I'd thought they were happy, which was why I had been so surprised when she said they had broken up.

Before I could say anything, he asked, "Did you send the cops to my house?"

I blinked. "What?"

"Officer Louter said you were the one who told them Samantha and I had broken up."

I didn't say anything. In my line of work, I had learned to wait and see what the other person had to say before speaking my mind. It served me well when dealing with criminals.

He threw his hands in the air. "How could you mislead them like that? Now they're looking at me as a suspect."

I felt a little bit of relief when he said that. At least I wasn't the *only* suspect as far as the police were concerned.

"Samantha said the two of you broke up," I said.

"We weren't broken up. We were on a break. All couples have breaks."

I knew that wasn't true, even if my own experience with Austin wasn't a good example. "The police have to look everywhere to find out who did this to her. Don't you want them to catch the person?"

He closed his eyes for a moment. "Of course I want that. I loved Samantha. I'm heartbroken over what happened." He reopened his eyes.

I studied him. There was no evidence of tears. He didn't look that heartbroken to me. "How did you find out?"

"The police stormed into a town council meeting this morning and practically accused me of running her off the road!"

I winced. "Officer Louter did that?"

"Yes, it was Louter," he snapped.

I wasn't surprised. Louter liked to make a scene

and throw around his authority as a police officer. In a small town like Herrington, there wasn't much opportunity for that except with the rebel kids smoking outside the high school.

"Where were you last night?"

He narrowed his eyes. "Do you think I'm a suspect, too?"

"The boyfriend—or in this case, ex-boyfriend—is always a suspect." I took a step back. "I don't have to tell you that."

He glared at me. "I was at home. Alone with my dog."

The dog wouldn't make any better a witness for him than my cat Gumshoe did to prove I was home when Samantha was killed.

He took two steps toward me. "Stop and think before you point fingers, Darby. If you're not careful, you could get burned."

I scowled up at him and refused to step back further. "Are you threatening me?"

"No, I'm warning you." He pushed me aside and stomped away, and for the first time, I actually thought Logan was capable of murder.

By the time I made it back to the agency, I was more than a little shaken. Inside the reception room, Gumshoe blinked at me, and I blinked back. How much time did I have before Tate found out that most of the agency and most of the building I stood in would be his?

I called Nat, who answered on the third ring. There was an audible sniffle. "Oh, Darby, I don't know what we are going to do without Samantha. She was the heart of that place."

"I know."

"Is it true the police think she was murdered?"

"That's what they told me," I said.

"Do they think you're responsible?"

I pang a stab in my chest. "Why do you ask that?"

"I mean, they probably figure you have the most to gain from Samantha's death—the agency and the house you live in." She sniffled again. "Another officer stopped by and asked me when was the last time I saw your car."

My breath caught. "What did you say?"

"That I couldn't remember. You hardly ever drive it."

The knot in my stomach that had been there on and off all day returned.

"I know you didn't do it, and I told the police that," she went on before I could reply.

"Who was the officer who asked you about the car?"

"Austin Caster. He interviewed me an hour ago. He had a lot of questions about your relationship with Samantha. I told him he should already know the answers to most of those questions, since the two of you—er—well, you know."

I did.

"I know this is tough, Nat," I said. "It's tough for both of us. Can you come to work tomorrow?"

"Of course."

"Good. I need your help. Tate Porter is in town."

"Samantha's nephew. I forgot about him. What's he

doing in Herrington? How'd he get here so fast? How long has he been here?"

The stomach knot tightened just a little. They were all good questions and ones I could've asked Tate when I'd stumbled upon him in Samantha's house. Had he been here long enough to steal my car and run his aunt off the road?

"He never paid much attention to his aunt," Nat went on to say. "After she raised him, too. It was a disgrace."

I took a breath and told her what Patrick had revealed to me about the will.

"What?" she yelled in my ear.

Nat was still in the middle of a rant over Samantha's will when I hung up. I hoped she would get most of her objections out of her system before she came into work the next day. I wasn't happy about this turn of events, either, but all we could do was accept it and prepare for what came next. I went back to searching for a reason that someone would want to kill Samantha.

An hour later, I was no closer to that answer. I sat in the middle of the main office floor surrounded by files, looking for something—anything—that would give me a clue as to what had happened to my friend and mentor. I slapped the folder I was holding on top of the others. There was nothing here. I had a long list of all the cases Samantha had worked in the last six months, but not one of them looked like they would lead to her death.

There was a knock at the front door and I frowned.

I had canceled all the appointments for the day, so I wasn't expecting anyone.

I stood up, and it took a moment to realign my spine because I'd been hunched over the files for so long.

The knock came again. It was different from the police knock that had woken me in the middle of the night. The *tap-tap-tap* came again, and I groaned. I knew who was at the door. I should have expected this. My mother.

I tried to push the files into some semblance of a pile before I stood up and walked to the front door. I saw her perfectly made-up face through the peephole. I let out a breath. I supposed I should have been happy that she'd waited until after work to come over. It must've driven her crazy, barely hearing from me throughout the day, and it must've been difficult learning about Samantha's death from library patrons and dealing with their questions about it. Other than Maelynn's coffee shop, the library was where the townsfolk went to get the latest news.

My mother bustled into the house. As always, she had a tote bag of books on her arm. She carefully set the tote by the door and enveloped me in a hug. Her blond hair was perfectly styled, and her figure was perfectly trim. Everything was perfect when it came to my mother—her appearance, her home, her library—and she wanted the same for her children.

Mom stepped back. "I took the liberty of pulling a number of books for you that will help. We have a nice section in the library about grief and dealing with adversity."

I nodded. I should have expected this. There was nothing that my mother didn't believe was fixable with the right book. "Thanks, Mom."

She peeked into the waiting room where my stacks of folders were all over the floor. "What happened in here?"

"I've been organizing." As a librarian, organizing anything was a project she could get behind.

My younger sister DeeDee walked in a few steps behind her. She was wearing a Herrington Cheerleader sweatshirt and leggings. Her silky blond hair was pulled back in a ponytail, and there wasn't a single flaw on her face. She was the queen of the high school. It was so different than the role I'd played there. I'd done whatever I could to blend in. I hugged her and she searched my face. "Sorry, Darb."

Words lodged in my throat. Her small condolence hit me harder than anyone else's had since I had heard the news about Samantha's death.

I hugged her again. My little sister was a head taller than me. She not only got our mother's looks, but our father's height. Genetics could be so cruel.

My mother was in the waiting room picking up files. She alphabetized them while she apprised the rest of the office. She couldn't help it. The need to put things in order was ingrained in her. She was the one who'd kept our lives together after my father's diagnosis. I couldn't fault her for being able to soldier on. She was a pro at that.

"Have you spoken to anyone about the funeral?" she asked.

I blinked at her, but then, I shouldn't have been surprised. "Samantha left instructions for me as to how she wanted the funeral to go."

My mother nodded. "That sounds like her. She was always so organized." She and Samantha had been on the same page when it came to perfectly orchestrated lives.

I needed to change the subject. "How's Dad?" Stress, or in this case, stress about his children, could bring on one of his seizures at any time. I hoped he wasn't feeling poorly because of what I was going through.

"He's fine. I told him," Mom said. "I didn't go into many details. It would help if you stopped by the house soon to reassure him you're all right."

I nodded. Dad would be worried about me. He would know of Samantha's death—at this point, it was doubtful anyone in Herrington had missed it—but I prayed the news about my being a suspect in her murder wouldn't get to him.

Mom and DeeDee helped me clean up the files, and I told Mom that Samantha's nephew was in town. I didn't add anything about Tate's inheritance. She didn't need to know that yet. It took some work, but I finally convinced DeeDee and my mother that I was fine. At least fine enough for them to leave.

Five minutes after they left, someone knocked on the door again. I sighed. I knew it was my mother again. She wouldn't give up that easily. I bet she wanted me to stay the night.

I threw open the door. "Mom, I don't—"

The words died on my lips.

Tate Porter stood on my doorstep—or should I say, he stood on *his* doorstep.

CHAPTER TWELVE

"**A**RE YOU GOING TO LET me into my own building?" Tate asked.

I squeezed the doorknob but didn't move. "Did Patrick tell you about Samantha's will?"

"Why yes, he did. What I don't know is why you didn't mention it when I saw you this morning."

I frowned at him. "It wasn't my place to do so."

He laughed. "I don't think that's your reason, but I'll let it go for now." He tried to peek around me. "Can I come in?"

As much as I didn't want to let him inside the agency, I didn't have much choice in the matter, as he did own sixty percent of it. I stepped back. "What did Patrick tell you exactly?"

Tate looked around the foyer and into the reception room like he was assessing the value of the space. Was he going to sell like Samantha had planned to do?

"Her home is mine, and her portion of the agency, including this building, is too. He wants me to think about what I want to do with it."

I stepped into the reception room, and he followed me. As soon as we walked inside the room, Gumshoe hissed and ran past Tate up the stairs to my apartment.

"What was that?" he asked.

"My cat."

"It looked like pillow filling with legs."

I scowled at him and folded my arms. "When exactly did you arrive in Herrington?"

He smiled. "Are you asking me if I arrived before my aunt was murdered?"

"Yes."

"I appreciate your honesty. I've been in western New York for a couple of weeks."

"Samantha didn't mention you were in town."

"I wasn't in Herrington, and she didn't know I was in New York. I was planning to come see her, but I just arrived the afternoon before she died."

"So you saw her," I said.

"No. I got to her house about four o'clock and let myself in with the hidden key. I planned to surprise her."

"Or scare her," I said, remembering how startled I had been when I'd discovered Tate lying on Samantha's couch. Before he could say anything to that, I added, "Samantha didn't go home at all that day? She left the agency in the afternoon, and that was the last time I saw her."

"Was she working a case?" He narrowed his stance and folded his arms.

I nodded. "She always was." I had to glue myself

in place to stop from stepping farther away from him. There were about seven feet between us. I could easily escape if he came at me, but I still felt the urge to put more distance between us. Tate had been in Herrington when Samantha had died. He checked two of the boxes: motive and opportunity.

"So you were in the village when she died," I said.

"So were you."

"What's that supposed to mean?"

"You were in Herrington, too, and you had motive to kill her. Patrick told me you didn't know she'd changed her will. He said you thought you were to inherit the agency."

I ground my teeth. Thanks, Patrick.

"In fact, you are the more likely killer because I didn't know about the will, so not knowing shows I didn't have a motive."

"You *claim* not to have known," I said. "There is no way to prove you didn't. Samantha could have told you."

We stared at each other. Neither of us moved. Looking at him, I noticed he had green flecks in his blue eyes. I found them disconcerting and looked away first.

Tate's posture relaxed. "Where do we go from here?"

"That's a good question."

He shook his head. "Come on. You're a P.I. Don't pretend you're not going to try to find out what happened."

I didn't say anything.

"I knew it. You are. If you are, so am I."

I put my hands on my hips. "You're not a private investigator."

He looked around the reception area. "Since I own this place now, I kind of am."

"You don't have a license."

"A mere technicality." He smiled. "Look, I want to find out what happened to my aunt just as much as you do, if not more. Maybe the best way to do that is work together, and we can keep an eye on each other at the same time."

I frowned.

"If you think I killed her, it will be your best way to keep tabs on me," he said.

He had a point there.

"Fine, but I take the lead. I'm the one with the P.I. license."

He held up his hands. "Sure thing, boss. Do the cops have any leads on who might have done it? Patrick was a little cagey when it came to that point."

I decided it would be best just to come and out and say it. "I guess Patrick was hesitant to tell you because the police think I was the one who killed her. Maybe he was showing a little bit of loyalty to me," I grumbled.

Tate nodded. "Since we've already established we both have motive and opportunity, who else is on your list?"

I pressed my lips together but then said, "It could be an old client. There are two potential business scams. Then there's the Multigrain case. It's the local health food store, and one of the partners in the store thinks the other is skimming money. He would like us to discreetly find out for sure. The other case involves a local stable. The owner thinks one of his trainers isn't reporting all her clients."

"Any others?"

"The open case is a woman in her forties, Quinn Stark, looking for her birth mother. I don't know how or why she would have motive to kill Samantha."

"What if the adoptive mom doesn't want her to know who her birth mom is and killed Samantha to stonewall the investigation?"

"That's a little farfetched. The adoption was decades ago." Before he could protest more, I held up my hand. "Besides, both adoptive parents of the woman are dead, which is what spurred her on to find out about her birth mom."

"Is that it?" Tate asked.

"Well," I paused. "There is also Councilman Logan Montgomery." I thought about my uncomfortable confrontation with Logan on the sidewalk earlier.

He snapped his fingers. "That's right. Her boyfriend. I should have thought about him first."

"Her ex-boyfriend," I corrected.

"Angry enough about the breakup to kill?" Tate asked.

"It's hard to fathom Logan doing that, but he was plenty mad when he thought I turned the police on him. He doesn't have an alibi."

"He's a keeper."

I frowned, suddenly feeling unsure about sharing my list with him. He was a suspect, too. I hadn't told him everything, though. I'd kept Samantha's connection to Lake Waters close to my chest for two reasons. I didn't want him talk to Billows before I got the chance, and I didn't want him to follow his aunt's lead and close the agency.

"You seem deep in thought," Tate said.

"Murder will do that to you."

"Listen," he said. "Let's talk this more over dinner. I'm starving and plan to head to the Fish Shack for some food. It was my favorite place to eat as a kid. Aunt Samantha used to take me there for special occasions. I could use the company. Maybe we can put our heads together and come up with more suspects."

"I—I'd better stay here and see if I can find anything more that might give us a clue as to what happened to her."

His mouth turned downward, and I immediately felt bad for turning down his offer. But how could I sit across from him and eat seafood when I thought he might have killed Samantha? What would I say? *Hey, can you pass the cocktail sauce, and did you kill your aunt?*

Tate walked to the door. "Well, the invitation still stands if you want to join me." He opened the front door.

"Thanks, but I do have a lot of work to do."

He stood in the open doorway and looked at me. "I didn't kill my aunt, Darby."

For some reason, I really wanted to believe him, but I said nothing. He closed the door.

CHAPTER THIRTEEN

S TARTING THE NEXT MORNING, NAT and I spent the entire day fielding calls from anxious clients who had heard about Samantha's death. I half-expected Tate to pop in the agency at any moment, ready to play detective. I had some regrets about not going with him to the Fish Shack last night. It might have been my one and only opportunity to grill him in a safe and public place. I had a feeling the offer would not be made a second time.

When the calls finally slowed, I went through the three open files. I started with Quinn Stark, the woman searching for her birth mom, and didn't get any further than that. Quinn worked at the front desk at Lake Waters Retreat. I smiled. This was the opening I had been waiting for to snoop at the resort.

I told Nat I was going out to follow up on a case, and she didn't even look up from her computer.

Instead of walking or running to Lake Waters Retreat, I decided to drive. The big problem was, my car was missing. So I hurried to Floured Grounds.

Maelynn smiled at me as I walked through the front door. "I've been working on the party for Samantha. You don't have to worry about a thing."

"Thank you. I heard from Pat this morning. The police have released Samantha's body to the funeral home. Do you think we can have the party tomorrow?"

"Not a problem," Maelynn said without batting an eye.

"You are the best. I don't know what I would do without you."

"You'd manage, but just barely." She grinned.

"You're right about that, because I actually stopped by to ask you another favor."

She nodded. "Okay. Anything."

"Can I borrow your car?"

Maelynn knew my car had been stolen, so I didn't have to explain why I was asking.

"You want to borrow the minivan? It's not a great getaway car."

"No one would think your minivan was any kind of getaway car. But I still need to follow up on some leads."

She nodded and poked her head into the kitchen. "Justin, I'm going outside with Darby!"

There was a muffled response.

She looked back at me. "He's testing a new cookie recipe. It's not a good time to talk to him."

I nodded. I knew how seriously Justin took his recipes. I followed Maelynn out of the front door of the café and around the side of the house that she and her husband had converted into a coffee shop. Just like at the agency, there was a small single-car garage behind Maelynn's shop. She opened the garage door, revealing the blue minivan.

Maelynn reached into her pocket and pulled out the van keys. There was a palm-size beaded turtle on the keyring. "Justin bought me that so I wouldn't lose the keys." She dropped them in my open palm.

"I don't know how you could lose these," I said. "And I'm an expert at losing car keys."

She laughed. "You need the wheels to find out who killed Samantha?"

I nodded. "I'm going to Lake Waters."

"You think that place is involved?"

I bit my lip and debated telling her about Samantha's plans to close the agency and work for Matt Billows. If I couldn't trust my best friend, who could I trust? I decided to tell her.

"Darb, that makes you look even more like a suspect."

"Please don't remind me."

She shook her head. "I don't like the idea of you out there alone trying to solve this case. Whoever killed Samantha went to a lot of trouble to steal your car and frame you. This is not a spontaneous crime."

I shivered. "I know, but I don't think anyone will expect to see me in this car."

She nodded. "You're going deep undercover. Soccer-mom style."

I laughed.

"I'd better get back to the shop. Justin hates to

watch the counter when he's in a creative mood." She turned to go and then stopped. "Be good to Berta?"

"Berta?" I looked around.

"The car. Rogan named her."

"I'll take care of her."

Maelynn headed to the front of the coffee shop, and I climbed into the van. It smelled like baked goods and old gym socks. The first was from her business and the second was from her eleven-year-old son, Rogan, who played every sport you could imagine. It seemed that Rogan's socks were always stinky.

I rolled down the window and started the engine. No one would expect to see me in this car. Maelynn was right. I was going undercover—deep undercover.

On my way to Lake Waters, I drove by Mrs. Berger's house and glanced at it. I didn't see Mrs. Berger, but Romy sat on the front porch rail twitching his long orange tail back and forth. I sighed. I suspected there was another feline rescue in my near future.

Lake Waters Retreat lay behind an iron gate and a stone wall. A sign that said *Beware of Dog* was affixed to the gate. Every time I'd driven, run, or walked by the gate, it had been closed.

There was a buzzer on the wall, so I stopped my car beside it and as I reached out to press it, I heard a noise.

"Psst!"

I dropped my hand from the keypad.

"Psst! Psst!"

The sound was coming from the trees to my left. I

poked my head out of the minivan window and started to look in that direction.

"Don't look at me. If you look at me, Lake Waters will be able see you looking on the surveillance cameras. We don't want that!"

"Benny B, is that you?"

"The one and only," he said back. "Also, I didn't know that you were a mom."

"What are you talking about?"

"The mom wheels."

I sighed. "I'm not. I borrowed the minivan from a friend."

"Because your car was stolen," he whispered back. "And possibly used in the murder of Samantha Porter."

"How do you know? You're a paparazzo trying to make a buck."

"A man's got to eat. Besides, I already told you," his whispered. "I prefer 'celebrity photographer.'"

"I would guess the celebrities you stalk at the retreat don't call you that."

"They don't," he agreed. "They use much more colorful language."

"I bet." I turned my head toward the bushes.

"Don't look at the bushes," he snapped. "How many times do I have to tell you?"

"What do you want?" I snapped.

"Your cooperation."

"What do you mean?"

"I think we can help each other. You help me get inside and get the photos I need to make my deadline, and I will tell you what I know about your friend."

My pulse quickened. "What do you know about Samantha?"

"No, no, no, that's not how it works. You get me in, and then I tell you."

The buzzer on the side of the stone wall sounded. "Can we help you?"

I jumped. "I—I'm looking for registration?"

The gate opened without another comment from the faceless voice on the intercom.

I hesitated before I drove through. "Benny B?" I whispered.

There was silence in return. Benny B was gone.

CHAPTER FOURTEEN

I 'D LIVED IN HERRINGTON SINCE I was ten, but I had only been through Lake Waters' gates a handful of times. Billows and his employees were very careful who they let inside in order to protect the clients who didn't want the world to know where they were. Honestly, I was surprised when I wasn't questioned at the buzzer about who I was and what I was doing there. Maybe the minivan made me look less threatening.

A long, tree-lined road led into the property, with thick forest on either side. To my right, I passed a narrow driveway, and I saw a mansion in the trees, Matt Billows' home. Lake Waters had stood on the shores of Seneca Lake since the 1920s, and the Billows family had always lived there.

The tires of Maelynn's van rolled over fallen leaves that were scattered across the road. Then the trees opened up and I could see the grand resort hotel with the sparkling lake in the background.

The main building was four stories high and built in the Greek revival style. Six fifty-foot-high pillars dominated the front of the building. In front of it curved a circular driveway. A limo was parked in the driveway, and an elderly woman wearing what I could only believe was a real fur coat stepped into the car. Her driver shut the door, and the limo rolled away. I parked the minivan in the small lot to the right of the building and surveyed my outfit: combat boots, jeans, leather jacket. Maybe I should've taken the time to change.

There was no time to worry about that now. I smoothed a wrinkle out of my T-shirt and walked toward the building.

The main foyer of the Lake Waters was gorgeous, with black-and-white marble floors. A chandelier hung high overhead and sparkled as light poured in from the floor-to-ceiling windows.

However, the most striking thing about the foyer was the stillness. I was trying to remember the last time I'd been there. It must have been five or six years ago. At the time, the main building had been bustling with staff hurrying about and guests checking in and out.

There was no one at the concierge's desk as I passed and headed to the main desk, which was also empty. "Hello? Hello?" I called.

No one answered, and then I saw a bell on the desk. I rang it, and a moment later a woman in a dark suit and pink blouse came out of the back room. She eyed me. I guessed I wasn't her usual guest by a long shot. "May I help you?"

"I hope so." I gave her my best smile. "I'm looking for Quinn Stark."

"I'm Quinn Stark." The woman raised a perfectly penciled-on eyebrow.

I held out my hand. "Darby Piper from Two Girls Detective Agency."

"Oh." Her face cleared, and she shook my hand. "I thought that my case was being dropped because, well, Samantha..."

"No, I'm Samantha's partner and will be taking over the case, but it would help if you brought me up to speed. Is now a good time?"

"Yes." She sighed. "I don't have any new guests coming in today."

I was surprised, but I reminded myself it was the middle of the week. Most of Lake Waters' registration probably happened on the weekend.

"Why don't we talk over in the waiting area?" She pointed at a cluster of expensive-looking couches across from the reception desk. "That way I can keep an eye on the desk just in case anyone comes in."

I walked over and sat down, and Quinn sat across from me with her eye on the door.

"Thank you for coming. I have been meaning to call the agency about my open case, but I wanted to give it some time. I'm so very sorry about Samantha."

"Thank you."

"Is it true she died at the top of the hill just a little ways from here?"

I nodded.

She shook her head. "I hate that curve. I go that

way home, but only when it's light out. I wonder if Herrington will do something about it now that there's been such a terrible accident."

"I think the town will take notice now." I cleared my throat. "Now, I have read your file, so I have the basics. However, I would like you to fill me in on your case."

She folded her hands in her lap and studied them. "I was adopted as an infant in 1977. My adopted parents, whom I loved dearly, are both gone now, and I have been thinking more and more about my roots. It's something I want to share with my eight-year-old daughter. She asks me all the time about where we came from, and I don't have the answers for her."

"Have you thought about taking one of those DNA tests to learn your ancestry?"

"I have. I actually took two from two different companies. They both said the same thing: that I'm mostly Northern European with some Arab ancestry as well. That was a surprise, and it got me interested in Arab culture, but I couldn't trace my birth mother from either."

I nodded. If no one related to her had taken the test, she wouldn't get very far with it.

"After I did those tests, I contacted Samantha. I had met her a few times here at the resort when she had meetings with Mr. Billows. She was always so nice."

I tried to hide my surprise to learn that Samantha had taken several meetings at Lake Waters. How long had she been talking to Billows about taking the head security job?

"When did you ask Samantha to look into the case?"

"Six months ago. She was very thorough, telling me every avenue she had taken to find my birth mom."

"And when did you first meet her?"

She frowned.

"I'm trying to get a handle on how long you have been working on this issue," I explained.

"Well, I suppose it was February. I know it was cold. The resort was desolate. No one wants to come here in February, even under the best circumstances."

That had been eight months ago. Samantha had been talking to Billows about working for him for that long? I'd heard about the possibility just a few weeks ago. What else had my business partner kept from me? And why did she keep *that* from me? I squeezed my hands in my lap and told myself to keep my cool.

Quinn twisted her wedding ring back and forth on her finger. "Do you think you can find her?"

"I'll try. It would be helpful if you could email the results from those DNA tests to my office." I removed a business card from my jacket pocket. "My cell number and email are on the card."

She took the card in her hands. "Thank you."

"When Samantha was here, did people at the resort know she was thinking of working here?"

She tucked the card into her jacket pocket. "Not at first. I thought maybe she was here to help Mr. Billows."

"Help with what?"

Before she could answer, the front door to the resort opened, and a man stomped inside. "Quinn, what is this about the front gate? It's working fine." He was a broad man who wore a dark suit. I realized that must be part of the uniform for employees at Lake Waters. There was no way I could work here based on the dress code alone.

Quinn jumped off the couch.

The man folded his arms. "Are you sitting down on the job? Aren't you supposed to be recruiting guests?"

"I was chatting with..." She trailed off.

Anyone who saw me would immediately know I wasn't a guest of Lake Waters.

"Who are you?" he asked.

I stood up. "I'm Darby Piper from Two Girls Detective Agency."

He stepped forward. "What are you doing here?"

"She's meeting with me, Cliff," Quinn said.

"You can't have visitors at work. You know how Mr. Billows feels about that."

"It's not her fault," I said. "I didn't tell her I was coming."

"That must be a habit with Two Girls," Cliff said.

"What do you mean by that?"

"Samantha Porter seemed to make a habit of dropping in whenever she liked."

"Who are you?" I asked him.

"Cliff Ritter. I'm the head of security at Lake Waters Retreat."

I stared at him. He held the job Samantha was supposed to get, which meant he had a motive. "How long have you been in that position?"

"Thirty years." He turned on Quinn. "What are you doing, taking a break on the job? You're part of the reason we're struggling right now."

Quinn stood as well. "There's no one here, Cliff. I think even you can see that."

"I was speaking to Quinn on a private matter," I said. "It has nothing to do with the resort."

Cliff glared at me. "In that case, I will kindly ask you to leave. This exclusive resort is for employees and guests only."

"I'll go. But before I leave...were you aware Matt Billows offered Samantha Porter the head of security job here?"

He glowered at me. "Yes, I knew. Mr. Billows thought he was doing me a favor and said I should be thinking about retirement at my age. He doesn't care that I'm not ready to go, or that his father would roll over in his grave over the way he's treated me. His father handpicked me as the head of security after the last one died."

"The last head of security being Samantha's father, Joshua Porter?" I asked.

"That's right. I took over right after he passed on. I've done an excellent job since then, and now Mr. Billows is trying to force me into retirement. He said Samantha had special skills to protect our celebrity clients from the paparazzi. I can do that. Who do you think has been doing it all this time since her father died?"

I couldn't help but wonder how far Cliff would go

to keep Samantha from taking his job. "When was the last time you saw Samantha?"

He shrugged. "I don't know. Two or three days ago."

"She was here Monday afternoon," Quinn said.

I suppressed a shiver. That was the day she died.

"I suppose in the end, it won't matter when this place shuts down. We'll all be out of work," Cliff said.

"Mr. Billows has a plan," Quinn argued.

Cliff snorted. "He's going to have to come up with a lot more than some high-priced rejuvenation center to convince people to come back here."

I glanced from Quinn to Cliff and back again. "Is the retreat struggling that badly?"

"Do you see anyone here?" Cliff asked. "If Lake Waters wants to compete with other rejuvenation retreats like it, it needs to up its game. The treatments and facials of the twentieth century aren't going to appeal to today's rich and famous. They haven't for over a decade."

This was an interesting piece of information, but it made it even more confusing as to why Billows would want to hire Samantha as head of security and why Samantha had been giving the struggling resort such serious consideration. Had she been talking to Billows for eight months because she'd been unsure how stable Lake Waters actually was? What had Samantha been thinking about all of this?

"Now, I will ask you to leave. Employees can't have visitors during work hours." He eyed his colleague. "And Quinn knows that."

She rolled her eyes, and I thanked both of them before I went out the door.

I'd wanted to snoop around the resort some more, but that was impossible with Cliff looking on. I would have to find a reason to come back. I could think of several, and one of them was called Benny B.

CHAPTER FIFTEEN

I WENT BACK TO THE AGENCY with two more suspects on my list: Benny B and Cliff Ritter. I couldn't think of a reason Benny B would want to kill Samantha. Just to snag a big story? Seemed unlikely. Cliff, however, looked more feasible, if only by a fraction. He'd been about to lose his job to Samantha. People killed for less than that.

I opened the front door to the agency and heard laughter coming from the reception area. I frowned and walked in to see Nat chuckling with Tate. I stood in the archway.

"Darby, there you are," Tate said. "Nat said you were working a case and would be back soon. I thought I would wait for you."

I forced myself to relax. I didn't want Tate to know how much it unnerved me to find him in the office joking with Nat. The fact that he already seemed at home here was unsettling.

"Where were you?" Tate asked.

I bit the inside of my lip. "I went to talk to the woman looking for her birth mom." I stepped into the room. "She was a dead end." I turned my attention to Nat. "Any calls come in while I was gone?"

She shook her head. "Unless you count your mother. Sometimes I think she calls the office to get you because she knows I will always answer the phone."

"Probably," I muttered.

Tate stood a few feet away from me with his arms folded. "I thought we agreed to work on this case together, and you went off and spoke with a suspect alone."

"Sorry. I didn't think to ask you to come along. I'm used to working cases alone. Even when working with Samantha, we rarely worked the same cases unless one of us needed help."

"This is a case where you need help," Tate said.

"Tate is right," Nat said. "You've never worked a homicide before."

"You too, Nat?"

She smiled and stood up. Then she pulled her purse out the large bottom drawer of her desk. "It's my lunchtime. I will leave you to it." She reached into her purse, came up with a penny, and dropped it into the jar on her desk. "Play nice, you two."

After she shut the front door behind her, I groaned. "What am I supposed to do if you two band against me like this?"

"What else did you learn?"

I sighed and I told him about Benny B as a possible suspect. "It's farfetched, I admit, but I can't rule him out just yet."

"Where do we go from here? Because I'm coming with you, wherever it is."

I studied him for a long moment. "I still have to visit the stables. You interested?" He nodded. "Let's go, then."

I sighed and walked out of the agency. Tate pulled up short when I unlocked the minivan, which I had parked in the middle of the driveway.

"You own a minivan?" he asked.

"I borrowed it from a friend."

He folded his arms. "Would that be because your car was stolen and might have been used in Samantha's accident?"

I stared at him. "How did you know that?"

"Why didn't you tell me?"

"The police don't know it was used in the accident. They won't know until the car is found. Now, who told you?"

"Nat and I had a nice chat," he said.

I rubbed my forehead. I should've told Nat not to tell Tate anything about the case. He was Samantha's nephew, but what did we really know about him? Besides, all she did was convince him I was an even better suspect for the murder.

Tate opened the passenger side door to the van and climbed in. Before he shut the door, he asked, "You coming?"

I stalked to the other side of the minivan and got in.

Twenty minutes later, I turned Maelynn's minivan into the gravel parking lot of Seneca Stables. Horseback riding was one of the favorite pastimes for vacationers around the Finger Lakes, and there were nervous-looking riders on horses ready to go on a trail ride. I guess most of them were vacationers. How many of them were staying at Lake Waters, if any at all?

While I parked, Tate unbuckled his seat belt. "Who are we seeing here?"

"Melinda Grimes. She's one of the trainers here. The owner thinks she's giving private lessons on his horses and pocketing the money."

"That's wrong?"

"Since she's using his stables and horses, she's supposed to turn the money in to the office. She's on salary as a horse trainer."

"Ahh.

What's the verdict? Is he right?"

I pulled a photograph out of a manila envelope and showed it to him. It was of Melinda with a young student riding a horse.

"Couldn't that have been part of her job?"

"The client isn't on the roster, and it was taken after hours," I said.

"Goodness." He reached for the photo, but I stuck it back in the envelope before he could grab it.

"Let's go. Follow my lead."

"Your lead?"

I nodded. "I'm the investigator here. I will be the one asking the questions."

He saluted me. "Yes, ma'am."

I shook my head. Inviting him along with me had been terrible idea. I had a feeling that he was going to joke the entire time. Maybe that's how he dealt with grief, but it wasn't my way. Murder was serious business.

I walked over to the fence around the corral, where the trail riders were getting instructions.

"If the horse starts to take off on you, pull on the reins and lean back."

A couple of the riders looked like they wanted to bolt right off their horses. And the horses shook their bridles and stamped the ground like they were laughing at the inept riders. A teenager in jeans and cowboy boots sat on the fence grinning at the scared riders.

"Do you know where I can find Melinda Grimes?" I asked.

He looked at me. "You need a horse?"

I shook my head. "I'm here to see Melinda."

He shrugged as if it made no difference to him. "She's in barn number four. She's shoeing." Then he turned back to the riders.

I walked toward barn number four. Fortunately, each building was clearly numbered.

"Shoeing?" Tate asked.

I glanced over my shoulder. "Putting horseshoes on a horse's hooves."

"Right. I knew that."

Sure he did.

In the barn, the stalls were filled with other horses, and they shook their bridles and neighed as Tate and I walked by.

In the middle of the barn, a slight woman hammered a horseshoe into the hoof of a horse five times her size. Even though she was small in comparison, it was clear who was in charge. I recognized her from the pictures as Melinda.

Melinda gently placed the horse's foot on the floor, and then moved to pick up the next hoof. "Can I help you?" she asked me. "If you're looking for the trail ride, it's in the first corral by the parking lot. You can't miss it."

"Actually, you're the person we were looking for."

"Who are you?"

"I'm Darby Piper, and this is Tate Porter. We're from Two Girls Detective Agency."

She eyed Tate. "You aren't a girl."

"Thanks for noticing," he said with a grin.

"Chet Horner hired the agency."

She put the horse's hoof back on the ground with its new shoe and patted the animal's side. "Why?"

I pulled one of the photographs out of the envelope. It was the same one I had shown Tate of her training a rider. "Do you recognize this?"

After glancing at the image, Melinda walked around to the other side of the horse. "That's me training someone to ride. It's my job."

"Look at the time stamp. It's after the stables are closed."

She raised her eyebrows at me. "So what?"

"Did you report this lesson to Chet and give him the money?"

"Listen, I don't like what you're implying here."

"I don't think your boss likes being cheated out of his fair share," Tate interjected.

I shot him a look and then turned my attention

back to Melinda. "Were you aware that Chet hired a private eye to follow you?"

"I had no idea. I've never seen that photo before."

"What's going on here?" A broad man stepped into the barn with a scowl on his face.

"Chet." Melinda frowned. "What are you doing, hiring a P.I. on me?"

He folded his arms. "So it is true. You are trying to rip me off."

"I took on a few other clients to train. I don't see anything wrong with that."

"She admits it," Tate whispered to me.

"You can't do that," Chet argued. "That's breach of contract."

Melinda threw up her hands. "Then why didn't you just fire me? Why bother with them?" She waved at us.

"Hey," Chet said. "One of you is a guy."

"Thanks for noticing," Tate repeated.

"The company I hired was Two Girls Detective Agency."

I stepped forward. "Two Girls Detective Agency is... was...Samantha Porter and me."

"That's right," Chet said. "The woman I spoke to was named Samantha. Why isn't she here?"

I shared a look with Tate.

"Was that the woman who drove off the road on Lakeshore Avenue and died?" Melinda asked. "My sister was telling me about that."

"It was, and she was investigating you at the time."

"Wait, what? Do you think she died because she was following me?" Melinda's voice went up an octave.

I glanced at Tate, and he shrugged. "Where were you two nights ago?" I asked.

Melinda spun around. "I was at home with my husband and kids. You can ask them."

"Did you ever speak to Samantha?" Tate asked.

"No!" Melinda insisted. "I didn't know she was following me. She must be good at her job." She turned back to Chet. "So now what?"

"You're fired," Chet said.

"But I have a family to take of," she protested.

"You should have thought about that before."

Melinda glared at us and then stomped out of the barn.

Chet shook my hand. "Thanks for handling this. I'm sorry about Samantha."

I cocked my head. "Can I ask you a question?"

"Sure."

"Why did you hire Samantha to look into this? Why didn't you fire Melinda when you knew what she was up to?"

"I've tried to fire her before, and she threatened to sue," he said. "I had to make sure I was right this time."

I handed him the photographs.

"If she does try to sue me, these will put it to rest." He held up the pictures.

Tate and I left the barn, and I shook my head. "I don't know how I expected that to go, but it wasn't like that."

"Nice work solving that case," he said.

"Samantha had done most of the work, and it

wasn't the case I came here to solve." We climbed back into the minivan. "I need to return this to Maelynn. She owns Floured Grounds, a few doors down from the agency. Do you want me to drop you off anywhere on the way?"

He shook his head. We rode in silence back down-town. I parked in Maelynn's garage and left the keys in the visor like she'd asked me to.

"Do you want a coffee?" I asked, pointing to the cof-fee shop.

He shook his head. It was his turn to turn me down. "I have some things to take care of."

"I can take you wherever you need to go."

"It's no problem. I have a rental car back at my aunt's, and I could use the walk."

"Okay."

He turned to walk down Maelynn's driveway.

"Tate?"

He turned around.

"I don't know if Pat told you, but your aunt's fu-neral is tomorrow at eleven a.m. There is a celebration of life party at Floured Grounds, the local coffee shop on Lakeshore Avenue, immediately after. It's a simple graveside service at the cemetery. It's what your aunt wanted."

He nodded. "She wanted to make things easy on people all the time. She knew you were the right per-son to handle the funeral. I'll see you after."

"You're not coming to the funeral?" I blurted out.

"I don't do funerals," he said simply.

"You can't bring yourself to come to this one to

pay respects to your aunt?" I was aghast. I knew how much it would hurt Samantha, had she known.

"Don't talk to me about paying respects." There was a sharpness in his voice that hadn't been there before.

I shuffled back a couple of steps.

"I respected Aunt Samantha and loved her more than an aunt, like a mother," he said. "I'm still not coming to that funeral. I can show my respect in other ways."

I was about to protest again but stopped myself. I didn't know this man. Who was I to tell him what to do? Samantha would have wanted him to be there, but maybe she *had* asked me to plan the funeral because she knew he wouldn't show. Samantha had said in her letter to me that Tate needed the stability of the agency, and his story was not hers, but his to tell.

"All right," I said giving up the argument. "But if you change your mind, you know where we will be."

He continued down the driveway, and I was left reeling from his sudden change of mood. One minute he was joking, and the next he was brooding. One thing was for sure: I didn't know my new business partner at all.

CHAPTER SIXTEEN

I WENT BACK TO THE AGENCY still worrying over Tate's shifting mood. "Nat?" I stepped into the reception room.

She looked up from her computer screen. "Did you and Tate have a nice chat? What does he plan to do with the agency? I couldn't get him to tell me anything earlier."

"We didn't talk about it," I said, shaking my head. "I had a question about Samantha's plan to dissolve the agency."

"What's that?" she asked, making a face.

"She told me I would have a position at Billows Security. That a job for me was part of the contract. I don't remember her saying anything about a job for you though."

"She told me I had one too. Something to do with the reception desk. I can't say I was very interested in taking it."

"Oh, okay," I said casually. I was more relieved than I cared to admit.

She eyed me. "Why do you ask?"

"I don't know what Tate plans to do with the agency, but there is a possibility he will want to follow through with Samantha's plan to dissolve it. I don't think he would go to work for Billows, but he might like to sell the agency and this house for cash."

"Did he say that?"

"No, but I think it's wise to consider the possibility that we might both be looking for work soon."

"You really think so?" Her expression was pinched.

I shrugged. "The main thing I've learned this horrible week is that anything is possible. If you need me, I'll be in my office. I want to follow up with some clients."

She nodded.

Sometime later, there was a knock on my door. I looked up from my computer, blurry-eyed from so much reading.

"I'm heading home," Nat said.

I stared at her. "Already?"

"It's five o'clock, Darby."

I checked my watch and saw she was right.

"I wouldn't worry about Tate closing the agency."

"Why not?" I asked.

She looked back at me as she opened the front door. "Because that would require him to make some sort of decision. I don't believe he is capable of that."

I blinked. "Why do you say that? Do you know something about Tate I don't?"

She sniffed. "He doesn't strike me as the decisive type, that's all."

I wanted to ask her more, but she left before I could say another word. Did she know more about Tate than she was letting on? If she did, why would she hide it from me?

After Nat left for the day, I could no longer stand sitting at the computer and decided to check out the organic food market that was facing trouble. Perhaps one of the owners would know something about Samantha's death. I peeked at the file again before leaving the office. Multigrain Market was owned by partners Edwin Yule and Pierce March. They had opened the store five years ago, and business had been good to the point that the market had begun sponsoring an outdoor farmers' market in the summers in Herrington. Even though it was small, our town was the kind of crunchy granola place, as my father would say, that could make such a market work. The locals were behind it, and the well-to-do visitors to Lake Waters Retreat found it charming. It was a recipe for success. That had been my impression, anyway. Meeting with Quinn had certainly opened my eyes to a new reality at Lake Waters.

Edwin and Pierce were partners in business and in life. Unfortunately, Edwin suspected that Pierce was skimming money off the top of the business for his own uses.

In my opinion, it would be much better if partners dealt with their problems directly rather than bringing in an outside party like my agency, but a surprising number of companies didn't do that, because the evidence that a private detective discovers holds up better in court. Also, if everyone followed my advice, I would be out of business. Edwin was a friend of Samantha's, which was why he'd come to her for help, and he was the one I knew better because of their friendship. I knew who Pierce was, because it was hard not to know your neighbors in a place as small as Herrington.

I closed the file, said goodbye to Gumshoe, who was lounging on the giant couch, and went out the door. Since my run that morning, the temperature had gone up, and the sky overhead was crystal blue. The lake across the road shimmered in the daylight. In some strange way, focusing on the murder investigation in the wake of Samantha's death was helping me. The mission I needed to accomplish—to find out who was behind it—was enough to distract me from my grief.

Real grief would come and would hit me hard, very hard, but in classic avoidance mode, I wanted to postpone that as long as possible.

Multigrain was in an old, red, converted barn at the end of Lakeshore Avenue before the road led out of town. It was the best place for it because there was enough room at the end of the street to have a gravel parking lot for fifty cars. Most of the locals walked around town, but there were enough people traveling about the Finger Lakes in all seasons that parking was needed.

The original barn, which held the market, had been condemned just about the time that Edwin and Pierce had purchased it and brought it back to life. Many people thought the couple would level it. Instead, the two men had restored the old barn as best they could while updating it for their purposes. It was a marvel.

Outside the market, Tate sat on the bench. He was wearing jeans and a rock band T-shirt. His hair was freshly cut, and his beard was trimmed close to his face.

I stood in front of him and put my hands on my hips. "I see you got cleaned up."

He rubbed his beard. "I thought it was time for a more civilized look. Besides, a beard that scruffy can be itchy. I've had ladies complain about it in the past."

I rolled my eyes.

Tate grinned. "I was wondering when you were planning to show up."

"You were sitting here, waiting for me?"

He cocked his head. "Naturally. Weren't the owners of this market some of the people you said were possible suspects?"

"Shh! You shouldn't say that out in the open." I looked around the parking lot. There was one young mother strapping her child into a car seat. "Someone might hear you."

"I doubt that. There's no one who can hear what we're saying right now, but if it makes you feel better, I'll keep my talk about suspects down to a minimum in public."

"What are you doing here? I thought you had things to take care of."

He laughed. "Taken care of."

"The new look? That's what you needed to do?"

"That was part of it," he said, giving no hint as to

what the rest of it might have been. "Are you ready to go in?"

"I guess." I wasn't sure what to make of Tate's surprise appearance outside the market, but I couldn't take any more time away from the investigation to find out. I left him on the bench and walked over to the front door.

The sign on the door read "Welcome to Multigrain Market. You are important."

Tate nodded to the sign. "I think they write that so they can charge ten dollars for a carton of milk."

I pushed open the door. "Cynical much?"

"Yeah, like I'm the cynical one in this friendship."

I scowled at him. Friendship?

He grinned, and I realized he'd wanted me to snap at him about the comment. I refused to give him the satisfaction, and instead I stepped into the small market. The smell was a mixture of herbs, vitamins, and freshly cut wood.

"It smells like a barn in here," Tate said.

I elbowed him in the ribs.

A woman at the cash register smiled at us. There was no one checking out at the moment, but the market wasn't empty. There were a number of people pushing carts around the market—young moms with toddlers in carts and older adults who looked like they might have danced at the original Woodstock.

The cashier smiled more broadly. "Can I help you? We're having a sale on probiotics today."

I opened my mouth, but Tate was faster. "I'm looking for some vitamins."

"Of course," she said happily as if he'd won a prize by saying the secret password. "We have a whole host of vitamins." She led us to the supplement area, which easily took up a quarter of the shelf space in the store. It seemed there was a vitamin or essential oil for every possible ailment a person could imagine.

"Is there a particular vitamin I can help you find? We have a special athlete's mix. I can tell you work out a lot. I think that might help you feel your very best and recover more quickly from a hard workout."

"You know," Tate said, "I was wondering if you have any vitamins or supplements for anxiety." He patted my shoulder like he would a team member at football practice. "My friend runs a little tightly wound and could use some calm."

"Of course," the woman said, and moved down the aisle.

"No, thank you," I said through clenched teeth. "We're looking for vitamins for him. I'm fine."

She pressed her lips together and inspected me over her glasses. "Everyone could use vitamins. It wouldn't hurt you to take some, too. I take ten different herbal supplements and vitamins every day. Fourteen on Sundays. You could use some of those. Everyone can."

I folded my arms. "I take a gummy vitamin every day. Thank you very much."

She peered at me. "A nice B complex is always a good option. Also, iron for energy. It's not unusual for women as they approach middle age to be deficient in this."

Approach middle age? I was thirty years old. I

opened my mouth ready to give her a piece of my mind, but Tate squeezed my arm lightly. I glared at him, but instead of telling the employee what I really thought about her B complex, I asked, "Is Edwin here? I was wondering if I could talk to him for a moment."

She frowned. "Is something wrong with my service?"

Tate shook his head. "No, no, it's nothing like that."

"It's not," I said. "Can you tell him Darby Piper is here?"

She wrinkled her nose as if she didn't like the idea of finding Edwin in the slightest, but she finally nodded and disappeared into the next aisle in search of her boss.

Tate held a vitamin bottle out to me. "This one will give you stronger hair and nails. Women always want that, don't they? Why don't you try it?"

I glared at him. "I don't need any vitamins right now. Thank you."

He shrugged and put it back on the shelf.

I didn't know what to make of Samantha's nephew. Didn't he know that his aunt was dead? How could he make jokes at a time like this?

CHAPTER SEVENTEEN

A FEW MINUTES LATER, EDWIN YULE stepped into the vitamin aisle, alone. He was a thin man with a precise goatee and round glasses. I didn't know where the assistant who had been so set on selling me vitamins had gone.

When he saw me, he adjusted his glasses on the bridge of his nose. "Darby, what are you doing here?"

"You've heard about Samantha."

He nodded and rubbed his bloodshot eyes. "I can hardly believe it. I've been crying ever since I heard the news. Maelynn told me about the celebration of life party at Floured Grounds. I think it's such a wonderful idea. Both Pierce and I plan to be there."

I smiled. "Good. I know Samantha cared about you both so much."

"She did," he said, while fighting off more tears. He glanced at Tate. "Who are you?"

"I'm sorry," I said. "Edwin Yule, this is Tate Porter. Tate is Samantha's nephew, and he will be working with me at the agency."

Tate's brows went up when I said that last part.

I lowered my voice. "I'm also here because I need to speak with you about the open case you have with Two Girls."

He looked around furtively. "We can't talk about that here!"

"I understand that, but I need to talk to you about it now. It's of some urgency."

"Let's go outside then, where we can speak more freely." He walked down the aisle and stopped in front of vitamin girl, who was back at the cash register. "Dory, I'm going out for a minute. I'll be back soon."

Dory nodded, but the sunny smile she'd had for Tate when we first arrived was gone.

Outside, Tate and I followed Edwin, who made a beeline for the lake. He stopped at a picnic table out of the view of his health food store. He pushed his glasses up his nose a second time. "What are you thinking, coming into my store and talking about my open case with the agency? What if someone overheard? That could ruin everything for Pierce and me."

"Have you confronted Pierce about your suspicions?" Tate asked.

"Oh, I could never do that. What if I'm wrong? It would ruin our relationship. I love him. When Samantha offered her help, it seemed like it would be the best solution. I never expected for her to be murdered!"

I flattened my hands on the tabletop. "You know she was murdered?"

"Your boyfriend was here this morning to tell us the news. It's horrible."

"Boyfriend?" Tate cocked his head.

"Austin Caster," Edwin said. "The police officer."

"Austin is not my boyfriend," I said.

"Good," Tate murmured, barely above a whisper.

I didn't allow myself a moment to wonder what *that* was all about. "What did he say?"

"That Samantha was forced off the road by another car and crashed in the ravine." He shook his head. "I can't believe it. Samantha was one of my dearest friends. She got her officiate's license because I wanted her to preside over my wedding to Pierce."

My mouth fell open. "You and Pierce are engaged?"

"Not yet. I want to ask him. I have the ring and everything." He removed his glasses and rubbed his eyes before putting them back on. "But before I propose, I have to know he's not cheating me out of the business."

I tried to keep my expression neutral. Actually, it wasn't uncommon for someone to hire Two Girls Detective Agency to make inquiries about the person they were dating before the relationship got too far along. It was a scary world out there, and the persona someone presented on social media or on a dating website could be much different than who the person actually was.

But Edwin and Pierce had been together close to a decade, and they'd started a business together. Why was Edwin doubting his partner now?

"What do you think Pierce is up to?"

Edwin sighed. "It seems strange to even focus on it now that Samantha is dead. Life is so fleeting. Maybe I should just trust Pierce to be the man he claims to be."

"You've paid the agency to look into this matter. And I know Samantha would want me to take the case seriously, not only because it's the professional thing to do, but because she cared about you so much."

"Just start from the beginning," Tate advised.

Edwin adjusted his glasses on his nose. "All right. About six months ago, I noticed there was money missing from our balance sheets. Usually, Pierce takes care of that end of the business. I know more about the products, like the food, vitamins, and other supplements. He knows more about business in general. I always thought that was why we made such a good team."

Clearly, Edwin had been the one to train Dory, the vitamin girl, who'd been dead set on sharing her vitamin knowledge with me.

Edwin sniffled but was able to hold his tears at bay. "For whatever reason, I looked at the books and noticed some money was missing from what I recorded when I closed the store the night before."

"How much was missing?"

"It was about five hundred dollars."

"For a store your size, that's a good amount of money," I said.

"It is," Edwin said with a nod.

"Did you approach Pierce about it?"

He pressed his hands together as if in prayer. "I did, and he told me I had to have been mistaken. He said the balance sheet was correct. I laughed it off and told him he must be right. He was always right when it came to money. He reminded me of some mathematical mistakes I made in the books in the past before he wholly took it over. They were all true, but I couldn't shake the feeling that something was wrong." He shook his head. "So when Pierce wasn't in the store, I started looking. I started keeping my own tally of our income every week, and every week, my numbers were just a little bit more than what Pierce recorded."

"How much more?" Tate asked.

"Every week it seemed to be off by a few hundred dollars here and there, but over the time, the money not recorded has been close to ten thousand dollars! I could see my business and life falling apart, so I spoke to Samantha. She suggested I hire a forensic accountant to look into it. She said a person in that field would do that best job, but I didn't want a stranger scrutinizing our books or my relationship with Pierce. I asked Samantha if she would look into it, and after some pleading on my part, she agreed."

Edwin looked at me. "Am I a terrible person for doubting Pierce? I have to know I can trust him before I get in too deep. Running a business together is one thing, but marriage, that's a whole other level. It's heartbreaking."

I shared a look with Tate. By the sound of it, I didn't have much hope for Edwin and Pierce's wedding ever happening.

"We will do all we can to get to the bottom of this," I promised. "But Samantha was right. A forensic accountant would be your best option."

"I'm not ready to do that yet. Will you take up where Samantha left off?"

I nodded.

"Thank you. Samantha spoke highly of you, you know. She even said to me recently that if anything happened to her, to see you for help, that you could be trusted one hundred percent."

I shivered.

Edwin covered his mouth. "That sounds like she might have known she was going to be killed."

"That's exactly what it sounds like," Tate said with a scowl. "Did she give you any other clue why she said that?"

Edwin shook his head. "I thought she was making conversation or telling me her backup on the case if she was away, or something like that."

"How has business been other than this situation?" I asked.

"Business has been incredibly good. The best we have had in years. We can't always keep everything in stock."

I frowned. "Why do you think that is?"

"Lake Waters Retreat has been our best customer. You would not believe how many vitamins and supplements they buy. They seem to want to try every new vitamin, and the newer stuff is always the most expensive."

I thought about my visit with Quinn at the retreat. It sounded like Billows planned to revitalize Lake Water by hiring Samantha for better security and buying expensive vitamins and supplements for his clientele. What else was he up to there?

Edwin shook his head. "When the police first came

to the store, I thought they were there to arrest Pierce and that Samantha forgot to tell me she'd found evidence against him for stealing. When they told me it was because Samantha had been murdered, I would've toppled over if Pierce hadn't caught me."

"It seems to me," Tate said, "that you have a lot of evidence already against Pierce to prove he is stealing from the company. What more do you need from us?"

"I *need* to know," Edwin said. "I'm praying he's innocent. If you don't find anything to incriminate him, I'm going to ask him to marry me, and I will never look at the finances for the store again."

I wanted to tell Edwin that was a terrible way to start a life with someone, but what did I know? My only real relationship had been with a cop who'd broken up with me at the drop of a hat. And what was worse, I'd taken back said cop dozens of times over the years. Ugh, I didn't even want to think about that.

"When does he tally the money?" Tate asked.

"At night, right after the store closes. There's a window in the back office. The computer screen points at it. I think you'd be able to see what he's doing from that spot without going inside the store."

"Why haven't you tried that?" Tate asked. "It would be just as easy for you to do."

"I could never do that. If I wasn't in the store tidying up for the night like I always do, Pierce would know that something was off."

"We can come tonight and do a stakeout," Tate said, looking to me.

Edwin shook his head. "Not tonight. A lot of the

staff will be working late because we offered to sup-
ply some of the food for Samantha's celebration of life
party. It's not a good night to be around Multigrain
Market and go unnoticed."

"Tomorrow night, then," I said.

Edwin nodded, but at the same time looked as if he
might be ill over the very idea. He stood up. "I have to
get back to the store. I don't want Dory to tell Pierce
I've been gone so long. The fewer questions I have to
field about this conversation, the better."

Tate and I stood as well.

Edwin nodded to Tate and me in turn. "Thank you
for your help. You would make Samantha very proud."

I bit my lip as he shuffled across the street to his
store.

Tate smiled at me. "Looks like you and I have our
first stakeout together planned for tomorrow night. Remember to wear black like they do in the movies." He
started to walk away from me.

I followed him. "Where are you going now?"

He looked over his shoulder. "Why so curious,
Piper? Are you going to miss me?"

"I—I thought you might want to come back to the
office to take a look at everything. Maybe we can find
something at the office that will point us in the direction of Samantha's killer."

"Haven't you already looked?"

"I have. Three times."

"Then that should be enough."

"Tate," I called after him. "Are you sure you won't
come to Samantha's funeral?"

His good humor was gone and his brow furrowed. "I'm more than sure." He continued on his way.

Standing by the lake, my shoulder slumped. I wished there was something I could do to change his mind. I felt like I would let Samantha down by Tate's absence, and I was positive it was a decision he would come to regret.

CHAPTER EIGHTEEN

I N THE MOVIES, FUNERALS ARE always on overcast days, but the day Samantha was laid to rest was one of the most beautiful fall days I had ever seen. The wooded cemetery was on a hillside that overlooked the lake. The brightly colored leaves reflected off the water's surface. It was a warm day for this time of year, in the seventies. I had to remove my jacket.

My parents were there. DeeDee was at school. My dad sat in the wheelchair he used for outings, and he patted my hand. I squeezed his.

The gravesite service was small. That was what Samantha had wanted, but I couldn't help but believe her life was worth so much more than this little gathering.

Maelynn was there as well. She was a true friend. Her husband was back at the coffee shop getting ready for the celebration of life party, and there were many more people at the party than who were at this tiny gathering.

Nat was also present, and she kept hiding her face in a ball of tissues as she cried. Logan Montgomery was also in attendance. I was relieved to see Logan. Samantha had spent a good part of her life with the councilman, and he should be pay his respects. He wouldn't meet my gaze, though. Was it because he was angry with me for talking to the police about him or was it because he was guilty?

Austin and his partner were there, but I knew that it was less about paying their respects than seeing who came to the funeral; they were looking for suspects. I feared that in their minds, they needed to look no further than me.

Edwin and Pierce were also at the gravesite. Edwin had his arm wrapped around his partner's waist, and you would never know by looking at the couple that Edwin had doubts about Pierce's honesty. Pierce was the bigger of the two men. He was tall and broad and carried himself with the confidence of a football player who'd just won the championship. I didn't know what would happen to them after Tate and I staked out Multigrain Market.

Thinking of the stakeout made me think of Tate who was, as promised, not there. I wished I could say I wasn't disappointed, but I was. I'd so hoped he would have changed his mind. Samantha had rarely changed hers, so maybe he was more like his aunt than I'd first thought.

The minister tossed a flower into the grave. I tossed the small bouquet I was holding in too. Others standing around the hole in the ground followed suit. The minister said one final prayer and with a quiet "Amen," the service broke up.

Dad squeezed my hand. "It was a lovely service. You did a good job."

I bent over to give him a hug. "Thanks, Dad. But I didn't do much at all. Samantha planned it before she died."

"Are you sure this is all she wanted?" my mother asked. "It's so small for a woman who was such a large part of this community."

"I know, but this is what she left for me to do. She was very particular. I need to respect her wishes. The party afterward will have a bigger crowd. Will you be able to come?"

"I wish I could," Mom said. "I have to get back to the library."

"And I should go home and rest," Dad added. "This has been quite an outing."

I nodded and understood, even though a small part of me was sad they wouldn't be at the celebration. I reminded myself that they'd come to the funeral, and of the two, that was the more important. I wished Tate had realized that and attended too.

I helped my father to their car, and then crossed to Maelynn, who was about to climb into the minivan I had grown to know so well. I gave her a hug.

"See you at Floured Grounds in fifteen," she said. "Don't stay out here too long and wallow. Right now, you need to be with the people who love you."

"I don't wallow."

She snorted. "Sure, you don't."

Logan was also walking to his car. I ran over to catch up with him. "Logan!"

He turned to me and scowled. "What is it, Darby?"

When his gaze met my eyes, I saw that his eyes were bloodshot, and there were dark circles under them. He had been crying. He loved her. I knew he did. I was looking into the eyes of a man with a broken heart. My chest tightened in sympathy for him. At the same time, I thought, it might be an act.

I didn't know how to ask the question without just putting it out there. "Why did you and Samantha break up?"

He studied me with those bloodshot eyes. "We didn't break up, she dumped me."

I blinked at him. "Why?"

"Because I asked her to marry me." His voice was low.

I stared at him. "But I thought neither one of you wanted to get married."

"Is that what she told you?"

I nodded.

"I have, for years. She was the one who didn't."

"What was her reason?"

He rubbed the back of his neck. "All she said was, her mission had to come first."

"Mission? What mission?"

He shook his head. "Her work. Samantha could be stubborn."

I knew that, and I knew how Logan felt too. I knew how it felt to want to marry the person you loved most in the world, but that person wasn't ready. Austin hadn't been ready for me after all that time, and Samantha hadn't been ready for Logan after well over a decade together.

I watched his car pull away. Could he have been so heartbroken over her refusal that he'd lost his mind for a moment and killed her? I rubbed my arms against the chilly air.

A crunch of leaves made me turn, and Tate stepped out from behind a tree. I was so relieved to see him, but I kept my face neutral. "You came."

"It was a nice service. You did a good job. My aunt would have liked it."

"Then why didn't you join us at the graveside?"

"I was here, just not up close. I could see everything from my tree. I don't care for funerals. I have had to attend too many in my life."

"I'm sorry to hear that."

I bit my tongue about paying respects to someone you loved. I couldn't know what it was like in his situation. My father was ill, but both my parents were living. I also didn't know what he had seen in the Army. I could only guess that death was something Tate Porter had had more than his share of in his young life. And realizing this, I again felt guilty for trying to pressure him in the first place. Who was I to determine how a person grieved?

"I'm glad you came, even if you watched from afar. Samantha would have wanted you here. She loved you. You were all she had."

"She was all I had too." He looked down at his feet. "I should have been a better nephew and visited from time to time."

What he said was true. He *should* have visited more. I didn't tell him about how much Samantha had worried about him while he'd been out wandering the planet. I suspected he knew, and it wasn't fair to tell him now since he no longer had the chance to make it right. Although, looking back, I knew that even while Samantha had worried, she'd also been very proud of Tate's independent streak, his honorable service in the military, the fact that he'd had the confidence to set out and see so much of this great big world.

"Wasn't that her to ask for a small service, so that she wouldn't inconvenience everyone?" he asked.

"She did all the planning and left everything with Patrick."

"She was awfully young to plan her own funeral, but Samantha was like that. She looked for ways to make things easier on the people around her."

Tears threatened at the corners of my eyes.

"I was thinking about tonight and..." Tate trailed off.

There was more crunching of leaves, and Austin Caster walked up to us. His body was tense as he approached. Tate looked over his shoulder to see what I was looking at and sighed. "Great."

I wrinkled my brow. I didn't know what that was about. I thought back to high school to see if I remembered the two of them having an issue, but nothing came to mind. How would I have known, though, when I'd been so caught up in ballet?

"Porter," Austin said.

"Caster," Tate said in reply.

I glanced from one man to the other. "Am I missing something here?"

Tate looked at me first. "There is nothing going on, Piper."

Austin scowled when Tate called me by my last name. "You've been in Herrington for two days, and as of yet, you have not come down to the station like we asked you to. We would like to talk to you about your aunt's death."

Tate rubbed his beard and then stopped as if he realized how short it was. Maybe he missed the long, scruffy beard after all. "I'll get around to it. I hope you don't think I'm behind my aunt's murder."

Austin pressed his lips together as if he was upset but accepting of that news.

"Here's what *I* would like to know," Tate continued. "You claimed my aunt was murdered by being run off the road, but you can't find the car that did it."

"We're looking for it," Austin said through clenched teeth.

Tate arched one eyebrow at him.

Austin glanced at me. "The white paint on Samantha's car matches the make and model of Darby's car. We need to find her car to make a perfect match."

I was being framed. I had never been so sure of anything in my life...but I didn't see how it would help to say so. I frowned. Why hadn't Austin arrested me yet? He had enough evidence to make the collar. No one would fault him for taking me in. I wouldn't fault him for taking me in. The circumstantial evidence was damning. He would not have to be a rocket scientist to put two and two together—the two and two the person framing me wanted him to see.

Tate glanced at me. "You okay there, Piper? You look a little green."

"I—I am. If you two will excuse me, I need to go thank the minister." I walked away toward the gravesite where the minister and funeral director were chatting.

I expressed my gratitude to the minister, and the action gave me enough time to collect myself. When I walked back to Tate, Austin was gone.

I checked my cell phone. It was well past the time I'd told Maelynn I would be at Floured Grounds. "Where did Austin go?"

He cocked his head. "Missing your lover boy already?"

"He's not my lover boy," I protested.

"Well, he still cares about you since he hasn't arrested you yet, that much is clear. Maybe he's hoping through all this he will win you back."

"What are you talking about?"

"Come on, Piper. I'm not an idiot. All the evidence is against you in this case, and now the white paint on Samantha's car matches your car. I saw the look on your face when Caster said that."

Was he right? Was Austin not arresting me because he still cared about me? It didn't make any sense. He'd broken up with me because he said he wasn't ready for marriage. I had told him I was tired of waiting, and that was the end of that—or so I thought.

I shook my head. Everything was all jumbled in

my head. "I have to hurry over to Floured Grounds, or Maelynn is going to blow a gasket. Are you coming?"

"I might drop in," he said, giving away nothing.

I turned to go, and then stopped. "Tate."

His posture was slouched and his hands were in his pockets. He looked like a little lost boy, and I had the terrible urge to hug him. I didn't let myself do that, though.

"If we're going to work together on your aunt's case, you need to come to the party."

He looked like he was going to argue. I could imagine that if he didn't like funerals or wakes, then "celebration of life" parties probably weren't much of a step up.

"Please, we both need to make an appearance, and there might be someone there who knows something. If you can't do it for yourself or for me, do it for Samantha."

He nodded and walked away, hands still in his pockets and posture still slumped.

I hoped I wasn't making a huge mistake by involving him in the case, but only time would tell.

I walked away from the gravesite as a police cruiser rolled out of the cemetery; I didn't have to see the number on the vehicle to know it was Austin's. He'd waited there until I left. I was under surveillance.

CHAPTER NINETEEN

I STEPPED INTO FLOURED GROUNDS. THE place was packed. Most of the people were there to pay their respects to Samantha, but there were a few stray tourists who looked around confused, like they hadn't expected a party in a coffee shop—and it was very much a party. A local folk band was playing, there was food everywhere, and I overheard so many positive conversations about Samantha, it was hard not to simultaneously smile and cry. As I made my way to the counter, people stopped me to share their condolences.

Maelynn waved from the counter, where she was filling a mug with free coffee. Justin stood next to her, a handsome man with a massive mane of black braids that made every woman jealous. Jealous that Justin wasn't available, and also jealous that their own hair wasn't as fabulous as his.

He came around the corner and gave me a quick hug. "Sorry about Samantha. It's such a shame."

I nodded. "Thank you so much for doing this. It

means so much to me. I don't know what I would do without the two of you."

"It's not a problem, and Maelynn loves to plan a party. She was more than happy to do it for you, and Samantha too. She loved you both, but most especially you."

Tears sprang to my eyes.

"I heard Tate is in town."

"He is," I said. "He was at the funeral."

"Is he coming to this?" Justin asked.

I shrugged. "I asked him to, but I really don't know."

He pushed a braid out of his face. "I haven't seen Tate Porter since we graduated from high school. We used to play football together."

I blinked. I had forgotten Tate and Justin had been in the same year at Herrington High School. It seemed like a lifetime ago. In many ways, it was.

"What's your take on Tate?"

"What do you mean?" He studied me, a curious expression on his face.

I shrugged. "It's just I can't seem to figure him out."

"Back when I knew him, he was always a straightforward guy. If he was upset about something, he was the type to deal with the person right in that moment rather than let it fester. He was a good athlete and could be a bit of a jokester. He had this running gag our senior year of hiding our coaches' shoes before every practice. Man, did that make Coach Rutherford mad." Justin laughed.

I scratched my head. I wasn't sure that described Tate Porter today.

As if he could read my mind, Justin continued, "But that was a long time ago. A lot can change in all that time, and he was in the Army, right? That sort of experience can change a person."

I nodded. I had a feeling Tate's Army experience had changed him a lot more than he was revealing to me—but why should he reveal anything to me? We'd really only met as adults yesterday. Even so, I felt nervous going into this partnership with him when I didn't truly know him. What if he was a loose cannon? That wasn't the type of person who would play well in the private investigation field. What if he decided to sell or close the agency? That would have the same result as if Samantha had worked for Billows at Lake Waters.

Someone tapped me on the shoulder, and I turned around to find Matt Billows standing directly behind me. Goodness, speak of the devil, and he materialized. "Darby, I'm so sorry." Billows enveloped me a hug, and I held my arms out like I was repulsed. Maybe internally I was, but not to be insulting, I patted him on the back and pulled away.

He looked me in the eye. "How are you holding up?"

I took a step back and ran into one of the stools at the coffee counter. It made a screeching sound across the tile floor that was barely audible above the band and the voices in the room.

"Everything okay, Darby?" Justin asked, eyeing Billows with open suspicion.

I patted Justin's arm. "I'm fine."

He nodded but his brow furrowed. Despite his concern, Justin left us alone. He knew I'd handled tougher

Amanda Flower

criminals than Billows in my career. There was no doubt in my mind that this man was crooked in some way. What crimes he'd committed, I didn't know. If they included Samantha's murder, I didn't know that either.

"I am very sorry for your loss. Samantha was a wonderful person and a top-notch detective. She will be sorely missed."

"Thank you," I said, because I didn't know what else to say.

"I would have been at the funeral today, but I had back-to-back meetings. I couldn't get away. I was so glad to hear you were having this event to celebrate Samantha's life. I can see all the people in town who really cared about her. The number here is quite impressive."

Sorry your meetings got in the way of coming to a funeral.

He took a breath as if what he was about to say next pained him in some way. "This might not be the best time, but I have wanted to speak to you about the offer I made to Samantha about coming to work for me at Lake Waters. She trusted you, and I wondered if you would consider the position I wanted to give her."

I eyed him. "It seems you've moved on quickly from Samantha."

He pressed his lips together. "I need someone in the job quickly."

"What about Cliff? He seems eager to stay."

If Billows was surprised I knew who his head of security was, he didn't show it. He forced a laugh. "It's

158

time for Cliff to retire. We both know it. He doesn't know how to outsmart the paparazzi like you do. When important changes are made at Lake Waters, I know registrations will increase and even more famous clients will be seeking out the retreat to rejuvenate and recover. We need to be able to promise them that their peace and privacy won't be disturbed while they are our guests. I can't make that promise with Cliff. If I am going to move the resort forward, I need to start with new staff in key positions. This is an opportunity for us to work together and be stronger together. We can help each other in the wake of Samantha's passing."

"I'm not interested in working for your company."

He pulled back as if I had slapped him.

"I don't understand. That was the plan all along. Even when Samantha was alive, I created a position for you. She would not take the job without you."

"That was your and Samantha's plan. I had no part in it. She didn't need my part in it to move forward, did she? Now she's gone and you suddenly need me to accomplish your goal. Isn't that funny?"

He held up his hands, with a look on his face as if my behavior completely bewildered him. Maybe it did. I had a pretty good guess that Matt Billows wasn't accustomed to hearing the word *no*.

"Did Samantha tell you all I had offered her, the benefits, the job security? You don't have any of that in your little detective agency."

"I like where I am," I said, leaving no room for miscommunication.

His face turned red. The overly friendly man who'd

given me a hug a few moments ago was gone. "So you are going to keep the agency as is. Do it all yourself and make no changes?"

"I can't answer that question for you."

He frowned. "The agency is yours now. Why not?"

"Because the agency's fate is mine to decide," a deep voice said.

Billows turned around, and there was Tate standing in the middle of Floured Grounds.

I had been so focused on Billows that I hadn't even noticed Tate standing there.

"Who are you?" Billows wanted to know.

Tate held out his hand. "Tate Porter. I'm Samantha's nephew, and I inherited her portion of the agency. Because of that, I assume any conversation you're having with Piper about the business, you should also be having with me."

"Samantha never told me she had a nephew," Billows said.

"I wasn't under the impression the two of you traded family histories." Tate arched his brow.

"Right." Billows smoothed his cuff. "Then I would like to talk to both of you about your aunt's plans to work for my company."

"I'm sure you would," Tate said.

"It would be my suggestion that you go through with the verbal agreement I struck with Samantha. The formal contract has already been drafted. We will have it revised now, of course, and put Darby's name on it. I would like her to work for me."

Tate glanced at me. "Is that what you want?"

"No, I'm happy where I am," I said.

Billows shook his head as if he couldn't believe how dense I was being. "Why would you want to stay at a struggling agency when you could work for a multimillion-dollar company?"

"The agency is not struggling," I protested. "And I wasn't under the impression that Lake Waters Retreat was doing all that well."

"There will be hiccups in registration during remodeling."

I wouldn't call a vacant resort a hiccup. What did Billows think he could do to save his retreat, and why was hiring Samantha, and now me, part of that equation?

"I would be interested to see what Lake Waters has to offer Darby," Tate said.

"Tate." I stared at him. "You can't be serious. It's a terrible idea. I'm not interested. He can't woo me away from the agency I love like he did Samantha."

"I didn't woo her away." Billows glared at me. "Samantha was the one who came up with the idea."

My mouth fell open.

"That's right," he said with a nod. "I suppose she never told you that part because she never wanted me to play the role of the bad guy. A role I am happy to perform when it comes to business, but it wasn't my idea. Samantha came to me and asked for the head of security position. At first, her suggestion amused me, which is why I entertained it for so long. However, over time I could see her point. Who better to stop the paparazzi from photographing my clients than a person who thinks like them? You and Samantha sneak around and snap photographs of other people all the time in your work as private detectives."

"He has a point," Tate said. "But before I encourage Darby to take the position, I would like to see everything that is involved, how much you would pay us, and the job offerings."

"Done," Billows said.

I couldn't believe I was hearing this. Tate had given me the impression he wasn't interested in selling to Billows, and here he was, asking Billows to list off the particulars. I didn't know which man I wanted to punch more, but I wanted to punch one of them square in the nose. I had a feeling it would be the only thing that would make me feel any better.

"And," Tate went on, "I want a tour of Lake Waters Retreat and your operation there."

Billow frowned.

"Not just for me either. For me and Piper. I want her to feel comfortable if that is the place that will become our new place of work."

I watched Tate as he spoke and realized that something was up.

Billows narrowed his eyes. "That can be arranged."

Tate nodded. "Glad to hear it."

Billows said goodbye and pushed his way through the crowd and out the front door of the Floured Grounds.

Tate watched him go with a smile.

"Tate, what are you up to?" I asked. "I don't want to work for Lake Waters."

He shrugged. "We need to get into that suspect's property, and I made that possible. You're welcome."

"So you don't plan to sell or dissolve the agency?"

"I never wanted to sell the agency. The longer I'm here, the more I want to stay and make a go of it."

"You want to run Two Girls Detective Agency with me?"

"I do." He smiled down at me, and deep in my chest I felt a little flutter. I tamped it down. I could not be attracted to my business partner. It was a recipe for disaster. Look what had happened to Edwin and Pierce, and they were a couple before they'd gone into business together.

Relief flooded through my body as I absorbed his words. "Oh."

He patted my arm. "You need to learn to relax and trust me, Piper. It would make your life a whole lot easier if you let yourself do that."

I had no doubt that was true, but trust wasn't something that came easily to me.

He squeezed my arm and walked out of the coffee shop.

I could still feel the warmth of his hand on my arm as he hit the door.

"Darby?" I heard Maelynn ask behind me at the counter. "What was all that about? Was that Matt Billows yelling at you just now? And was that Tate? My, my, time has treated him well. I don't remember him being that handsome in high school."

I waved away her questions and ran out of Floured Grounds after Tate.

I got outside and saw him a little way down the sidewalk. "Tate!"

He turned and waited for me to catch up with him. "Did I forget something, Piper?"

"No, I—I..." I couldn't think of what to say. I couldn't think of a reason I had run out of Samantha's celebration-of-life party to find him.

"Go back to your party," he said with a sympathetic smile.

I folded my arms. "Aren't you coming back in?"

He shook his head. "It's too crowded in there. I'll pay my respects in my own way."

Before he could go, I asked, "Are we still on for the stakeout tonight?"

"That, Piper, I wouldn't miss for the entire world." And he strolled away.

CHAPTER TWENTY

T HAT EVENING, I WAS ALONE in the office when there was a knock at the front door. I knew it was Tate. This was when I had asked him to come for the stakeout. Multigrain Market closed at eight, so we wanted to be in position before the market closed and in view of the window Edwin had told us about.

I walked to the front door and opened it.

Tate stepped inside, looking around. "Nat said you live here."

I nodded. "I live upstairs. My office is to the right, but the main reception area and Samantha's office, which I suppose will be yours, is to the left. I guess Nat would have already told you that when you were here before."

He followed me into the reception room and promptly lay down and stretched out. "Wow, I can never find a couch long enough for me. This is amazing. More comfortable than any bed. Care if I stay here the rest of my life?"

I stared at him and the couch. "This is why," I murmured.

He sat up. "You look like you've seen a ghost."

"Maybe in a way I have." I pointed at him on the couch. "This is why. You are the reason why."

He held up his hand. "Now, Piper, I will admit you are freaking me out a bit by pointing at me and saying I'm the reason why. Reason for what?"

"The couch!"

"You're bananas."

"No, listen. Samantha bought this couch for you. When she bought it, I was upset because it was so huge and expensive. The front door had to be removed from its hinges even to move it in the house. She did it all for you, because she knew you would fit on it. She hoped you would come here and lie on it. In a way, she thought if she bought it, it would bring you home."

"Whoa." He held up his hands. "You got all of that from me lying on a couch."

I nodded.

"Oh-kaay. Maybe I could take the first shift at the stakeout."

I didn't care what Tate thought. I was right, and something about knowing why she had bought the couch made me miss Samantha even more. It was as if she'd always known what was going to happen and what the next step was. Had she known she was going to be killed?

Gumshoe walked into the room with his plume of a tail held high.

The cat marched right over to Tate and sniffed his

legs. Tate patted the couch cushion next to him. Gumshoe lifted his nose as if considering and then jumped up on the couch next to Tate. Instead of staying on the couch cushion, he stretched his long body over Tate's legs.

Tate held his hands in the air. "I've been fluffed."

I laughed. "You were the one who invited Gumshoe to sit with you. He will always take that as sit *on* you."

"I'm covered in cat hair."

"Are you allergic?"

"No," he said grudgingly.

I smiled. "Then you will survive, and that's good too, because Gumshoe is the agency cat."

Tate ran his hand along Gumshoe's back. "He feels like cotton."

The cat began to purr. He loved compliments on his coat.

"We should probably head out," I said, "so we can be in position outside of Multigrain Market."

Tate shook his head. "I can't move. Your cat is holding me captive."

Gumshoe burrowed down farther in his lap, and his purring picked up too.

"Just move him."

"I can't do that," Tate said. "He will hate me. Do you know what happens when a cat hates you?"

I cocked my head. "Enlighten me."

"They scratch your eyes out when you're sleeping."

I snorted. "No, they don't." With the exception of Romy, of course, but I didn't say that.

"It's true. There was a guy in the service who told me it happened to his uncle."

I squinted at him. "Are you really afraid to move Gumshoe?"

He nodded.

I laughed and scooped up the cat. I buried my face in his soft fluff before I put him on the floor. The cat flicked his long tail in Tate's direction before he sashayed out of the room.

"Are you ready to go now?"

Tate stood, and cat hair floated to the floor from his lap. "You must have to vacuum every day."

"When Gumshoe is shedding in the spring, it's twice a day."

Tate shook his head, and I opened the front door.

The walk to Multigrain Market was quick. When we reached the gravel parking lot, I pulled Tate around the other side of the building. I peeked in the windows until I found the one that was clearly the office. Just as Edwin had said, the computer screen was pointed toward the window.

Edwin came into the room and saw us looking in. His eyes went wide and he glanced behind him.

Tate waved him over, and Edwin walked over to us. Tate made a gesture for Edwin to open the window. Edwin did as he asked.

"You two can't be in clear view of the window like that," he said. "What if Pierce saw you standing there looking in? You scared me half to death. This isn't the time for practical jokes."

"Who said anything about practical jokes?" Tate grinned.

I elbowed him in the ribs.

"Hey!" he whispered. "That hurt."

"Edwin," I said. "Can you leave the window open a crack so we can hear what's going on inside?"

He looked over his shoulder. "Only a crack."

"Edwin!" a voice called from outside the office.

Edwin jumped. "That's Pierce. I have to go." He closed the window, leaving it open half an inch, and left the office.

"Jumpy fellow, isn't he?" Tate said.

I removed my camera from my pocket. It was a simple point-and-shoot digital camera, but I liked it more than my SLR for this type of situation because it was light and fit into the back pocket of my jeans just like a cell phone. What's more, it had a great zoom, so it was the perfect camera to get detailed shots from far away. I focused on the computer screen to set up the zoom perfectly before Pierce came in.

I stepped away from the window and pressed my back against the side of the building. Tate didn't move. He looked inside like he was mentally cataloging everything in the room. Perhaps he was.

"You should probably get away from the window," I said.

"I have reflexes like a cat. He won't see me."

I rolled my eyes and checked my smart watch. It was five till eight. The sun had set and the temperature was dropping. I zipped up my leather jacket. Turning my collar up on my jacket, I wished I had thought to bring a scarf.

"I know, I know. Let me settle the books for the night, and we can leave," a male voice said.

Tate ducked under the window. I crouched down next to him.

It's Pierce, he mouthed.

I had my camera at the ready. Tate shook his head and gestured that he was going to look. He peeked over the edge, and then waved me up.

As I was much shorter than Tate, I stood up straight, and my eyes and nose just reached over the windowsill. That was all I needed, though.

Pierce was at the desk with his back to the window. I could clearly see the computer screen with a balance sheet on it.

I lifted the camera up, at the ready.

Edwin stepped into the room. "I have the income sheet for the day right here for you," he said speaking extra loudly and pointing at the piece of paper. He turned the paper to the window, and I snapped a photograph of it. I hoped he would have had the foresight to make a copy of his own.

"What are you doing?" Pierce asked, and his head snapped around in the direction of the window. Tate and I ducked below it just in time. "Are you okay, Edwin? You're acting very strange."

From the sound of his voice, Pierce had turned away from the window again and was looking at his partner.

I dared to poke my head above the windowsill again.

Edwin adjusted his glasses and licked his lips. "You know I've been broken up over Samantha. The funeral and party today was a lot to absorb. It's difficult to go back to normal life."

Pierce rubbed Edwin's arm. "I know. She was a good friend to you. Let me finish what I have to do here, and we can go home."

Edwin relaxed a tad. The way his eyes darted around the room, I knew it was taking all his concentration not to look at me in the window.

"That would be nice. I could use a little nightcap. I think it'll help me sleep."

"Then that's what we'll do," Pierce said gallantly. "You close up the front of the shop, and I'll finish up here." He turned back to the computer, and Edwin couldn't fight it any longer. He shot me a pleading look.

I shooed him away. I wasn't going to snap the photos we needed with him hovering over Pierce like that. If Pierce was stealing from Edwin, he wasn't going to do it right in front of him.

Edwin left the room. Pierce shook his head and went back to the desk. He had the cash register drawer with him. He carefully counted out the money. I snapped photos as he worked. Then, he removed a small stack of mixed bills. I saw fives, tens, and twenties. Those he folded together and put in his pocket. I kept snapping, while my heart sank for Edwin. He loved Pierce, and now he would have to face the fact that Pierce was stealing from the market, and from him.

A gust of wind came off the lake, over Tate's and my heads and through the window. The open curtain on the inside fluttered.

Tate and I ducked down.

"Why is this window open? Doesn't Edwin know it will kill our electric bill to open the windows?" Pierce muttered above us.

Tate and I were flat against the building below the window. If Pierce glanced down, there was no way he could miss us.

The window slammed closed, and the lock clicked over for good measure. I let out a sigh.

Tate put a finger to his lips, and we waited in the spot for a full minute. Then, he peeked over the windowsill again. As he lowered himself back down, he said, "Pierce is gone."

I rested my head against the building. "Poor Edwin. It's going to break his heart when we tell him."

"He already knows. We just got the proof." He slid away from the window and stood, and held his hand out to me.

I hesitated, and then kicked myself for stalling. What was my problem with accepting help from Tate? From anyone, really?

I was brushing off the back of my jeans when a man came rushing around the market with a tennis racket over his head, ready to crack both of ours. It was Pierce. He stopped in front of us. "What are you doing here?"

CHAPTER TWENTY-ONE

"I KNEW I HEARD VOICES," PIERCE said. "Answer me, or I'll whack you both on the head!"

I held up my hands. "Pierce, it's me, Darby!"

Pierce glanced at me but didn't lower his tennis racket. "Who is this man? Is he hurting you? Should I whack him?"

"No." I waved my hands. "Pierce, this is Tate Porter, Samantha's nephew."

He lowered his tennis racket. "Okay, but what are the two of you doing? And why were you outside my window just now?"

I racked my brain for a viable excuse as to why Tate and I would be creeping around the market after closing. I had to think of something to cover for Edwin.

"Oh, no." Edwin said as he ran around the building. "He found you!"

I groaned. So much for making up a story to cover for him. He'd let the cat out the bag himself.

"You knew they were here?" Pierce asked. "Edwin, what's going on?"

Amanda Flower

Edwin looked at me, and I shrugged. He had to tell Pierce now. It wouldn't do any good to their relationship to continue this lie.

"I—I hired them. I hired Samantha, actually, to look into a matter I was concerned about regarding the store."

Pierce narrowed his eyes. "What concern? If you had a problem, you should have come to me instead of hiring a private detective."

"I couldn't," Edwin blurted out. "Because it was about you."

Pierce gaped at him. "What on earth are you talking about?"

"I think you're stealing money from the store," Edwin blurted out. "The balance sheets aren't adding up, and I had to know for sure." He looked to Tate and me. "Was I right?"

I held up my tiny camera. "I have photos of Pierce pocketing money from the cash register."

Edwin flushed and turned to Pierce. "How could you do this to me? How could you do this to our business?"

Pierce pulled the wad of bills out of his pocket and held it up. His face softened. "This is what you're upset about?"

"Yes. We might be a couple, but that doesn't change the fact that you have been stealing from the market for months."

Pierce dropped the tennis racket on the ground. "Edwin," he pleaded. "You have to listen to me. I did it for us, for our business."

Edwin's face crumpled. "How can stealing from me be for our business?"

Pierce walked toward Edwin with his arms stretched out.

Edwin held out his hand in the universal stop sign. "No, don't come any closer. I don't even know you anymore."

"I took the money because I knew you wouldn't approve of what I had to do with it to make Multigrain Market thrive," Pierce said.

"What did you have to do?" Tate asked.

Pierce looked over his shoulder at us and then back at Edwin. "I was paying Matt Billows."

"What?" I yelped.

Pierce turned his attention back to Edwin. "Billows owns Lake Waters, and he's the main reason we've seen an uptick in the number of Lake Waters' guests who are shopping in the market. I'm paying him to use us to order the vitamins and supplements for his clients. I swear that's all I used the money for. It was for the business."

"Billows was making you pay him?" I asked.

"No, no, nothing like that. It's more like he's taking money to endorse our business to his clients."

"Did he threaten to not shop here if he wasn't paid?"

"Not exactly..." Pierce looked at each of us in turn. "It's not illegal to take payouts to ask for endorsements. Celebrities make most of their money that way."

"It might not technically be illegal, but it sure

sounds shady," Tate said. "And if Billows threatened you in any way, it is extortion."

I couldn't have agreed more.

There were tears in Edwin's eyes. "You should have told me."

"If I did, what would you have done?" Pierce asked.

"I would've told you not to do it. We can make our own way without Billows' guests."

"See, you're proving my point. I'm the one with the head for business. We need Lake Waters' clients, and with the changes he's planned, Matt promises the business will grow even more," Pierce said. "The townsfolk of Herrington would never buy that much at one time. We're lucky if we can talk them into a boost of vitamin C! Besides, I should be the angry one. You hired people to spy on me. What does that say about the trust in our relationship? Nothing good, I'll tell you that."

"I wanted to check what was going on because I love you and I want to marry you. I couldn't go through with it if I thought you were doing something illegal."

Pierce blinked at him. "You want to marry me?"

"Of course I do. You're the man of my dreams. I forgive you for your mistake, but I insist that next time, you talk a decision like this over with me. Even if you don't like what I have to say, it's what partners do. It's what spouses do."

Pierce stared at his shoes. "Edwin, I'm so sorry. I should have told you about my agreement with Billows. I thought by not telling you, I was saving you from worry. Now I see that was a mistake. I'm sorry."

Edwin hugged his partner with tears in his eyes.

Tate tugged on my sleeve. "I think we should leave them alone now. It looks to me like the matter is settled."

Edwin peeked over Pierce's shoulder and mouthed *thank you* to Tate and me.

I followed Tate out of the parking lot and onto the sidewalk along Lakeshore Avenue. We walked in silence for a few minutes. I spoke first. "I'm glad Edwin's problem is cleared up, but there is something off to me about Billows asking a small business in Herrington for money to endorse them to his clients. I wonder if other shops and businesses have been approached in the same way."

"It's worth looking into," Tate said. "And it seems to me that a more serious chat with Matt Billows is long overdue."

"Might be something to do on the tour you are insisting on having."

Tate grinned. "That was clever of me, wasn't it?"

I rolled my eyes. "You have your moments."

The next day, I slept in until seven. Usually my run was underway by that time, but after the eventful day of the funeral, I couldn't work up the motivation.

I would have slept even longer if Gumshoe hadn't been standing on my chest, batting at my nose with his paws. I supposed I should be grateful that he didn't extend his claws. When I opened my eyes, the Ragdoll was staring right at me with his blue eyes. He meowed loudly, and I covered my ears.

He meowed again and I scratched him between the ears the way he liked. He leaned into the caress. Then, I gently pushed the cat off me. He stood at the end of the bed, looking offended. Sunlight streamed into the room through the window; it hurt my eyes. I hadn't fallen asleep until four the morning. My head had been reeling from the funeral, Tate being here, and what we'd learned last night from Edwin and Pierce.

What was Billows' game exactly? Was it all interconnected? It was beyond odd, and I couldn't make heads or tails of it.

Even though I was getting a later than normal start, I fed Gumshoe and went for a run. It was the only way I would be able to clear my head. Since Samantha's death, I had avoided running. The more days I went without running, the harder it would be. It was time for me to face my fear and take my space back, and that meant running to the top of the hill where the accident had happened.

I was breathing heavily as I reached the crest of the hill. Not so much from the exertion, although that was part of it. I had run up here so many times before that my body was used to the climb. The heavy breathing came from facing my fear of being at the site of the accident. It was something I had to do for myself. I didn't want to be afraid to go back to any place, and certainly not one that had been so important to me until now.

The skid marks were there. The turf that was torn up on the side of the road and the mangled undergrowth down the hill was still there too. As was the scar in the large tree.

I heard the rhythmic footsteps of a runner behind me. I turned and saw Tate Porter crest the hill. Part of me should have known it would be him. He seemed to pop up everywhere I went.

Tate wasn't even sweating as he made it to the top of the hill.

"What are you doing up here?" I asked.

"Same thing I think you are. I wanted to see the scene of the accident, and there is no better way to get some thinking done than to go for a run."

I nodded. At least we had something in common outside of the agency. "I run up here every day."

He peered down at the town below on the lake. "Are you insane? Now that I see how sharp the curve is and how steep the drop, I'm questioning why I did. I must be crazy too. It might serve us both well to have another route."

"It has the best views," I said, defensive again about my need to run this path.

"Yeah, with a one-way ticket to the Grim Reaper." He studied me. "Why do you really run up here?"

I frowned. "What do you mean?"

"I think you know."

I thought about it for a minute. "I play it safe."

He nodded encouragingly.

I hesitated, not sure I should tell a man I really didn't know this about myself, but it was too late to back up now. "I play it safe in all aspects of my life. I follow the rules. I always have. You have to be a rule follower, in a way, to be a good dancer. Running is different for me. It's my time, and I want to take a risk. Running here makes me feel alive and a little out of control when the rest of my life is so controlled." My cheeks burned. "I can't believe I said all that."

"I'm glad you did," he said quietly and then looked down at the road, probably to give me a moment to compose myself. He examined the two sets of skid marks on the road. "This is where it happened, then."

"Yes."

He walked to the edge of the road and stared down the hill. His gaze stopped on the scarred tree where Samantha's car had finally stopped, just as my gaze had the first time I had seen it.

"Wow, this is where it happened." His voice was quiet.

I stood next to him.

"You really shouldn't run up here. It's got bad vibes now. Plus, if a car came around the curve too fast, you would never see it, and the driver would never see you."

"You sound like Maelynn."

"Maelynn is a smart woman. I've always liked her, and she makes one killer cup of coffee. I think she will double my habit."

"She has for most of the people in town. Myself included." I paused. "You and Maelynn are right. I may change my route. There are many places to run around Seneca Lake. After what happened, this spot has lost some of its appeal to me. But I still had to come back one more time to face it."

"I get that." He squinted at me in the sunlight. "You're a lot braver than a lot of people I know, Piper. Other people run away from what makes them sad, but you ran to it." And then, he added in a quieter voice, "You're braver than I am."

"I'm not any braver than you. You're here too."

He reached out like he was going to touch me and then pulled his hand back like he'd remembered something. Perhaps that we were supposed to be business partners, maybe someday friends, but nothing more than that. "I suppose that's true," he said as he dropped his hand.

"Race you back down the hill?" he asked, and then took off.

"Hey!" I cried, but my competitive streak kicked in and I ran down the steep hill after him.

He was six yards in front me. I knew that the chances of my catching him were slim to none, but that didn't stop me from trying. At the bottom of the hill, the road flattened out, and Tate and I ran by the imposing iron gate of Lake Waters Retreat.

I yelled at Tate to stop, but he either didn't hear me or chose not to, because he kept running. When we reached Mrs. Berger's house, Tate did stop, because the elderly woman stood in the middle of her driveway, waving her arms widely.

"Help! Help!" she cried.

CHAPTER TWENTY-TWO

"W HAT'S WRONG?" TATE ASKED, ALARMED.
I staggered to a stop beside him.
As I had predicted, she said, "Romy
is up the tree again, Darby. Can you get him?"

My shoulders sagged.

"Who's Romy?" Tate asked.

I was happy to see he was panting now. At least my
running had pushed him to break a sweat. Even if I
couldn't beat him in the footrace, I was glad I was fast
enough to make him work for his win.

"Romy is Mrs. Berger's cat, and for whatever reason, he likes to climb a giant tree in her backyard.
Unfortunately, he's either too chicken or not able to get
down by himself."

"Romy is not a chicken," Mrs. Berger said, offended.

Uh-oh.

I waved my hands at her. "I didn't mean it in a bad
way."

"He is a distinguished Maine Coon cat and should
be treated with respect." Mrs. Berger adjusted the

pillbox hat that matched her lavender pantsuit. She tended toward pastel in her color choices.

"Ummm..."

Tate stifled a laugh.

Mrs. Berger narrowed her eyes at him. "I don't appreciate the laughter, young man." Then she pulled up short. "Oh my stars! It's Tate Porter." She grabbed him by the face and squeezed his cheeks together.

Tate looked at me and whispered, "Help."

I grinned and shook my head.

Tate narrowed his eyes. I suspected I would later pay for not rescuing him, but I was enjoying his discomfort too much as Mrs. Berger gave him the once over.

"You've turned into a very handsome young man. It's no wonder Darby chose you as her running buddy. I would chase you down too if I was twenty years younger. That was before I got my new hips too!"

Now I was the one who was scowling. Tate was *not* my running buddy.

Tate smirked, or it looked like he did. It was hard to tell because his face was being squished together by Mrs. Berger's wrinkled hands.

Gently, he took her hands from his face and held them lightly. "It is so good to see you again, Mrs. Berger. I had no idea you still lived in this house."

"I do. I've scared off every developer who's wanted to buy this place."

"Good for you, Mrs. Berger. Stick to your guns," Tate said and carefully let go of her hands.

Mrs. Berger pointed at him. "I like him. Excellent

running buddy, Darby. Much better than Austin Caster. That boy is too stiff, like he has a stick—"

"You said Romy was stuck up the tree," I interrupted before she could finish.

"Oh yes, the poor old dear." She picked up her cane, which she'd dropped when she'd taken hold of Tate's face. "Come with me." She turned down the long driveway toward the house.

"She's moving pretty fast," Tate said as he followed. "And do you notice the cane isn't even touching the ground?"

"It's less support and more of a weapon," I whispered back.

"Great," Tate muttered.

Mrs. Berger led us back to the tree I had climbed so many times before. Up on the same branch, over twenty feet from the ground, was a large orange ball of fluff.

"How'd he get up there?" he asked, his neck craned back as far as it would go.

"He's a cat," Mrs. Berger said. "Cats climb trees."

Tate eyed me. "I don't think your cat would climb a tree."

He was probably right. Gumshoe would be too worried about mussing up his fur. I was pretty certain Romy never worried about that.

The cat let out a great yowl.

"He sounds like a mountain lion," Tate said. "Are you sure that's a housecat? Even from down here, he looks very big."

"He's twenty-three pounds," Mrs. Berger said proudly.

He gaped at her.

"I will have you know that is a perfectly acceptable weight for an adult male Maine Coon." She poked at his leg with her cane.

Tate jumped back as if the cane had a Taser on the end. I covered my grin. I was really enjoying his discomfort more than I should.

Romy yowled again. I think he was frustrated he wasn't receiving his mistress's undivided attention.

"I'd better get up there before Romy throws a complete fit." I grabbed the lowest branch.

Mrs. Berger poked my bottom with her cane. "No," she said, eyeing Tate. "We need to know what this running buddy is made of and if he really can keep up with you. Tate Porter, you go up the tree and fetch my cat."

Tate held up his hands, and for the first time since he had returned to Herrington, I would say he looked scared. "No, no, no, I'm not the one who you want to climb up a tree to rescue a cat. Piper is perfect for this job. She's small and compact, and can shimmy up there like a little spider monkey."

I scowled at him. "I think it would be good for him to give it a go." I might have let him off easy if it hadn't been for the spider monkey comment. I could be a little sensitive, I admit, when someone referenced my size in such a way.

"Good, good," Mrs. Berger said. "Then it's settled." She pointed to the boughs of the tree. "Up you go."

"Wait," Tate said. "I know, let's ask the fire department to rescue your cat. That's their job, isn't it? It's what you pay municipal taxes for. You don't want to be cheated out of services the city owes you by having Darby or me fetch him. You already paid for the service; you might as well use it."

"The fire department is volunteer and in the next town over." My mouth twitched up in a smile. "They don't suit up for cat rescues in Herrington."

"No, they do not," Mrs. Berger agreed.

Tate gave me pleading eyes.

I shrugged. "Watch out for his claws. He scratches when he's upset."

Romy yowled, making it clear to everyone in a three-mile radius that he was a very upset feline.

Tate groaned and put his hand on the lowest limb.

He climbed up the tree with ease, much easier than I ever had. I attributed this to his training in the Army—didn't he have to climb over things all the time there?—and the fact that he was over a foot taller than I am. He didn't have as many tree limbs to climb to be at the same level with the cat.

When he was a foot away from Romy, the cat hissed in his face. When he reached out to touch the cat, Romy swiped at him with claws out. Tate screamed and swore a string of curse words I hadn't heard in years.

"I should have made popcorn," Mrs. Berger said with a mischievous smile.

I couldn't agree more.

"The view isn't bad either," she continued.

I blushed.

"Are you okay up there?" I called.

"Just fine!" Tate snapped. Clearly, he wasn't fine at all.

I took pity on him. "Maybe I should tell him to come down and go up myself. I don't want him or Romy to get hurt."

Mrs. Berger shook her cane at me. "No. When a woman is picking a running buddy, she must know he is worthy of her in all ways. What if your cat got caught in a tree? Shouldn't your running buddy be able to retrieve him?"

Like Tate had said, there was no way diva Gumshoe was going to be climbing a tree. He refused to even go outside when the front door was wide open and no one was in his path to block him. Also, I wasn't sure where Mrs. Berger had gotten this "running buddy" thing. Was running buddy even a term for, what...boyfriend? Was that what she was trying to imply? Because Tate was *not* boyfriend material for me. Ever.

"He doesn't even have a towel. Why don't we get that to help him? Do you still have the towel I used in your mud room?" I started for the house.

"I got him!" Tate called from the tree as if he was as surprised by this turn of events as the rest of us.

Mrs. Berger and I peered into the tree. Sure enough, Tate stood precariously on a branch with a hissing and swiping cat in his hands. Because he was holding the cat with two hands, he wasn't holding on to the tree.

I cupped my hands around my mouth. "Tuck him

under your arm like a football, and hold on to the tree with the other hand."

"That's easier said than done," Tate shouted back.

"Trust me. He will calm down if you do that."

"If he takes my arm off, I'm blaming you, Piper."

Mrs. Berger clicked her tongue. "That's ridiculous. Romy is a dear. He would never take a man's arm off."

I was beginning to wonder how well Mrs. Berger knew her cat.

Tate finally did as I instructed and tucked Romy under his arm. The cat stopped fussing and trying to scratch him. Romy wasn't happy by any stretch of the imagination, if his continued hissing and spitting was any indication, but at least Tate might survive.

Tate carefully climbed down the tree. When he reached lowest branch, he let himself drop to the ground, landing on his feet...like a cat.

Mrs. Berger held out her arms to Romy, and Tate quickly passed off the animal. She rubbed her face in Romy's ruff. "You poor creature. I'm so sorry you've had such a fright. I hope the big man in the tree didn't scare you."

Tate shot me a look, and I covered my mouth to fight back a giggle.

"Why does your cat keep going up the tree, Mrs. Berger?" he asked.

She looked up from Romy. "I don't know exactly. He has a lot of reasons, I'm sure. Romy doesn't always share his plans with me before he takes action. Today, I know he went up there because those fools from Lake

Waters Retreat were back again. Every time they come, they make Romy nervous, and up the tree he goes."

I perked up. "What fools?"

"It's that Matt Billows fellow and a few of his men in black."

"Men in black?" Tate asked.

"His henchmen."

"Why were they here? It must have been very early. It's eight thirty now," I said.

"They were here at six sniffing around my property."

"Why?" Tate asked.

"They said they were measuring my dock because they needed to expand the resort's access to the water. They have a meeting with the city council about it and can claim eminent domain because it would be good for the success of the city if Lake Waters could accommodate more guests. They want to tear down my house!" She took a breath and held Romy closer to her chest. "I told them, 'Over my dead body.'"

I shivered as I thought of what had happened to Samantha. I didn't know for sure that Billows was the one who'd killed my mentor and friend, but I knew in my gut that Lake Waters had something to do with it.

"There's a town council meeting about it tonight?" Tate asked.

"Yes, and you'd better believe I'm going to be there."

I glanced at Tate. "We'll be there too."

Mrs. Berger's eyes shone. "Thank you both. I'm not afraid. I have been able to fight them off for decades and I will continue to do that. That place is a nuisance." She glared in the direction of Lake Waters. "It's no matter. I need to get Romy inside so I can warm up his milk and tuna. That's what he loves most for breakfast. You two stick together. I approve of this match." With that, she went into her house.

"What do you think of that?" Tate asked.

"I think we need to go to that council meeting and learn what Billows is up to. I have a feeling all the odd things happening are related to him."

"Me too," he said, and then there was a pause "So," he cocked his head. "How do I measure up as a running buddy?"

I rolled my eyes, but I ran all the way home with a smile on my face.

CHAPTER TWENTY-THREE

N AT WAS IN THE OFFICE when I got back. She eyed my sweaty clothes. "You were out for your run a long time. I was beginning to wonder what became of you. You can't do that now, with what happened to Samantha. It gives me a scare."

"I got caught up with Mrs. Berger and her cat again."

She dropped two more pennies from her wallet into the half-full jar on her desk. "I thought it was something like that, which is why I didn't call Austin."

Thank goodness for that. I started to make my way to the stairs when Nat cleared her throat. "Is there something else?" I asked.

"I've been so upset over what happened to Samantha."

I stepped back into the room and sat on the arm of the extra-long couch. "We both have. The whole town has, actually."

She nodded. "I could tell that from the party at

Floured Grounds. She was beloved and well-respected. I just..."

I leaned forward. "What is it, Nat?"

"I don't think I can work here any longer. There are too many memories."

I almost fell to the floor. That was the last thing I'd thought she'd say. Nat had been with Two Girls from the beginning. Samantha had hired her as the office manager even before she'd offered to partner with me.

"This has been a very difficult time. I don't think either of us is in the right frame of mind to make any big decisions right now."

"My mind is made up," she said firmly and patted a letter on the corner of her desk. "I have an official resignation letter right here. I wasn't sure if I should give it to you or to Tate, but I hardly know him. I don't feel comfortable giving him the letter. I assume you will share the information with him."

I stood in the middle of the office, my mouth hanging open. "Are you sure? I don't want to you to regret this decision down the road."

"I'm sure. What happened to Samantha reminded me that life is short. It's time for me to move on. I've been thinking for a long while that I need a change. I have been here from the beginning, and I care about you and Samantha so much. However, I want to do my own thing now, and with her gone..." She trailed off.

"Is there anything I can do to change your mind?" This was the worst time for Nat to leave. I didn't have a handle on managing the agency alone, and I didn't know what Tate's role would be in all of it. I needed her steady hand.

"No."

That was the truth. When Nat made up her mind about an action or a person, it was made up. In all the time I had known her, I had never seen her change her mind.

"Okay. I hate to see you go. You have been such an integral part of Two Girls, and I'm going to miss seeing you every day. If this is the best decision for you, I won't try to talk you out of it. Do you already have a job lined up, or do you need a reference from me?"

"I don't need a thing. I got everything I wanted from working here. I have you and Samantha to thank for that."

"Okay," I said and backed away.

I shook my head all the way upstairs to my room. What was I going to do without her?

A little while later, I came back downstairs and told Nat I was headed to the library to research one of the open cases. I didn't tell her the case I was working on was Samantha's murder. Because of her resignation, something had shifted between Nat and me.

As I did with most places in town, I went to the library on foot. Not that I had much choice to travel any other way. I didn't want to borrow Maelynn's minivan again, and my car was still missing, presumed stolen. At least, that was what I presumed. I didn't know what the police thought had happened to the car.

When I stepped through the automatic doors into my mother's library, it felt like coming home. I had spent most of my childhood in this building. It was where I'd come every day after school, and where I'd spent the bulk of the summer. I knew the building as well as employees did.

Even so, the building had changed in the last twenty-some years. There were new fixtures, carpet and paint, and the books were constantly being replaced or weeded to make room for newer titles, but the children's room was in the same place, and the bean bag chair where I'd spent ninety percent of my time was still there. It had been re-covered at least three times since, though.

The library circulation desk was near the front door, and my mother was there, her eyebrows raised. "Darby, what brings you here? You haven't been in the library since the third of last month."

I sighed. My mother did this to all her patrons- reminded them of the last time they had been in.

My mother had a near-photographic memory, which was helpful in her profession. She could remember exactly where she had last seen a missing book or where it had gone on the shelf. It wasn't helpful as far as having her as a mom because she remembered with excruciating detail every mistake I had made throughout my life, and I had made a quite a few.

"How is everything going now that the funeral is over? How is Tate settling in? Does he plan to stay?" She asked in rapid succession.

Leave it to my mother to cut right to the chase. "I thought librarians were supposed to answer questions, not ask them."

"You can only answer a question if you're willing to ask a few first," she replied breezily.

I was so relieved I had never told anyone about Samantha and my plans for the business in case anything happened to either one of us. That especially went for my mother. Had she known, she would have held it against Tate. As much as I didn't like his being here, and as much as I would have preferred to operate the agency under my own rules, I didn't want him to be disliked for something he didn't do.

"What brings you in today? You don't have anything on hold at the moment."

"I was wondering if I could use the microfilm to look at some old newspapers." This wasn't an unusual request for me to make. As private detectives in Herrington, Samantha and I had been both heavy users of the library. Because of my familiarity with the resources and the equipment from having worked there, I usually was the one who did the library research. I suspected the same would be true with Tate as with my former partner.

"Can I help you find a particular article?" she asked eagerly.

I shook my head. I didn't want her to hear my suspicions about the Billows family. "I should be fine on my own. I want to know if it's okay to use right now if you didn't have anything else going on in there."

She sighed, and I knew I'd disappointed her because I didn't need her help.

"The local history room is open. If you need any help, I'm happy to pop in."

I smiled.

The local history room was in the back of the main floor. It was enclosed in glass. The lights were on, but the room appeared to be empty.

It was where the town stored its historical documents, a few artifacts like the first mayor's pen set, and local newspapers dating back to the nineteenth century.

The newer newspapers were in digital form, and the library was starting to digitize the oldest issues of the local paper for preservation. As far as I knew, they were still working on the nineteenth century. Papers from the 1960s were in paper form or could be found on microfilm, which was what I was looking for.

Lakes Waters Retreat, according to its website, had opened in 1968. Before that, it had been a large private estate owned by the Billows family. I was curious why the resort had come about. Up until that time, Herrington had been a sleepy little lakeside town in the hills. However, the resort had changed everything. I was betting there had been a lot about it in the local paper at the time. I decided to start with 1967 to gather a background.

I stepped through the glass door carefully and closed it behind me. There was one woman in the room poring over old maps. She was tucked in a corner behind a bookcase, which was why I hadn't seen her through the window. She had a magnifying glass out and leaned in so close that she appeared to be slumped over, asleep. When I took a closer look, I saw that she was asleep. That was a no-no in the library, but I decided to let her be. Knowing my mother, she would be in here before long and she'd wake the woman up herself. I think my mom got some perverse pleasure in doing that, so who was I to take it away from her?

The sleeping woman was on the right side of the room, and the microfilm cabinets, holding the films and the single microfilm machine, were on the left. The library only had one machine, because there wasn't a large demand for microfilm any longer. I couldn't remember ever using it in high school or college. The only reason I knew how to operate the machinery was because I'd worked in the library and had helped patrons, most of whom had used it to trace dead relatives.

My mother, bless her, had made an index of the newspaper, printed in a giant binder next to the microfilm machine. The binder was so huge I had to stand up to turn the pages. I flipped to the Lake Waters Retreat entry. The first mention of it was in 1966. That would be an even better place to start, I decided.

I opened the drawer that held the 1960s. The film was organized in neatly labeled boxes. I removed the one I needed and sat at the machine. Using a microfilm machine was like wrestling an octopus. There were so many arms and the moment you thought you had it handled, you lost control. Also, the film had to go in just so around the spool. If it didn't, you could very well get slapped in the face with it.

I scrolled until I got to the page mentioned in the index. The headline read, "Billows plans exclusive resort." The next headline said, "Town in Uproar over Billows Build."

I read the article more closely.

Jameson Billows says Lake Waters Retreat will bring more income into the community of Herrington and make it a major tourist destination for the elite who would like to rest and recuperate after private procedures, such as plastic surgery and clinical exhaustion. Some locals protest that the resort is too exclusive. The rates start at eight hundred dollars a night.

I whistled. Eight hundred dollars a night was a lot of money in the late 1960s. Who was I kidding? Eight hundred dollars a night was a lot of money right *now*. I would never pay that to stay anywhere.

I kept reading.

Josh Porter, head of security at the resort, says Lake Waters will have the added benefit of top-notch security, so that wealthy guests can feel secure and happy during their stay.

I started at the name. Josh Porter. That was Samantha's father, who'd been killed when she was a child.

The door opened.

I heard some muttering coming from the woman with the maps.

"I wasn't sleeping," she mumbled. Clearly, she was barely awake now.

"No one said you were," Tate said.

I peeked over the microfilm cabinet that blocked my view and watched as the woman packed up her things and bustled out of the room.

He grinned at me. "I think I would make an excellent librarian, had I been so inclined."

I shook my head. "I'm guessing you're the kind of person who thinks he would be great at just about everything, had he just been given a chance."

Tate shrugged. "It doesn't hurt to be confident."

"How did you know where I was?"

"Nat told me you went to the library, and then your mom pointed me in the right direction. I didn't have to use my super detective skills to track you down. Find anything interesting?"

"As a matter of fact, I did." I paused. "Your grandfather's name was Joshua Porter, right?"

"Yeah," Tate said and walked around the cabinet to stand by me.

"Did you know he worked for Lake Waters Retreat?"

"He did? What does that have to do with my aunt's murder?"

"I don't know yet. It might have nothing to do with it, or it might have everything to do with it. We need to find out which."

CHAPTER TWENTY-FOUR

"WHAT DO YOU HAVE THERE?" Tate asked. I pointed at the screen. "Your grandfather's name appears right there. He was killed, wasn't he?"

"That's what Aunt Samantha always said, but the case was never solved."

I looked up at him. "Maybe she was cozying up to Billows because she wanted to solve her father's murder. It is why she became a private investigator."

He nodded. "It would make more sense, her wanting to work at Lake Waters, if it would lead to solving his murder."

"That's what I was thinking," I said, and finally, after all this time, I understood why Samantha had been trying to get in with Billows. It had been to find out who killed her father, and why. Relief swept through me. She hadn't wanted to throw our agency away, but felt she had to close it and work for Billows, so that she could discover the truth.

"Can you pull up the story about my granddad's death?"

"Sure. Will that be hard for you see?"

"Whether it's hard or not isn't the point. I need to see it."

I nodded and flipped through the massive index my mother had created until I came to the name "Porter, Joshua." There were sub-entries, because my mother was nothing if not thorough. The subcategory was "Porter, Joshua, murder investigation." It had happened in 1991. Samantha would have been a preteen at the time.

I went to the cabinet and removed the correct roll of microfilm, scrolled through it, and searched for the article. All the while, Tate looked on. He stood lightly on the balls of his feet as if he were tempted to bolt. Perhaps he was.

I glanced over my shoulder. "I found it."

I read the article, and Tate read over my shoulder. Part of me wanted to swat him away, but I resisted.

July 17, 1991. Joshua Porter, Sr. (48) was found dead last night. He was stabbed in his home with a kitchen knife. Porter's wife and young daughter were out of state visiting friends at the time of the murder. There was evidence of a forced entry into the home. The police believe that Porter interrupted a burglary in progress.

Porter was the head of security at Lake Waters Retreat. The resort refused to comment on his death. Investigation is ongoing. The police ask anyone with information to come forward and notify the Herrington police department immediately.

Tate swallowed hard. "I didn't know any of this. Aunt Samantha never told me. She didn't like to talk about her father much."

I glanced at him. "She didn't talk to me much about him either."

I saved the pages and printed them.

Tate wouldn't look me in the eye. "I knew my grandfather had died tragically, but I never spoke to my parents or aunt about it. After my parents died..."

I stood up. "You were a kid then. I'm sure their deaths were all you could have handled at that age."

"I should have asked." Regret and sadness settled on his face. "1991 wasn't that long ago. There have to be people in town and in the police force who remember this."

"I wonder if the police have made the connection between the two deaths," I mused.

"We'll have to ask Officer Caster to find out. It might go better if you ask him, not me."

I glanced at him. "Why?"

He smiled. "I don't think he likes me all that much, and I'm sure he doesn't like how much time we spend together, either."

I gathered up the articles I had printed from the machine. I had also sent copies to my email in case these were misplaced. It was helpful to read the difficult script printed out rather than on the screen.

"What time is it?"

"Close to five."

"Good. I didn't know I was here so long, and I don't want to miss the city hall meeting."

"Me neither. Mrs. Berger is taking on Lake Waters. That will be worth the price of admission. I'll bring the popcorn."

Outside the local history room, the main part of the library was busier now that school and the work day were over. Adults browsed the shelves, and all the computers were in use. High school students sat at a couple of long tables, pretending to study. Mostly they were giggling. Not much had changed since I was a teenager, when it came to studying with friends.

My mother walked around the library, pushing in chairs and picking up forgotten scraps of paper, while her teenaged staff collected books left on tables and at the end of the shelves onto a cart. She smiled at us. "I hope I will see you again soon with that library card, Tate. We have so many great things going on at the library you will enjoy."

I stopped in front of the desk. "You got a library card?"

He held up the bright blue-and-yellow card, the color scheme chosen when they'd been the colors of the local school system. "Hot off the presses."

A library card meant he planned to stay, didn't it? Was he going to really give this a go? He said he was, but I couldn't say I believed him. There were so many times Samantha had told me Tate had said he would stay in this place or that place, but it had never stuck. I couldn't take the library card as a promise that he was here for good.

I glanced at my mother. "I thought you had to have proof of residency to get a library card."

"You do, but I trust he will bring it in when his living arrangements are settled." She smiled at him.

Tate put his library card back into this wallet. "Trust me. I got the full inquisition. Your mother asked me what my life plan was. If I was married or had children. The works."

I grimaced. I knew for a fact those questions weren't on the library card application. That was my mother, the expert at gathering information from books and from people.

My cheeks flushed. "I'm sorry. You know you didn't have to answer any of those questions, don't you?"

He grinned. "I didn't mind. I don't have anything to hide."

My mother patted her hair. "I like him, and he has a lot more personality than Austin ever did."

"Mom!" I yelped.

She looked back at Tate. "She doesn't like it when I give her librarian real talk."

"Is that what that is?" Tate asked with a chuckle. "I have never heard of library real talk before."

I yelped.

Mom folded her hands in front of her. "I'm glad Tate was able to find you. Did you find everything you need?"

I held up the sheaf of papers in my hand, but took care not to show my mother what they were about, because the interrogation would *really* commence if I did.

"Good. I always like to see a satisfied patron." She

picked another book off a table and set it on her cart. "Tate, what do you like to read? I like to know all my patrons' interests."

"History mostly."

"Very good. I will have some options for you the next time you come in."

I tugged on Tate's arm. "We had better go or she will load you up with books right now."

My mother ignored my comment. "We have a family dinner once a week. It's the only time I can get Darby to commit to. We would love it if you could join us for it tomorrow. We are all very curious about Darby's new partner."

I stared at my mother. I had forgotten about family dinner tomorrow night. And I hadn't expected her to invite Tate. What was she up to?

"Mom, don't put him on the spot like that. He's very busy dealing with his aunt's affairs and learning the business."

Tate smiled. "I would love to come. All those other things can wait. I haven't sat down at a family dinner in a very long time."

My mother smiled. "Good. We will see you at six sharp tomorrow." She glanced at me. "Don't be late."

CHAPTER TWENTY-FIVE

"I CAN'T BELIEVE YOU AGREED TO have dinner with my parents," I said to Tate when we hit the sidewalk.

"What's wrong with that?"

"Nothing," I muttered.

He stopped in the middle of the sidewalk. "That sure doesn't sound like nothing."

My cell phone rang, and I pulled it out of the back pocket of my jeans. The call was from Maelynn. I could have ignored it, but it was a good excuse to stop talking to Tate about dinner at my parents' house.

"Darb, you are going to want to come down here right now." Maelynn was breathless.

"What's going on?"

Tate watched me with concern.

"They are pulling a car out of the lake right in front of the coffee shop, and it looks a lot like yours."

My heart stopped for a second. "I'm on my way." I ended the call and started to jog in the direction of Lakeshore Avenue.

Tate ran alongside me. "Piper, what is it?"

Without missing a step, I repeated what Maelynn had said.

His mouth fell open and then he grabbed my wrist and sprinted along the sidewalk. "We have to know for sure!"

When we reached Floured Grounds, we were out of breath from running. In front of us, a cluster of emergency vehicles was parked on the grassy area in front of the lake, with officers and divers milling around. A large tow truck, bigger than the one that had pulled Samantha's car out of the ravine, was winching in a long, taut chain that extended into the water. I could see the white hood of a small car above the water's surface.

Maelynn met us on the sidewalk. "I can't believe this is happening."

"How long have they been here?"

"The tow truck got here ten minutes ago when I called you. There had diving crews in the lake all afternoon, but I didn't even stop to think they might be looking for your car. I thought they were surveying the lake or something. Had I known, I would have called you a lot sooner."

I smiled at her, even though my stomach was in knots. "Don't worry about it. Who knew my car would be found here, of all places?"

"This is one of the busiest places in Herrington. How did the car get in the water without anyone seeing it?" Tate asked.

"Whoever dumped it must have done it at night," Maelynn said.

"And was extra quiet," he said.

The winch on the tow truck screeched, and the officers and divers stepped back as the car rolled onto the grass. I didn't need to see the license plate to know it was my car. I could tell from here that it was the right make and model. My stomach turned, and I covered my mouth.

To the left of the tow truck, I saw a flash of metal and a glimpse of a baseball cap.

"Oh no, he doesn't!" I broke into a run.

"Darb," Maelynn called. "Where are you going?"

I didn't stop to answer, and ran around the police vehicles and the tow truck until I found Benny B. "What are you doing?" I demanded.

"Working on my story," he smirked. "Do you have any comment on the car?"

"What's going on over here?"

I glanced over my shoulder and saw Austin marching toward us. Dark circles hung under his eyes, and his pants were wet up to the knee. Most likely from wading in the lake to help pull out my car.

"What's going on?" he asked again.

"He was taking photos," I said.

Tate jogged over to us.

"Can I see those pictures?" Austin asked.

Benny B grinned. "Not without a warrant."

Austin narrowed his eyes. "Get away from the scene."

The man shrugged. "Fine. I got what I needed." He

slung his camera strap over his shoulder and walked away.

After, Benny B was gone, I asked, "How could no one see the car go in the water here? This is a major street."

Austin shrugged. "We didn't get any reports about anyone seeing it happen. Something like that would have been reported, I'm sure." He glanced at me. "It's your car."

I nodded. "I know." I had known as soon as I'd gotten the call from Maelynn.

"The front fender on the right passenger side is dented. There is black paint there."

He didn't have to remind me Samantha's car was black.

"If the paint on the car is a match to what was found at the scene of the crime..." Austin trailed off.

"So it's likely this car ran my aunt off the road, and it's Darby's car," Tate said. "But that doesn't mean Darby did it. She reported the car was stolen. Someone stole the car to frame her."

I looked at him, and my heart swelled. Did he believe I was innocent after all?

Austin didn't say anything.

Tate folded his arms. "Come on, you think Darby would sink the car she killed Samantha with in the lake right in front of the agency? How stupid would that be? There are hundreds of places to unload or hide a car in the Finger Lakes. Whoever drove it into the lake here wanted you to find it."

Something like a ray of hope started to grow in my

chest. Tate was right. I smiled at him, and he smiled back at me. He believed I was innocent. He really did, and that meant more to me than he could possibly know. For the first time, I thought we really could be partners.

But I looked away. Did I think he was innocent too? I still didn't know why he'd been in Herrington the day Samantha was murdered.

"Darby, if you are dead set on finding out who killed Samantha, do it soon," Austin said. "I'm afraid time is running out."

"Officer Caster!" one of the divers called.

I grabbed Austin's arm. "What do you mean, time is running out?"

Austin looked down at my hand on his arm and frowned. My heart constricted. There had been a time when I'd thought he loved me, that he wanted me to touch him. That time had passed. I let go of his arm. Austin joined the rest of his officers.

Tate rocked back on his heels. "I really don't know what you saw in him. I mean, yeah, he has the looks. Blond hair, dreamy blue eyes. But what else does he have?"

"I'm not in the mood, Tate," I said.

"What he doesn't have is loyalty," he went on, ignoring my comment. I turned to face him. "If he loved you, he wouldn't seriously consider you as a suspect."

I wasn't sure that was true. Didn't loved ones surprise their friends and family all the time? Even so, I said, "Thank you." If I said anything more, I was afraid I would cry.

CHAPTER TWENTY-SIX

I N HERRINGTON, THE TOWN HALL and city office were in the old schoolhouse, which had been built in the early 1900s. Although the building was picturesque, it wasn't a good place for a meeting with a big crowd, and the expansion of Lake Waters Retreat was sure to attract that. Instead, the meeting was held in the high school auditorium.

Fifteen minutes before the town council meeting was to begin, Tate and I stood outside the auditorium door. He wasn't moving.

"You okay?" I asked.

He gave a sharp shake to his head, as if trying to dispel a memory. "I never expected to go back into this building. Ever."

A few people walked around us to get inside.

"Was high school tough for you?"

"It wasn't great."

I was surprised to hear that. When I was a freshman and Tate was a senior, he'd always seemed so confident. I'd thought he was the big-man-on-campus type.

There was so much I didn't know or understand about my new business partner and so much I wanted to know. I wanted to know what kind of partnership I was in for. Was Tate here to stay? Would he take this job seriously? Was he amusing himself with my agency before he moved on and found something more exciting?

We'd just met again after over a decade apart, and he wasn't very forthcoming. My life was out there on display for him. He'd met my mother, my cat, and would meet the rest of my family tomorrow at dinner, apparently. Goodness, he even knew my ex-boyfriend.

I knew next to nothing about him.

"Are we going to go in?" I asked.

"Yes, right." He opened the door for me. "I want to grab some good seats to see Mrs. Berger tell Billows what's what."

I wanted that too.

The auditorium had theater seating, and it was half full. On the stage, the mayor, other town officials—including Samantha's ex-boyfriend Logan Montgomery—and Matt Billows sat on metal folding chairs in a straight row. Billows and Mayor Brenda Granada chatted while they waited for the meeting to begin.

"This is quite a crowd," I said.

"There's your mom," Tate said and waved at her.

I'd expected to see her. Since the library was dependent on the town for funding, she usually came to every meeting she could. She said it was because she had to be a presence for the library, even if she didn't say a word in the meeting.

Mom waved back at Tate and me and gestured for us to sit with her.

I shook my head. It was more important to find Mrs. Berger. She had to be here already. "She's probably near the front," I told Tate.

I was right; we found Mrs. Berger front and center, glaring at Billows on the stage. Her pantsuit was pressed, her hair perfectly curled, trusty cane at her side.

"There you are." Mrs. Berger patted the seat beside her. "I knew the two of you were coming, so I saved you each a seat. Running buddy, you sit right here next to me. Darby, sit on the other side of him."

Tate gave me a panicked look, and I just smiled. It appeared to me that Mrs. Berger was a wee bit enamored of Mr. Porter, and I was going to enjoy every minute of it.

We took our seats as the mayor stood and walked over to the podium. "Thank you so much for coming. I hereby call this special meeting of the city council to order." She paused. "As you all know, we are here this evening to discuss the expansion of Lake Waters Retreat two hundred feet west of their current property. Matt Billows, owner of Lake Waters, is here to explain how this expansion will benefit both his company and the town of Herrington as a whole. We will begin with his presentation." She looked over her shoulder. "Matt?"

Billows stood up. "Thank you, Brenda."

Mayor Granada simpered. I didn't take that as a good sign for Mrs. Berger winning her argument. It seemed the mayor was already on board with Billows' plans.

Billows walked up to the mic. "It is such a pleasure to speak to you tonight about the wonderful opportunity Lake Water Retreat and, by extension, the town of Herrington has to attract more guests to this area. There will be little or no negative impact on townsfolk to make this minuscule expansion."

"Liar!" Mrs. Berger shouted and waved her cane in the air. She almost whacked Tate in the head.

He leaned over and whispered to me. "If I don't make it out alive, tell Gumshoe I much prefer him to Romy."

I snorted.

"Mrs. Berger," Billows said breezily. "I can understand your concern, considering the location of the expansion, but I will ask you to wait until the end of my presentation for any comments and questions."

Mrs. Berger stood up and waved her cane in the air again. "Tell them where this expansion is going to be, then."

Billows scowled down at his notes. Apparently, Mrs. Berger had caused him to skip ahead in his planned speech. "If we can wait to the end—"

She smacked her cane on the edge of the stage. She was having none of it. "Tell them where the expansion will be *right now*."

Billows jumped back.

The mayor stood up. "Mrs. Berger please have a

seat, or I will have to ask Office Caster to escort you out of the high school."

I closed my eyes for a moment. Austin was here. I hadn't seen him, but of course he would be, especially if whatever happened in the auditorium tonight was related to Samantha's murder.

I wished I could stop myself from doing it, but I turned around in my seat and looked for Austin. I saw him at the rear of the room beside the doors, holding his hands behind his back. He caught me looking, and I wanted to slide right under my seat and never come out again.

Mrs. Berger shook her cane. "You haven't heard the last of me." Then, she settled back into her seat next to Tate.

"I didn't know this show was going to be quite so violent," he whispered.

Billows pulled on his collar. "Now then, as I was saying, this expansion will be of great benefit to the town of Herrington. What I am seeing is an elite health and wellness complex for our clients. In order to be competitive in the rejuvenation business, we have to have the best of the best. This will bring an enormous amount of tax revenue to the area that can benefit the schools, town, and parks."

Murmurs rolled through the auditorium.

"What do you need from the council?" the mayor asked.

"Approval to build," Billows said with a small smile. He glanced down at Mrs. Berger, who was glaring at him so fiercely, I would have melted if she stared me down like that.

"We also need Herrington's support because in order to make this great addition to the area, we must purchase the land adjacent to Lake Waters. We have offered the owner three times its worth many times, but as of yet, she refuses to sell."

Mrs. Berger leaped out of her seat. "You'd better believe I refuse to sell. I built that house with my late husband and have lived there for over sixty years. Do you think I want to move? It's the prettiest spot on the lake, and I won't let you steal it from me. If you buy it, you will level the house I shared with Mr. Berger and tear it apart brick by brick." She raised her cane higher. "I know what your sort is like!"

"Sometimes," Billows said, flushing with anger, "it is more important to do something for the good of the entire town than for one person. I'm sorry, Mrs. Berger, but that's a fact. This market has the potential to bring millions upon millions of dollars into Herrington. Don't you want the town to flourish after you're gone?"

"I don't much care what happens to it after I'm gone if people like you are living here."

"How much money did you offer, Mr. Billows?" the mayor asked.

"Two and a half million."

There was a gasp in the audience. That was a lot of money to anyone who was sitting in the room. Lake Waters might be in Herrington to serve the wealthy, but there was no one living in town who could afford to spend one night at the resort.

Mayor Granada directed her next comment to Mrs. Berger. "That seems like a generous offer. Are you sure you don't want to take it? It is very likely the money you will receive for your land will be considerably less if the council votes for eminent domain."

"What am going to do with two-point-five million dollars?" Mrs. Berget stamped her cane on the floor. "I ask you. I'm ninety years old. I don't have the time to spend that money, and there is nothing on this earth I want to buy with it. I have my house and Romy. There is nothing else I need. I'm not from one of these younger generations that buys, buys, buys. Why can't he wait for me to die so I don't have to watch my home being destroyed?"

Tate winced as Mrs. Berger stamped her came on the ground again, barely missing his toe. He tucked his feet under his seat.

"Yes, well, Mrs. Berger..." She trailed off. "I don't think anyone wants you to die. We all understand why you are upset, but we have to do what's right for the town's future."

"Well, take it to a vote then. Let the people decide."

The mayor grimaced. "That's not how it works. The community elects officials to make decisions like this for them. That is representative government."

Mrs. Berger stamped her cane on the ground. "It's not my representative government. No, ma'am."

Logan spoke up. "I think if we wait until Mrs. Berger is no longer in any need of the house, it will be better for everyone."

"No!" Billows said. "No, that would be a waste of

time. If Herrington doesn't do this, it's a missed opportunity. The town will be kicking itself in a few years for not going for it."

"He wants to say that I refuse to die." Mrs. Berger cried. "And he's quite right on that point. I will stay alive forever if that means I can keep his grubby little hands off my house. It's not just my house either. It's Romy's home too."

"Who's Romy?" Mayor Granada asked.

"He's my cat. I just know that when they tear down the house, they will tear down Romy's climbing tree too. That breaks my heart; Romy loves that tree. He loves to climb it, and it's how he can spend the most time with Darby," Mrs. Berger said.

The mayor walked to the podium and edged Billows out of the way. By the expression on Billows' face, it was clear he wasn't used to being pushed aside. "We will take the suggestions and concerns of all parties to this matter into consideration. I propose that the council looks over the proposal from Lake Waters and puts the matter to a vote at the next council meeting."

"But that's a month away," Billows said, still standing on the stage, having not taken the hint from the mayor to sit down. "That will lose valuable time. In a month, it will be mid-October. We need to break ground before winter so we can be open for the summer season."

She eyed him. "I can understand your concern, but the council is not going to take lightly the act of demolishing a member of the community's home. We will review and put it to a vote one month from today." She slammed her gavel down on the podium for emphasis. "Now, I would like to move on to the next item on the agenda."

"This has definitely been worth the price of admission," Tate said to me.

"Admission was free," I said.

"I would have paid money to see Mrs. Berger stand up to Billows like that any day," Tate said.

I smiled. "Me too."

CHAPTER TWENTY-SEVEN

W HEN THE MEETING FINALLY WRAPPED up, after reports from the sanitation department, lake patrol, and others, I knew more about Herrington than ever before. I knew not to mess with Mayor Granada, for one. If she didn't like what you had to say, she shut you down fast.

Tate stood up and looked at his watch. "That's two hours I'll never get back."

"Nope."

"You were such dears to come and support me." Mrs. Berger patted my cheek. "I will be sure to tell Romy you were here sticking up for us."

"Any time, Mrs. Berger." I glanced at the stage and noticed Billows having an animated conversation with the mayor. Neither of them seemed happy about what was being said. "I think the council will vote in your favor."

Her eyes sparkled. "You do?"

I bit my lip, praying I wasn't getting her hopes up.

"You have a good chance, Mrs. Berger," a deep male voice said behind me.

I glanced over my shoulder and saw Logan standing there.

Mrs. Berger squinted at him. "How do you know, young man?"

He smiled. "Just know there are members on the council, myself included, who are on your side. We don't like the idea of you losing your home."

"I'm glad to hear it," she said. "I don't think you killed Samantha. You couldn't have if you want me to keep my house."

I winced, but to my surprise, Logan laughed. "I'll take that as a compliment." He glanced at me. "And I didn't kill her. I loved her." He said this so sincerely that I believed him. Still, I didn't know for sure that he was innocent, even though I didn't know how he could have stolen my car.

Mrs. Berger patted his arm.

"Excuse me," Logan said and left us to speak with the mayor. I watched him go, wondering what he knew about Samantha's movements at Lake Waters Retreat.

"Piper is right," Tate chimed in. "Herrington is a sleepy little lakeside town and always has been. From what I remember of this place, I don't think they want to lose that. I don't think anyone who lives here would like to see that, no matter how it might help the town. Herrington is fine the way it is."

"Well said, running buddy. Oh, I'm so glad you and Darby found each other. It does my heart good." She picked up her cane. "Now, I must be off home. Romy will be worried as to what became of me. I will be pleased to tell him we lived to fight another day."

"Do you need a ride home?" I asked.

She shook her head. "Don't be silly, I can drive fine, thank you." She marched away. Her cane never touched the ground.

I shook my head. "I think Mrs. Berger has the wrong idea about our relationship."

Tate waggled his eyebrows. "But does she?"

I was tempted to step on his foot, but I restrained myself.

Austin walked up to us. "I wish I could say I was surprised to find you here, but I'm not."

"I'm not surprised you're here, either," I said.

Austin didn't say anything.

Tate nodded to Austin. "Caster."

Austin nodded back. "Porter."

"What is it with the two of you?" I asked.

Austin shook his head. "It's a long story, and it shouldn't even be an issue anymore, with all the time that's past. I guess old grudges die hard."

"What is it?"

"Doesn't matter," Tate agreed.

I scowled at them.

"Tate!" My mother waved at him. "Come here."

Tate raised his eyebrows at me.

"Go," I said.

He glanced at Austin and walked away.

After he was gone, I turned to Austin. "Are you go-ing to tell me what's going on with you and Tate?"

"No." Austin changed the subject. "Billows said he offered you the head of security job at the resort."

That seemed to be an odd bit of information Billows would share with the police if he had any hope of hiring me. "Why would he do that?"

"He wanted to know if you would be a good fit for the job."

"Did you tell him, 'No, don't hire her, because she's a murder suspect'?"

"I didn't. I said you would be great."

"You did?"

He nodded and glanced toward Tate, who was in the middle of an animated conversation with my mother. They both appeared to be having a grand time. It didn't bode well for me if he and my mother were so chummy.

"Are you here because you suspect Billows is involved in Samantha's murder?" I asked.

"You know I can't answer that."

"Maybe not," I said. "But your presence here is telling."

He pressed his lips together. "I know you would do a great job for Billows, and he asked me to encourage you to take the position."

"Is that what you're doing?"

"No, I'm telling you to be careful. Very careful."

"Do you think he could be behind Samantha's death?"

Austin frowned. "He's never done anything specifically illegal, but he's not an honest man. He gets through loopholes in the system."

I thought about what had happened at Multigrain Market, but stopped myself from telling Austin about it.

Austin said, "I know you're a P.I. and you think you can handle just about anything or anyone, but Billows is different. Please remember that."

"Have they tested the paint from my car yet to see if it's a match?"

He looked pained. "The county lab is backed up, but they promised to get me the results tonight since it's a murder investigation." He paused. "I would be very surprised if the paint wasn't a match to your car."

"I would be too," I said in a low voice.

"You need to be careful until the case is closed."

"What do you mean?" I asked.

"If you didn't kill Samantha..."

I opened my mouth to protest, but he was quicker. "If you didn't kill Samantha, someone went to a lot of trouble to frame you for the crime. Stealing your car, using it as a murder weapon, and sinking it in Seneca Lake is a well-thought-out plan. Watch your back, and have Porter look out for you too. Not that I know what good he'd be to you, considering..."

I wanted to ask him for specifics, but he continued. "I want to believe you didn't do it, Darby, but the evidence is strong. If that paint comes back as a match, I will have to arrest you."

Austin cleared his throat. "Don't leave town."

I sucked in a breath.

His cell phone rang, and he checked the screen. "It's the station. I have to go." He walked away.

Across the auditorium, Tate waved me over to where he stood with my mother.

I tried to compose myself before I joined them. If Austin arrested me, I risked losing my private investigator license, not to mention my reputation. I took a breath and walked over.

"I was asking your mom what she remembered about my grandfather's murder," Tate said.

"Oh?" I hadn't planned to share that detail of the investigation with anyone yet. I hadn't even finished my own research on it.

"It was horrible." Mom adjusted the strap of her library tote bag on her shoulder. "Everyone in Herrington was on edge because the police believed it was an interrupted robbery. It seemed like Josh was completely caught off guard. Thank heaven your grandmother and the children, Josh Jr. and Samantha, were all away at the time of the break-in. I felt so bad for your grandmother! Her spirit was crushed after that."

Tate frowned.

She squeezed his arm. "Tragedy has hit your family very hard. Sometimes it seems that's the way of it. One family takes one hit after another, while another seems perfectly fine. Although that's rarely true. If there is something I've learned in my thirty-some years as a librarian, no one has a perfect life."

Tate's brows knit together as my mother spoke, and I realized how accurate her statement was. Perhaps Tate's family history was the reason he'd left for the Army and never come back until Samantha died. Then why had he left the service?

My mother smiled. "I need to get back to your father." She pointed at us. "I will see both of you for dinner tomorrow night. No excuses."

At this point, most of the auditorium had cleared out.

"When they said meeting adjourned, people really bolt around here," Tate said.

"I'm pretty sure when they got to the sanitation department's presentation, everyone in the room wanted to make a break for it."

Tate laughed. "While you were talking to lover boy—"

"Austin is not my lover boy," I said through clenched teeth.

"O-kay. There's no reason to get so testy about it."

I sighed.

"While you were talking to the very attentive police officer..."

I groaned. If he only knew that Austin had threatened to arrest me.

"I was thinking we need to get into Lake Water Retreat," Tate said.

"I thought we were going there on the pretense that I was considering Billows' job offer."

"We could, but the more I think about it, he's not going to show us anything bad about the resort. Also, I wonder if your job offer still stands. It was clear you were here on the side of Mrs. Berger. That had to rub him the wrong way."

"Good point." I nodded. "But then how will we get inside?"

"I might have another way."

"Are you going to tell me what it is?"

He thought about this for a moment. "I will tomorrow, if I can set it up. It's a delicate situation."

"If you tell me what it is, maybe I can help you. I'm great with delicate situations."

"Not this one you wouldn't be, trust me. In fact, having you involved will make it ten times more difficult."

I glowered and followed Tate, still pestering him to tell me what the delicate situation was. Before I left the auditorium, I looked back at the stage and spotted Billows standing there by himself, staring at me.

CHAPTER TWENTY-EIGHT

T HE NEXT MORNING, I WAS in the office after my run, and Tate waltzed in. "You want to go to Lakes Waters Retreat?"

I looked up from my computer. "Yes."

He grinned. "Then you are going to love me. I have an in for you."

"What's that?" I closed my laptop and folded my hands on top of it.

"Billows' ex-wife."

"Matt Billows' ex-wife can get us in Lake Water Retreat? How?"

"She lives there."

I stared at him.

"I'm serious. She got the house in the divorce and a ton of money. She really took Billows to the cleaners."

"And she still lives there after the divorce is settled? Why doesn't she move?" I leaned back in my chair.

"They have a son. I think she's staying for his sake. That would be my guess."

I shook my head. It wasn't the kind of relationship I

would want with my ex-husband, if I had one. I would want to get as far away from him as possible. I wanted to get as far away from Austin as possible, and we'd never even gotten engaged. I supposed with a child, though, everything changed. You were tied to that relationship through the child no matter how much you would like to escape it.

"Are you in?" Tate grinned, looking like a kid who'd won the school spelling bee.

"I'm in." I stood up. I wasn't getting anywhere with my computer searches about Joshua Porter's murder anyway. It was too long ago. The internet had barely existed when he'd died. If I wanted to find more information about him, I would have to go back the library and use my mothers' printed index and the microfilm. Some technology would never die.

Nat came in the room then. "Darby, I have a message for you from Edwin Yule. He called about forty minutes ago."

"Why didn't you patch it through?" I frowned. It wasn't like Nat to keep information about clients from me.

"He asked me not to. He just said he wanted to thank you for your help and, I quote, 'Pierce said yes.'"

"I hope we're invited to the wedding," Tate said. "There's a happy ending for you."

I nodded. "Thank goodness for that." I grabbed my jacket off the back of the chair.

"Are you going out?" Nat asked.

"Tate and I are going to Lake Waters Retreat to speak with Matt Billows' ex-wife."

"Why? What good will that do?"

I shrugged into my jacket. "We don't know, but we are running out of places to look for Samantha's killer. It seems all roads lead to Lake Waters and Billows. We have to at least rule them out."

"What about Logan?" Nat asked.

"You think her boyfriend is behind it?" Tate asked.

She shrugged. "He would be at the top of my list, much higher than Billows would be. She broke up with him. Darby and Samantha always said you should suspect the significant other first when there's a crime."

She was right, but I couldn't shake the feeling that Logan had really cared about Samantha. He'd said he wanted to marry her, but did I have any proof other than his word that that was the reason they'd broken up? Nat was right. I should take another look at Logan, no matter how much I liked him and sympathized with him about wanting to get married. I couldn't let my own situation with Austin color my opinion of him as a suspect.

She shook her head. "You're on a wild goose chase. There is no way you will find who did this to Samantha. It will even be difficult to prove Logan was the killer without evidence. All the evidence points to the same person."

I hung my head. "Me."

"Don't count me out," Tate said. "I make a good suspect too."

I didn't count him out, but I didn't say that aloud.

"Or," Nat said, "it could have been someone from a long time ago seeking revenge."

"Revenge for what?" Tate asked.

She turned to him. "Any number of things. Samantha was a private detective for nearly twenty years. She put of a lot of bad men and women in jail. They could be harboring a grudge."

If that was the case, it would be impossible to find Samantha's killer. Even so, I didn't think it was one whom she'd collared years ago. Why go to all the trouble of framing me if you knew you were going to take off? It didn't make any sense.

Nat interrupted my thoughts. "You promised to go over a list of my job duties before I left."

I had forgotten. I was having a serious case of denial that Nat was leaving Two Girls Detective Agency.

"I'll do that when I get back." I looked to Tate. "Are we going to the resort?"

He nodded. "Now that I have permission, it's best not to keep Portia waiting. She can be difficult..."

Tate and I said goodbye to Nat and walked outside. "I suggest we drive," he said.

"I guess I can ask Maelynn if I can use her minivan again."

Tate pointed at a luxury red convertible parked on the street. "No need. I got us a ride."

I nodded to the car. "Yours?"

"It's a rental. Pretty nice though."

"Not very practical for hills and sharp turns around the Finger Lakes."

"Are you kidding? It's made for sharp turns." He unlocked the car with the key fob. "Get in."

I climbed in the car.

"How did you afford to rent a car like this? I'm not sure I should even sit in it. I might get it dirty."

"Stop being a ridiculous. It's a car. They're meant to be driven and ridden in."

I shook my head. "Not cars like this. When did you rent this?"

He shot me a look. "When I got to the airport. Any other pressing questions?"

"Yes. When you got to the airport, you didn't know about your inheritance. Where did you get the money for this?"

"Whether or not I can afford something like a rental car doesn't have anything to with the money I received upon my aunt's death."

"This is a terrible vehicle choice for a private investigator. You want to blend in in this business, not stand out."

"Maybe I'm a different type of private detective." He winked. "And as you have told me, I'm not really one yet since I don't have a license."

Tate revved the engine. Before I could warn him about not driving fast through Herrington, he shifted the car into gear and took off. I buckled up and held onto my seat. We reached the gates of Lake Waters Retreat much faster than we would have had I been driving. We also wouldn't be suffering from mild cases of whiplash and tangled hair.

He stopped outside the gate and pressed the

buzzer. My gaze fell on the "Beware of Dog" sign I had seen the last time I'd come to the resort. I supposed I should be happy that Cliff hadn't let the dogs loose on me when I left. It reminded me of Benny B popping out of the bushes too. I looked around but didn't see him. That didn't mean he wasn't somewhere nearby.

Tate reached over and moved my hair out of my eyes. It was a windblown mess. Nothing short of a rake was going to get it untangled.

"It's a good look for you," he said as he dropped his hand.

The gate remained closed.

I finger-combed my hair the best I could. "I thought you said you have a way to get in. If the head of security sees me with you, he will stop you. When I came here before, he told me to leave."

"I've got this. You really need to learn how to relax, Piper. You're wound so tight most of the time, you're on the verge of snapping."

"That's not true."

He cocked his head.

"Maybe I have been a little tightly wound," I admitted, "but I think under the circumstances it's understandable."

He rolled down the window and hit the button on the gate. It buzzed, and he said, "Tate Porter to see Portia Billows."

There was no response but a loud buzzing sound as the gate opened.

"See?" He smiled at me. "Easy-peasy."

I regarded him suspiciously as the car rolled

through, and the gate immediately closed behind us. My head snapped around to watch it. Tate had gotten us in, but could he get us out? I didn't think that would be so easy-peasy.

"Portia's house is the one in the front," Tate said. "The main building is farther away on the water."

I knew where the main building was from my last visit to the resort, but that didn't explain how he knew. "You say that like you've been here before."

He gripped the steering wheel a little more tightly. "I haven't. Portia told me." He glanced at me again. "Everything will work out. Don't worry."

I hated it when people told me not to worry. It only made me worry more.

Portia's home was a giant white Georgian affair with wide pillars in the front that were as large as century-old trees. The front door was black. The only color came from the yellow mums that marched across the front of the house.

I stared up at it. This was what money could buy. Old money. The Billows family had plenty of that. Perhaps that was what had made the family go into the elite resort business?

I felt more self-conscious of my mussed hair than ever. This was not the place to come with hair that looked like you'd stuck it in a blender. I fished in my jacket pocket and was rewarded with an elastic hair tie. As Tate and I walked to the front door, I knotted my hair into a bun on the back of my head.

"Better," Tate said.

I glared at him. It was his fault my hair was in knots in the first place.

He rang the doorbell. A butler, a living breathing butler in a suit and tails, opened the door. "Mr. Porter." He nodded and then looked at me. "Who is this? We weren't expecting anyone else."

"This is my business partner, Darby Piper."

"I don't know that Mrs. Billows will want to speak with anyone other than you. She was very firm on that point, that she would speak to you and you alone."

Tate shrugged. "I can be firm too, and Darby either comes in with me, or I leave. We both need to speak to Portia."

The butler looked me up and down, and I wondered if he was taking my small size into account. If he needed to, he could throw me out the door. What he didn't know from looking at me was that if he tried it, he might come out with a broken arm.

He stepped back. "Very well. Mrs. Billows is eager to see you. However, there is always a chance she will ask Miss Piper to leave if the two of you discuss more personal matters."

Eager to see Tate? How did she even know who he was? And why would Tate discuss personal matters with Matt's ex-wife? All of these questions were on the tip of my tongue, but I couldn't ask a single one of them, because the butler was there. I was sure whatever he heard was reported to Portia, if not to Matt Billows too.

"You're awfully quiet," Tate said.

"How did you get us in here, really? Something is up."

Tate looked like he was deciding whether or not to answer when he was saved from making that choice by the butler. "Mrs. Billows will see you in the drawing room," the man said.

CHAPTER TWENTY-NINE

A S TATE AND I FOLLOWED the butler down the hall, I leaned close to Tate. "It's interesting that she continues to go by Mrs. Billows."

He didn't say anything. There was no eye roll or smart remark. I pulled back as if I had done something wrong. Something was different with him. I had never seen him so tense.

The butler stood off to one side and gestured us to enter the large room.

The drawing room was straight out of the game of Clue, with a dark wooden chair rail, a stone fireplace, and a pair of pewter candlesticks on the mantel that looked like they could do their share of damage. I glanced back at the butler. In the drawing room, by the butler, with the candlestick. It was surreal and a far cry from my usual cases that had me sitting in my car freezing to death outside of a motel watching for evidence of a wayward spouse's latest dalliance.

The butler bowed—he actually bowed—and backed out of the room. I felt like I was in a weird remake of

Downton Abbey, minus the nice British accents. Up-state New York voices didn't have the same character.

After he was gone, I turned to Tate. "What's going on?" I whispered.

"Portia is an old friend, but we didn't part on the best terms. I'm not sure how she will react when she sees me."

I eyed him suspiciously and was about to ask him how they were friends, when a woman floated into the room wearing black silk pajamas and a match-ing cape. She finished the outfit with black stilettos, and her black hair cascaded down her back in elegant curls. Wearing silk pajamas as clothes was a fashion trend, so I supposed that was what the woman was going for. No matter what she was wearing, she was gorgeous, with her black hair and dark blue eyes. Not many women could pull off caped PJs, but this woman could.

On the flipside, I wore my favorite boots, jeans, and a sweater I had owned since high school. It was like we were from two different planets.

"Tate, honey, I heard you were here and couldn't believe it." She floated toward him with her hands out-stretched. "It has been too long."

Whoa, *honey*—let's back up for a moment here. What on earth was going on?

Tate refused to look at me. When we got out of here, he was getting an earful, probably two. How could he hold out on me that he knew Billows's ex-wife?

"And who is this?" Portia asked. She scrutinized me up and down, and I wondered what my boots and black jeans said to her. That I was trouble, that I was tough? That I was trying too hard because I was small...?

"Tate, I wouldn't think she was at all your type. I know you have been away from town for quite some time, but this is a giant leap."

I glared. "At least I'm not wearing pajamas."

Tate groaned. I didn't feel the least bit bad about saying it. He could have warned me it was going to be like this with Portia, because it was clear he knew her very well.

She looked down at her outfit. "This is the latest fashion."

I straightened my back to add another half inch to my height. Even though she was taller than me by a good six inches, I could take her. She was wearing high heels and I was wearing boots, after all.

"This is Darby, and she is a friend of mine."

Friend? That was how I was introduced, as his friend. I ground my teeth. "Darby Piper from Two Girls Detective Agency. Tate and I are here to ask you a few questions about Samantha Porter." I used my firmest voice because it was time to take charge of the situation.

"Oh, I see. You are the one who was working with Samantha. She wasn't my favorite person."

Tate took a huge step back.

"Oh, Tate, I am sorry. She was your aunt, wasn't she? But the two of you couldn't have been all that close. You have been gone for ages."

"Samantha was all the family I had," he said sharply.

"Oh, excuse me for speaking out of turn. I'm so embarrassed. I'm sure she was a fine woman, but she had bad taste in men. It gets the very best of us. I made poor choices too until I met Matt."

My head snapped in Tate's direction. He wouldn't look at me.

"What a dream he was," Portia went on. "He swept me off my feet. We were married in a whirlwind romance, six months after we met. Six years later we were divorced, which all and all I thought was a good run for a marriage. Who has the stamina or the desire to make it a lifetime or even a decade? Wouldn't it be boring to be married to one person for that long? As always, I landed on my feet and got this house and Chatham for good measure."

"Chatham? Is that a pet?" I asked.

She laughed and doubled over in her mirth. "Oh Lord, no, and please don't let him hear that. Wait, on second thought, do tell him. It will be a great laugh when his ears grow red. They do that when he's particularly upset, and being confused for a pet would just be the ticket. Chatham is my butler."

"I'm sorry," I said. "I didn't mean any offense."

"None taken, by me. And if he is told, he will get over it. He's paid handsomely by my ex-husband to put up with me."

"So you still live here because of the butler?"

"I stay here for my four-year-old son. It's much easier on him not to be carted between two different homes. Here he can move freely from my house to his father's. It's like he's being raised in a two-parent home, and I wouldn't want it any other way."

"Why don't we sit down and talk," Tate said.

Portia nodded. "Chatham will be back in a moment with coffee and tea. I would suggest something a little bit stronger, but as I remember, Tate, you never indulged in spirits."

I shot him a look when she said this. What else didn't I know about Samantha's nephew? I felt like in the last five minutes I had been presented with a brand-new person, and I didn't like it in the least. It made it hard to expect what was coming next.

Portia sat on a long velvet sofa. "Sat" was the wrong word. She settled on it like a leaf falling silently from a branch. She flung her right arm over the back and slouched with one foot on the floor. Had I attempted that position, I would have looked like a jellyfish that had washed up on the beach, but Portia made it appear elegant.

Tate perched on a straight-backed chair in the corner of the room. The chair was still within hearing range, but he couldn't have been farther away from Portia in the massive drawing room if he tried. If Portia noticed this, she made no comment.

I took the seat in between, on a leather armchair that was so deep, my feet didn't touch the floor when I sat. Feeling like a child, I scooted to the edge. What I wouldn't give for a few more inches to even the playing field between me and the rest of the tall world.

"How do you know each other?" I asked.

"Oh, Tate and I go way back. We dated in high school and then we ran into each other when he was in the Army. He was stationed in Europe, and I was traveling. I wanted us to date again, but Tate wasn't interested. Broke my heart twice over." She sighed and winked at Tate.

Tate folded her arms. "We are better as friends, Portia. I couldn't see you as an military wife."

She shrugged. "I guess we will never know now. I met Matt, and that was the end of that."

Chatham entered the drawing room pushing a tea cart—like, a legit tea cart with a steaming teapot, china, and tea sandwiches on a three-tiered dish.

She nodded at the butler. "Thank you, Chatham. That looks absolutely lovely. I couldn't have done it better myself." She laughed. "Not that I would have tried."

Chatham poured the tea, and held out a cup to me. "Milk or sugar?"

It seemed impolite not to accept it. "Plain is fine. Thank you."

He nodded as I took the cup.

Portia asked for milk in her tea, no sugar. Tate refused the drink all together, and I wished I had done the same. There was no table near me and I awkwardly held the hot cup and saucer, wishing I could put them on the floor. I blew on the tea. "How did you meet Matt?"

"I went in for an interview at the resort. I was hoping to get a job at the front desk. I heard they paid their employees well. I aced the interview, and the rest was history. Matt whisked me off my feet. He was so handsome and charming, and rich. It was enough to make the strongest of girls swoon. When we were married, I wanted for nothing." She sighed wistfully.

I couldn't help wonder what else she could want here. She had a butler, after all.

"I hope this separation is only temporary," Portia said.

I frowned. "But I thought you were divorced."

She laughed. "To be honest, I would like to remarry him."

The confusion must have been obvious on my face.

"We love each other, we just can't be married. Matt is not the marrying type. Some men are not built for that. He needs his freedom. I let him have it as long as he doesn't become too attached to the woman he might be seeing at the time. I will always be the number-one woman in his life." She glanced at Tate. "That's why I wasn't fond of Samantha Porter. That was the longest he's been enamored of anyone."

"They were dating?" I couldn't keep the disbelief from my voice. Samantha would never date a person she'd consider working for—or cheat on her boyfriend. Did Logan know about this? It would give him even more motive to kill her in a jealous rage. Had he asked her to marry him, and she'd said no because she was with Billows? Logan went up another notch in my suspect list.

"Yes, and it seemed to me he was growing more attached to her than he had women in the past. In the end he would come back to me. He always did, but I will admit I was beginning to become frustrated by his attentions to her." She waved her hand.

I wished I could see Tate's reactions while she said all this, but he was sitting behind me.

"I see that look on your face, Tate. I know she was your aunt, but Matt was the love of my life. We are meant to be together. I would do whatever I needed to keep us together."

"Does that include murder?" I asked.

She sat up straight. "Who said anything about murder?"

"The police believe Samantha was murdered." I held my rapidly cooling tea in my hands. I still hadn't sipped from the cup.

"Matt told me she died in an accident. I knew nothing of murder." She glared at me. "You came here because you think I killed her?"

I didn't say anything.

"Your silence makes it true." She reclined on the couch again.

"Portia," Tate said, "What proof did you have that they were dating? I find it very hard to believe my aunt would do that. He was going to give her a job."

"I was told. I have spies all over town keeping an eye on Matt to make sure he's behaving himself."

"He was trying to convince her to work for him as the head of security. That could be the reason your spies saw them together so much," he retorted.

Portia chuckled. "Like I believe that."

She glanced from me to Tate and back again. "If you are wondering if I killed her, I will tell you again, once and for all, I did not. I didn't even know she had been murdered."

I wasn't sure I believed her, but there something else I wanted to know from Portia Billows. "Why is your husband so dead set on building this complex at Lake Waters?"

She sat up on the couch, as if she was no longer set on impressing us with her elegant posture. "Why else? Because Lake Waters needs the money.—I can tell by the looks on both of your faces that I have surprised you."

Remembering the empty lobby and the conversation I'd had with Cliff two days ago, I was more surprised that she'd come out and said it.

"Matt would be pleased. He wants everyone in Herrington to believe that Lake Waters Retreat is still the premier destination in the Finger Lakes for the rich to renew themselves."

"But it's not?" Tate asked.

"Not at all. You have to remember, the resort was built in the 1960s. Over the years, it was the place for the wealthy to come. Matt's father and grandfather put all they could into the business, and it had all the latest amenities for the time."

He nodded. "When my aunt did speak about it, she said it was very glamorous."

Portia nodded. "But today, celebrities want more and they want exotic locales. Who wants to come to Seneca Lake when they could go to Dubai or an exotic island to renew body and soul? If Matt wants to convince famous clients to come here, he must do more."

"Like what?" I asked.

"All the buildings need to be updated, and so does the spa." Her tone was much more businesslike than it had been before.

I realized that Portia knew more about the business than she had let on.

"The spa and rejuvenation center are completely out of date," Portia said. "It would be more expensive to bring them up to today's standards than build an all-new facility, which is what Matt would like to do. The rich do love their treatments, and they are always looking for the next best thing. Lakes Waters hasn't offered the next best thing in over a decade." She patted her flawless skin. "I don't even use the spa for myself. Instead, I fly to New York City, where I can get all the services I need."

"If his resort doesn't appeal to those clients any longer, why doesn't he just open it to other people? Families? He might not be able to charge as much—"

She held up her hand. "You can stop right there. He would never do that. Matt is too much of a snob. He would rather run the business into the ground on the premise that it's for the ultra-elite. Matt is determined to take the resort back to its former glory." She shook her head. "The resort has been refinanced four times, which has given him enough money for the construction. He wants to offer something new and shiny to bring all the wealthy customers he lost. He can't open the resort again with the same services, only updated."

"And Mrs. Berger?" I asked.

She shook her head. "Matt is beside himself over

that woman. He can't even afford to pay her what he's offered, and still she refuses to sell that little eyesore of a house. I'm not worried about it, though. I know he will prevail. Matt has his way of getting what he wants from people."

"He corrupts them," Tate said.

She laughed. "No, no."

I took that as a "Yes, but let's not call it that."

"Did you know Mr. Billows wanted to hire Samantha as the head of security?"

"He said that was his reason for being with her so often. We have in the past had a terrible time with paparazzi taking photos of guests. We can't have that if we want those kinds of clients. Who wants a photograph of themselves in a glossy magazine while recovering from a facelift? Matt didn't think Cliff was the man for the job. He thought Samantha was a much better fit. He told me she came to him, which is why I thought she had plans for him other than work."

Even though Billows had said the same to me, that it had been Samantha's idea to work at Lake Waters, it still surprised me. "Samantha always said it was Billows' idea."

She shrugged. "Then one of them is lying. Even so, I don't think my ex-husband is involved in her death. What could he have gained from it if he wanted to hire her to work for him?"

It was a fair question, and one I had asked myself several times.

She turned to me. "If you would be so kind, Darby, I would ask you to give Tate and me a minute alone."

I stood and set my still-full teacup on the tea cart Chatham had left in the room. I glanced at Tate.

"Wait for me outside, Piper," he said.

As if out of nowhere, the butler appeared at my side.

"Chatham will show you out," Portia said. "My advice, Miss Porter, is to leave Matt out of this and concentrate on who killed Samantha."

"Go ahead," Tate said. "I'll be a minute."

I frowned at him, and then I followed Chatham through the rambling house and out the front door. I stepped outside, and the door closed behind me even before I could thank him.

CHAPTER THIRTY

I STARED AT THE CLOSED DOOR for a moment. Tate had said he would only be a minute, which meant I didn't have much time.

This was my chance to take a look around the estate. I walked around the large house, and there was a huge English-style garden in the back that this time of year was awash with oranges, reds, and other autumnal colors.

A small puffball of a dog was in the back garden. It lifted its nose in the air and turned around. When it saw me, the little dog bared its teeth and charged. I yelped and ran into the woods that surrounded the property. The dog stopped on the edge of the yard. Perhaps an electric fence held it back. In any case, I didn't think I wanted to return that way and risk being bitten. Maybe I would walk around the house in the woods.

As I walked through the trees, I was careful to keep my eye on the back of Portia's home, I didn't want to lose my way. I came upon a path I could only assume led to the main resort building, where I had met Quinn.

The land Lake Waters lay on was vast. What I thought would be a brief walk turned into a longer one as the path meandered to the clearing where the large white Greek revival building stood.

I took more time to inspect the area around the grand resort. The building and grounds were beautiful, but now that I knew the real state of it, I could see the wear and tear of time. Some of the paint on the shutters was chipped. There were cracks in the blacktop that led to the front door. The weathervane sat crookedly at the top of the building. These were all small cosmetic details, but they spoke of larger problems.

A black luxury car pulled into the circular driveway, and Billows got out. I slipped into the woods and went back the way I came. I would need to speak to him soon. However, I didn't think sneaking up on him was the best way to go about it.

If I'd oriented myself right, Mrs. Berger's property, where Billows wanted to expand, was to my right. I waited until Billows was inside the building and then I scurried to the back of the resort. From there, I had a lovely and unobstructed view of Seneca Lake. A set of wooden stairs led to the pebbled beach below. The most striking thing about the view was that there was no one there. Not that I expected sunbathers on the beach in September, but I thought at least a guest or two would be walking about and enjoying the scenery.

I glanced back at the house. Tate would be wondering what happened to me if he left Portia's house and found me gone. I shot him a text about where I was and walked down the steps to the beach. If I looked down the sand to my right, I could see the edge of Mrs. Berger's dock. Her property really did butt up against Lake Waters. I knew Billows was infuriated that she wouldn't sell. However, seeing the view she would have to give up, I couldn't blame her. I walked down the beach about a quarter of a mile, and when I paused at that point, I could see Mrs. Berger's house clearly. If I peeked through the trees, I could also see Romy's grand oak. I hoped he wasn't up there at the moment.

I headed back to the resort.

"Piper!" Tate called.

I stepped out of the woods.

He grinned at me. "Doing a little snooping?"

"It's my job." I shrugged.

When we were in the car, I turned to Tate, who said, "I'm beginning to wonder if the resort was involved at all. What would they get out of killing Samantha? I can't think of a single benefit to the resort."

"But who else do we have for viable suspects?"

"The horse trainer?"

I decided it was best to ignore his tone. I shook my head. "Doesn't seem likely. Did you learn anything else from Portia? Or did the two of you discuss old times?"

"Am I sensing a bit of jealousy, Piper?"

"Jealousy? Of her? Don't be ridiculous."

He stared back at Portia's house and then shook his head. "For the record, not that I feel the need to clear it up with you, but Portia and I went on a few dates after I graduated from high school. She doesn't look it, but she's four or five years older than I am. It was nothing serious; I was going into the service. Then, years later we bumped into each other in Europe while I was traveling after leaving the Army. There was nothing to it. I think she made it seem more serious because she was irritated at me for bringing you to her home."

"Oh."

"After you left, she told me more about the history of the resort. Her father-in-law was the one who ran Lake Waters into the ground and refused to put any money into updates or let Matt do it. He ruled the family with an iron fist. He died two years ago, but by that time, the resort was in such a mess, it would take a major overhaul to bring it back to life, which is why Matt hatched his plan to expand the retreat and build a new state-of-the-art facility."

"And Mrs. Berger stands in the way of that."

"Right."

"What about that stuff she said about Samantha dating Billows?"

"That's hard for me to believe," Tate said.

"Me too. She sounded like a jealous ex-wife."

"She didn't just sound like it. She is a jealous ex-wife. She may be afraid that if Billows remarries, she will be asked to move."

"That would be a shame, because she really loves that butler."

Tate laughed. "I think Chatham is stuck with her. Poor guy."

CHAPTER THIRTY-ONE

AFTER TATE AND I LEFT the resort, I went back to the office to finish some paperwork, and he promised to meet me at my parents' house for dinner. I had conveniently forgotten again about dinner with my parents. Okay, maybe I hadn't and wished I could.

When I stepped into the office, Nat was packing a box of her things.

I stood in the doorway of the reception area. "You're packing already?" My voice wavered.

She looked up. "I thought I would get this done while it was quiet."

I nodded, but I couldn't hide my disappointment. "Do you want to meet to go over your job duties now?"

"Now is a good time as any."

I pulled a rolling chair up in front of her desk.

"Do you care if I pack as we go over this list?"

I shook my head.

She picked up one of her jars of pennies and carefully wrapped it in bubble wrap, then set it into the waiting box. "My number-one most important job was to keep the master calendar of where you and Samantha were at all times so I would know where to send someone if either of you needed help." She peered over her glasses. "It wasn't an easy task, because neither you nor Samantha were good at telling me what you were up to. Every morning I had to quiz you."

I was guilty of this. "Which is why I told you when Tate and I planned to go to Lake Waters this morning."

"How did it go?"

"All right. But I am becoming more and more convinced that Billows might not have anything to do with Samantha's murder."

She looked up from her box. "Why's that? I thought he was the best suspect you had. You seemed more sure before."

"He was and still is, but I can't figure out what he had to gain by killing Samantha. He wanted her to come in as head of security. Why would he kill the person he wanted to recruit?"

"Who does that leave you with?" Nat asked.

"Logan Montgomery."

"You don't sound happy about that."

"I'm not. I like Logan."

"He's a good guy, and he put up with Samantha for a long time."

"What do you mean that he put up with her?" I asked.

"He told me on more than one occasion that he wanted to marry her, but Samantha was having none of it."

Her words stung. "Did he say why Samantha didn't want to marry him?"

"Only one time. He said something like she was too focused on something else."

"What was that?" I asked. "Work?"

"He didn't say. I'm not sure he even knew."

She shook her head. "You look like you could use some coffee. I made a fresh pot." She pointed to the coffee maker in the corner of the room.

"Thanks." I walked over to it and filled my mug, and then sat across from her.

"So where does the investigation go from here?" Nat asked.

"That's a good question. I'll need to talk to Logan again, that's for sure." I paused. "But I'm starting to wonder if this is about her dad. In my research, I stumbled upon Joshua Porter, Sr.'s murder. I knew of it, of course. Samantha would sometimes mention that she wanted to solve her father's murder. She never believed it was an unknown intruder. Her father worked at Lake Waters Retreat. Matt Billows and his ex-wife Portia told us that Samantha approached him about the head of security job. I think her father's death was connected to Lake Waters in some way, and she wanted to work there to get to the bottom of it."

"That's crazy. How could she solve a case that's over twenty years old?"

"She was a great investigator. Maybe she did solve it. Or maybe the killer felt like she was getting too close."

She rolled her eyes. "Sounds like a conspiracy theory to me."

"Me too," I admitted. "But that doesn't mean it's not true."

"If it is true, I think you should stop looking into it. If you are right and Samantha was killed over this, you will be putting yourself in danger too. I don't want anything to happen to you."

I stood up. "I can't do that. Samantha was my friend and my mentor. I owe it to her to find out what happened."

"You should think less about the murder and more about what you will do with the agency. Do you have a plan?"

"I guess that depends on whether or not Tate stays."

"You're a good investigator, Darby. You don't need anyone else. If Tate leaves, strike out on your own. You might lose this office, but you can find somewhere else to live and work."

I hadn't thought of that, but I realized she was right. Whether Tate stayed or left, my career wasn't over, just as it wouldn't have been over if Samantha were still alive and had gone to work for Billows. I felt a lot better now.

"Thanks, Nat," I said, and sipped the coffee.

After our meeting, I went back into my office, but I couldn't concentrate.

I called Logan and asked him to meet me at the boardwalk. To my surprise, he agreed.

By the time I met him, it was late afternoon. The sun was low over the hill, and there was an ocher hue to the surface of the lake. Two older women, clearly sightseers, were on the boardwalk taking photos of the lake and the autumn foliage.

I beat Logan there and was relieved when I saw him walk down the boardwalk toward me. When he was within five feet of me, I saw that his eyes were blood-shot.

"Thanks for meeting with me," I said.

"I'm glad you called. I know you must think I had something to do with Samantha's murder, but I did not. I loved her. As her death becomes more and more of a reality, I realize just how much."

"It would be easier to believe you if you had an alibi."

He studied me. "I'm a smart man. Don't you think if I did kill her, I would have been smart enough to se-cure an alibi?"

He had a point, but I didn't know what to believe when it came to Samantha's murder.

"I want to show you something to prove I'm tell-ing the truth." He reached into his jacket pocket and pulled out a velvet ring box. He opened the box and held it out to me.

Before I could say a word, the two elderly sightseers strolled by.

"You should say yes, miss. He looks like a keeper," one of them said, and the other chuckled.

I closed my mouth, unable to speak. I didn't explain to the passerby that this ring had been for Samantha, not for me.

"I could tell you didn't believe that I asked her to marry me. Here's my proof."

I wished I could say that seeing the diamond ring convinced me of his innocence, but it didn't.

He closed the box with a snap and tucked it back into his pocket.

"Logan, why did she say no?"

He studied me. "She said she had to take care of something first."

"What was that?"

He paused as if considering his answer. "She wanted to know who killed her father. She was obsessed with the case, and it had grown worse in the last few weeks."

"Do you think that's why she was killed?"

He shook his head. "Maybe." He swallowed like he was fighting back tears. "I need to get back to the office."

I nodded and watched Logan walk away. He was a heartbroken man. What I didn't know was whether or not he'd caused his own heartbreak by killing the woman he had loved.

I wished I could believe him. Tate came to mind. In the last couple of days, I had grown fond of him. I wished I could believe him, too. Maybe I would, if he would tell me what he'd been doing in Herrington the day Samantha had died.

CHAPTER THIRTY-TWO

T HAT EVENING, I DROVE TO my parents' home. They lived away from the town center. Mom said she'd picked the location of the house because she didn't want to see library patrons when she was sitting in her own backyard. Their ranch home was on three acres, and the property was more affordable for them because it was out of the view of the lake, which was over three miles away. They'd bought the ranch because my father needed a home all on one level for mobility. The acreage was for his passion for plants.

It was nearing the end of the growing season, but he would be outside every waking second until the snow began to fall.

I was happy to see Dad wasn't in his wheelchair. It meant he was having a good day, and the dizziness brought on by his disease was mild. He stood in the middle of the front yard with a potted yellow mum in his hands.

"Hi Dad," I said, as I walked up the driveway.

"There's my favorite eldest girl," Dad said with a

smile. "You mother said you and Samantha's nephew were coming for dinner. She's very enthusiastic about this dinner." His eyes twinkled. "She came home early from the library and had been cooking up a storm ever since."

I didn't like the sound of that.

He held up the pot. "Where do you think this one should go?"

Even this late in the season, his garden was bursting with flowers.

"What about next to the orange mum there?" I suggested. "I think the yellow and orange will look very nice together."

"A wonderful idea. Would you mind? I'm feeling good today, but I'm not as steady on my feet as I would like. At least not steady enough to get on the ground and be able to get back up again."

I took the pot from his hands and picked up the trowel on the edge of the flower bed. My father had taught me when I was a child the proper way to plant. I dug a hole the depth of the pot, removed the mum from the pot, loosened the roots, and placed it into the hole. I smoothed the dirt around it. It was the simplest problem I'd faced all week.

"Are you all right, Darby?" Dad asked. "You look concerned."

I stood up and brushed the dirt from my hands. "It's everything to do with Samantha's death. The investigation has hit a major dead end, and I don't know where to go from here."

"What do the police say?"

I looked down at my feet. "To be honest, the evidence against me is bad. I wouldn't believe I was innocent if that's all I had to go by."

He squeezed my hand tightly. "But you are. Of course you are."

"I am." I shrugged. "But honestly, I'm sitting on pins and needles waiting for the police to arrest me. I don't know why Austin hasn't done it yet. He claimed to be waiting on evidence from the car, but he has enough now to take me in."

"Austin." My father wrinkled his nose. "What does that boy know? He doesn't have any taste."

I smiled and patted his shoulder. My father had liked Austin just fine when we were dating, but every time we'd broken up, he'd hated him again. He was a good dad that way.

"Austin is a good cop," I said, coming to his defense. "I've worked with him on several cases, and he's always been fair despite our personal history."

My father grunted. "He's out of his league for this investigation, just as he was way out of his league with you."

"The same could be said for me, that I'm way out of my league too."

"No, I've seen your work. You are a top investigator."

Leave it to my father to give a super pep talk.

"Are you ready to go in?" I asked. "It's starting to get chilly."

"I'm afraid it is. I'm not looking forward to winter.

Those are the cruelest months. I miss my flowers so much. I always wonder if I will see them again."

"Don't talk like that. You will see them again, year after year. There is always the promise of spring," I said.

He patted my cheek. "It seems you have been listening to me after all."

"I always listen to you, Dad."

"That's why you're my favorite eldest daughter."

I laughed and helped Dad walk toward the house.

He gripped my arm. "I'm glad you're here to lend me a hand. I suppose I became a little stiff from playing in the dirt for so long."

I squeezed his hand.

"It must be difficult for you to run the business now that Samantha's gone, but I have faith you can do it. You do need to give yourself time to mourn though, and process the loss. The two of you were very close."

I wondered how very close Samantha and I had been. It seemed to me the longer this investigation went on, the more I was learning about her that I hadn't known. I didn't mention that to my father. "Mom agrees with you on that. She wants me to read about grief. She checked out the entire section in the library. The books are at my house right now."

He laughed. "That sounds like your mother, and she is trying to help you the best way she knows how. She wants to empower us with information. But there is a point that we have to come to acceptance of something. That's where I'm at."

"Don't give up, Dad." I felt tears in my eyes again. I hated when he talked about his disease in this way.

"Give up? I would never. I have too much to enjoy in this life. My wife, my garden, and my two beautiful and feisty daughters. Now, let's go see what you mother has made for dinner to impress Tate."

I groaned.

As soon as I stepped into the house, I volunteered to set the table. I wasn't much use in the kitchen, but this was a task I could handle. I had a stack of plates in my hand. It was the good china, because Mom had insisted we use the good china for Tate's first home-cooked meal back in Herrington.

I began setting out the plates when DeeDee shouted from the front door.

"Darby, your guy is here!"

A moment later, she came into the dining room, Tate in her wake. Tate rubbed his beard. "I didn't realize I belonged to anyone."

"You don't," I said. "DeeDee, Tate is Samantha's nephew, and he's helping me out at work for a little bit."

DeeDee looked unconvinced before she left the room with her phone in her hand.

"I wonder what she sees in us not to believe the truth?" Tate teased.

I wasn't going to get into this conversation with him.

"Oh!" My mother stepped in the room, carrying a giant lasagna tray. "I didn't know that our guest had arrived." She shot me a look. "It's nice to see you again,

Tate." She set the lasagna on the table. "I hope you like lasagna. I also made a salad, garlic bread, and berry trifle for dessert."

"It all sounds wonderful," Tate said. "You didn't have to go to all this trouble just for me."

"It was no trouble." Mom pushed a stray hair out of her face. "It will just be a moment."

"Is there anything I can do to help?" he asked.

"Oh, aren't you sweet. Come with me to the kitchen, and I'll put you to work."

Tate followed my mother out of the room. "I'd love to help. I happen to be an excellent cook." He winked at me.

I'll bet.

I finished setting the table and poked my head in the kitchen to see Tate tossing the salad like a pro. It seemed he did know what he was doing, at least as far as the salad was concerned.

A few minutes later when we were all sitting at the table, my mother set a heaping plate of lasagna and salad in front of Tate. "Here, eat up."

Tate picked up his fork and knife. "This looks great. Thank you."

My mother beamed. "Good. Come over any time, and I will feed you. See if you can get Darby to come with you. She doesn't stop by as often as we would like. Maybe you can be a good influence on her in that regard."

"Subtle, Mom. Thanks." I picked up my water glass. "And how can Tate be a good influence on me? He's spent the last few years traveling the world."

"Where did you go?" DeeDee asked with bright eyes.

"A better question is where I didn't go," Tate said.

"I love you, honey," Mom said to me, warming up to her subject. "We want you to be happy."

"You know, there is a nice new doctor at the hospital where I get treatment," Dad said. "He moved here from Pakistan. Smart as a whip, and handsome too."

"Dad," I said, "I'm not looking for a boyfriend. Besides, I don't have time for any of that. I have to figure what do to about the agency." I pushed my food around on the plate, not eating anything. My stomach hurt. It was probably the stress from the investigation.

Tate looked at me. "*We* have to figure out what to do with the agency. Together."

I sipped my water.

"Are the two of you still interested in Joshua Porter's murder?" Mom asked.

"Yes," Tate and I said in unison.

"After I left the library, I did a little more digging."

"And?" I asked.

Mom shot a glance at Tate. "I don't want it to be hard for you to hear, Tate."

He shook his head. "I never knew my grandfather, so whatever you have to say won't upset me."

"There was a filing back in the early nineteen seventies by a woman who claimed she was the mother of one of Joshua's children and she wanted child support."

"She was the mother of my dad or aunt?" Tate asked.

"No, of another child, Penelope Wring."

"Who was Penelope's mother?"

"Georgia Wring. She claimed she and Joshua were married for three months and the marriage was annulled because Joshua's family didn't approve of the match. After they split, she had Penelope."

"How did you find this?" I asked.

"I had some time, and I flipped through old county court documents for Joshua's name. It was fun."

Tate glanced at me. "Now I know where you get your inquisitive nature."

"What happened to the case?" I asked.

"It was dropped," Mom said. "After the initial filing, there was no more mention of it."

"They settled out of court?"

Mom nodded. "That would be my guess."

"Wouldn't there be a record of the marriage?"

"I couldn't find one. My guess is they got married out of state. I'm still looking, though."

"What happened to Penelope and her mother?"

"I don't know what happened to Penelope, but I did find the obituary for her mother." Mom stood up and opened a drawer from the secretary desk tucked in the corner of the living room. She removed a piece of paper from the drawer and handed it to me. It was Georgia Wring's obituary.

She had died in 1976. The only living relative mentioned was her daughter. The obituary was two lines long. Birth, death, daughter, that was it. My heart sank. I felt unexpectedly sad. I handed the paper to Tate. "What happened to Penelope?"

Mom shook her head. "I haven't found out yet. I'll

keep searching if you want me to. I'm already trying to track down the marriage certificate."

"I do. I don't know how this relates to anything that is happening today, but it might be a clue as to what happened to Joshua."

Tate handed the obituary back to me. "And I'm certain that's what my aunt was working on when she died. She was trying to find her father's killer."

"It could have been someone wanting revenge for Georgia's death," DeeDee chimed in.

"That's not a bad point, DeeDee," Tate said. "But there is nothing to say she died of unnatural causes."

My younger sister glowed under his praise.

"It's a terrible thing," Dad said. "I am curious now to know what happened to Penelope. I hope she turned out all right." I hoped so too.

The doorbell rang. Mom looked at my father. "Alan, have you been online shopping again? Are you expecting any packages?"

"No," Dad said, indignant. "I haven't bought a thing since I got that turkey platter." He nodded at Tate. "It'll be perfect for Thanksgiving. You should join us this year. The more, the merrier. I never like the idea of someone alone during the holidays."

I shook my head. My parents had already decided to adopt Tate into the family. There was no reason to fight it.

DeeDee jumped up from the table. "I'll go see who it is."

From the dining room, we could hear the front door open, and there was a murmur of voices. DeeDee hurried back into the room with wide eyes. "Darby, it's for you."

Austin and his partner stepped into the doorway. They were in uniform, and this wasn't a social call.

CHAPTER THIRTY-THREE

I JUMPED OUT OF MY SEAT. "Austin, what is it?"

He swallowed and his shoulders drooped. "Can we speak to you in private for a moment?"

My mother jumped out of her chair. "Whatever you have to say to Darby, you can say in front of her family."

I lifted my hand. "Mom, it's okay. You all wait here, and I will go see what they need." I dropped my hand at my side when I saw it begin to tremble. I wasn't kidding anyone by saying I would see what they needed. I knew what they needed. Austin could no longer ignore the evidence mounting against me.

I stepped into the living room. Louter was quiet and stood by the front door with his arms folded over his chest. He looked like a statue. In reality, he was a guard. He was there to make sure I didn't run away.

Austin frowned. "Darby, we are going to have to ask you to come to the station. We have a few questions to ask you about Samantha Porter's murder."

"Is she under arrest?"

I looked over my shoulder and saw Tate and my entire family standing in the doorway to the living room. I shouldn't have expected them to stay put. None of them were good at following directions.

"Not yet," Austin's partner said.

Austin shot him a look, then looked back at me. "We have a few more questions. We need help solving this murder and believe you are the key to cracking the case open."

"Because you think she did it." DeeDee pushed her way through the doorway.

"Dee," I said. "Don't be ridiculous. Austin is doing his job."

She scowled at Austin. "I'm glad my sister broke up with you. You were never good enough for her."

Austin winced.

"DeeDee!" I exclaimed. "I'm sorry, Austin. We're all upset over everything that's been going on. She didn't mean to say that."

"She's wrong. I did mean it," DeeDee declared.

"I'm coming too," Tate said.

Austin frowned. "If you have questions about the case," Tate added, "Darby and I are working it together. I can help too."

"Fine," Austin said. "You can come, Porter, but you will have to wait in the lobby while we speak to Darby."

Tate folded his arms. "Works for me."

I hoped it wouldn't come to that. "I need to call my lawyer and ask him to be there too."

Austin glanced at me with a frown and appraising cop eyes. "That is your right.

"Mr. and Mrs. Piper, I'm so sorry to have interrupted your dinner like this."

My parents glared back at him. Even if I wanted to, there was no chance now of Austin and me getting back together with my entire family against him. *Not* that I wanted to. And the realization was actually quite liberating—ironic, considering the circumstances.

"Let's go," Austin said. He took me by the arm.

Gently, I removed my sleeve from his grasp. "I can walk on my own, thanks."

He nodded.

I followed him to the door and then turned back to my family. "I'll be fine. It's just a formality. Don't worry."

They looked worried, and I most certainly felt worried. I tugged on Tate's sleeve. "Can you call Patrick for me and ask him to meet us there?"

He nodded. "I'll be right behind you."

I knew he would.

Austin walked me to his car, put me in the back seat, and climbed behind the wheel.

Through the car's back window, I saw DeeDee and my parents standing in the front door. I had to look away. I dug my nails in my hands again to hold back the tears.

The Herrington police station was a tiny, box-shaped brick building tucked behind the small and historic mayor's office. The station was built in the 1970s and was a modern sore thumb that stuck out in a cluster of two-hundred-year-old buildings.

It wasn't the first time I had been to this building.

I came to the police station often in my work as a P.I. It was, however, the first time I'd been there as a suspect. I knew Austin said I wasn't under arrest, but that could change. I had to be careful about what I said. I could very easily incriminate myself if I wasn't careful. I had been able to keep it a secret from him that the last time I had seen Samantha alive, we'd fought. I planned to keep it that way.

I was ushered into a small meeting room with a table and chairs. That was all, and it was intentional, so a suspect didn't have anything to throw at the police if he—or she—got too upset. I stood behind the table.

Austin and his partner stepped into the room. "To start, I'll speak with Darby alone," he said to the other officer. "Go check on Porter and make sure he's not causing any trouble in the lobby."

Louter nodded and shut the door behind him.

"Darby, can you sit down?"

I sat and folded my hands on the table and stared Austin in the eyes. I refused to be intimidated by him or this situation. "How did you know I would be at my parents' house tonight?"

His face grew red. "I knew it was your family dinner night."

"Using information from when we were together for the investigation. Nice, Austin."

He sighed. "Darby, don't make this more difficult than it has to be."

"If you have questions for me, why did you have to bring me here if I'm not under arrest? You could have spoken to me at my office or somewhere more neutral, like Floured Grounds."

He chuckled. "Floured Grounds isn't neutral, with Maelynn glaring at me from the coffee counter, and I know she switched me over to decaf as payback for whatever happened to us."

"'Whatever happened to us?' You sound like you don't know."

"I don't, not really."

I scowled at him. Now was not to the time to rehash our latest and final breakup. It was over, dead and buried. "So why am I here?"

"We need to talk. The case against you is very strong, and my chief won't let it go on much longer. It's very likely he will want me to make an arrest this weekend. I have been able to convince him you're not a flight risk."

"What's going on?" I asked.

He took a breath. "I wanted you to hear it directly from me. The paint on Samantha's car and at the crime scene is an exact match to yours. Your car was the one used in the accident."

A heavy sense of dread fell over me, but it had been what I expected to hear since I realized the car was stolen.

"Then why not arrest me?"

"I'll probably have to arrest you, but I'm buying time. I told the chief I have another lead I need to follow up first." He ran his hand through his blond hair. "I'm in a difficult position."

"So am I," I said quietly. "So you brought me here to warn me? That's a strange way to do it."

"I brought you here to prove to the chief I am taking the evidence against you seriously. I don't think you're aware of how much trouble you're in. You have a great motive, you have no alibi, and you had easy access to the murder weapon, since it's your car. I could arrest you right now, and the D.A. would have no trouble at all building a case."

"I know that," I said in a quieter voice. "But I didn't kill her." I wished Patrick would show up already. What was taking so long? Had Tate gotten hold of the attorney? "What other suspects do you have?"

"That's the problem, Darby. I don't have any others...you're it."

"What about Billows? He was trying to convince Samantha to work for him."

"So it makes no sense for him to kill her."

"And he's trying to get Mrs. Berger's house demolished," I added.

"Which has nothing has to do with the murder that I can see."

"And he—"

"And he has an alibi. He was with his ex-wife at a charity event in Rochester. The event went until two in the morning and was over an hour away."

"Why would he take his ex-wife to an event like that?"

"She still does some of the philanthropy work for the family. In any case, I spoke to a dozen people, and they all remember him being there."

"Oh," I said in a small voice, as I realized that Portia Billows, my other suspect and Billows's ex-wife, also had an alibi for the same time. That was unfortunate.

"It has to be someone else."

He pressed his palms on the table and leaned forward. "Who?"

"Samantha was trying to solve her father's murder, and I think that's what got her killed. Logan told me that's why she wouldn't marry him."

"You spoke to Logan?"

"Of course I did. I assume he's still a suspect."

"He is," Austin admitted. "But the evidence still points directly at you."

I didn't like the sound of that, but continued with my theory. "Samantha's father was killed twenty years ago, and according to the reports it was an interrupted robbery. The police at the time believed it was someone who was passing through the Finger Lakes."

"You know they said that to the public to calm fears over the murder."

He tapped his fingers on the table. "It could also be true, though."

"Samantha didn't think so. I know that, but she was never happy with that answer to explain his murder. She talked about it all the time. She was determined to solve that case." I paused. "And I think she was finally getting close when she was killed."

"That would mean the person who killed Joshua Porter was local and may still be in Herrington."

I nodded. "That's exactly what that means, and we need to find out who it is."

"*I* need to find out who it is. You need to stay as far away from this investigation as you can possibly get."

"You have to be joking."

"If you keep poking your nose in it, you will appear even guiltier." He leaned back in his plastic chair. "I'm trying to protect you."

I stopped myself from making a sarcastic response. It wouldn't help. "Will you look at the connection to Joshua Porter's murder?"

He sighed. "I can pull the file, but I don't know what good it would do."

"Can you pull it now?"

He stared at me. "Right now?"

"I can wait." I smiled.

He sighed and walked out of the room.

While I waited, I went over in my head what I knew about Joshua Porter's murder. He had been the head of security at Lakes Waters Retreat, which seemed like an odd coincidence to me, but I decided not to think on that part for the moment. He'd been married to Samantha's mother, Gina. They had two children: Tate's father, Joshua Jr., and Samantha. Joshua Jr. and Samantha were ten years apart.

Joshua Sr. had been murdered in his own home thirty years ago when he'd interrupted a robbery in progress. His wife and daughter had been out of the house at the time. Joshua Jr. had been an adult and was no longer living at home. And then Joshua Jr. and his wife, Tate's parents, had been killed in a boating accident on Seneca Lake twenty years ago.

When I looked at all the facts, it was one the most

tragic family histories I had ever heard, and now, Samantha was added to the list of losses.

He came back into the room about forty minutes later, just when I was really regretting my decision to ask him to pull the file, because the stomachache I'd had at dinner was so much worse now. I felt like my insides were being twisted.

He set the box on the table.

"That's quite a file," I said.

"It's the only other murder Herrington had ever seen up to this point." He lifted the lid off of the box. "You have to keep in mind that Joshua was stabbed, so some of these images will be hard to look at."

I stood up and peered into the box. "Are you still trying to protect me, Austin?"

He lifted an envelope from the box. The photographs were inside. He took them out and set them on the table.

I swallowed hard. They were difficult to look at, as he'd said. I made myself do so anyway. Joshua had been killed in the kitchen. I pushed the photos aside.

"I have the interview with Gina, his wife, right here. She said she didn't know who could have done this to her husband. He didn't have any enemies. He was well loved. He never had any arguments with anyone."

"That's not true," I said.

Austin riffled through the papers in the box. "There is nothing in here about another kid in the family or about anyone named Penelope."

"Could Joshua have purposely buried the story?"

"Maybe. I'm sure if there is nothing mentioned here, his wife was in the dark."

"Tate didn't know anything about it, but he was born long after all of this went down."

Austin frowned when I mentioned Tate and began to repack the box.

"I wasn't done looking at that."

"There's nothing else to see," he said shortly. He closed the box. "Heed my warning, Darby. Stay out of the investigation."

"Or?"

He didn't answer.

CHAPTER THIRTY-FOUR

T ATE WAS WAITING FOR ME in the police station's lobby just like he'd promised. He jumped out of his chair when I came out. "They let you out. You were in there for so long, I thought for sure you were going to be thrown into a cell."

I peeked at my watch. I had been at the police station for nearly an hour and a half. My shoulders slumped.

"I called Patrick like you asked. He wanted to come down here, but I told him to hold off. However, if you had been arrested, I would have driven him here myself."

"Thanks. I need to keep the police on my side as much as possible. The paint matches. It was my car that was used to kill Samantha."

"It's what we expected," Tate said. "Why didn't Austin arrest you?"

I shook my head. "He said he will have to this weekend if there's not another break in the case. I told him about Samantha looking for her father's killer, but

I don't think he took me seriously." I felt like all the energy had been sucked out of my body.

"You look beat. I'll take you back to the agency. You and Gumshoe can chill out then."

I was too tired to argue. "Okay."

"Yikes. Let's get you home. I know when you are so agreeable you really are spent."

I followed him out. Before I went through the external glass doors of the station, I looked back and saw Austin watching me from the office. There was a scowl on his face. He wasn't happy with me, but then again, I wasn't happy with him either.

Tate still had the top down on the convertible.

I pointed to the folded roof. "You might want to put that up in case it rains tonight."

"Let me worry about my rental car and the rain, and you concentrate on getting into the car without falling over. You look like you might drop."

I blinked, and the world seemed to spin in front of me. "Now that you mention it, I don't feel very good. I'm kind of dizzy."

Tate was immediately at my side. "Dizzy how?"

"Like I'm going to fall over." My words were coming slower. "Like any minute I could fall right down." I wanted to say more to better explain what was going on, but I couldn't.

"Did you eat anything strange? Did someone give you something?"

"N—no." My eyes closed, and all I saw was blackness.

My head throbbed. I lifted my arm to touch my head and felt a sharp pinch. I opened my eyes. Everything was so bright. I closed my eyes again.

"Darby?" a gentle voice asked. "Are you awake?"

I squeezed my eyes shut and wished that whoever was asking me that would go away. My head throbbed.

"Darby? Darby?"

Slowly, I opened my eyes, and as my vision came into focus, I realized I was in the hospital.

My father leaned over me. "She's awake."

There was a rustle of activity, and I found my parents and DeeDee looking at me with concerned expressions.

"You gave us a scare," my mom said. Her voice was so loud. All their voices were loud. It took all my strength not to wince every time they spoke.

My dad touched my cheek like Gumshoe did when he needed to be comforted.

"What happened? Are you okay, Dad?"

"I'm fine, Darby girl. Don't you worry about me."

"Don't you remember what happened?" DeeDee asked.

It came back to me. "I wasn't under arrest. Austin had to ask me some questions."

"Because he thinks you killed Samantha," she said.

"Dee, you are not helping," my mother said.

"I think Tate brought me here. Where is he?"

"He met us at the emergency room door and said he had to leave," Dad said. "We were so concerned about you that we didn't ask him where he was headed. I'm sure he will be back soon. He must be worried."

There was a knock on the door, and it swung inward. To my surprise, Austin stepped into the room carrying flowers. "Can I come in?"

"No, you're the reason Darby is in the hospital," DeeDee snapped. "Get out of here."

"DeeDee." I sighed. "You can come in, Austin."

He set the flowers on the blond wood dresser in the corner of the room.

"Tell me what happened, Austin," I said.

"Did you take any aspirin lately?"

I blinked at him. "No. I don't know the last time I did."

"There was a large amount in your system, which caused the dizziness and stomach pain, according to the doctor."

I struggled to sit. "But I didn't take any."

"Someone gave it to you."

I gasped. "You think I was poisoned?"

"It's possible. Unless you can think of another reason there would be that much aspirin in your system."

"Now do you believe I didn't kill her?" My voice was hoarse.

"If you're asking me if you would to poison yourself to remove blame from yourself, no, I don't think you would."

I guessed that was the closest thing to a straight answer I was going to get out of him.

A nurse bustled into the room. "She needs to sleep a bit more as the medicine works its way out of her system. We don't induce vomiting for aspirin because the medicine is corrosive. They will release her in the morning, most likely. All of you can go home and visit again tomorrow."

"No," Mom said. "I want to stay here with my girl."

"Mom, you heard the nurse. I'm going to be sleeping. Go home and get some rest," I said. "I promise you can fuss over me once they release me."

She frowned. "I'm going to hold you to that."

I had no doubt she would. Austin stayed back for a moment.

The nurse frowned at him.

"I have to ask her a few questions for my report," he said.

She scowled. "Be quick about it. She needs her sleep." She left the room.

"I like that nurse," I said.

"That's because she's tough like you."

I chuckled. "I don't feel very tough right now. I feel like I have the mother of all hangovers. What happened?"

"Tate took you from the police station and then came running back inside saying you passed out in the parking lot. We couldn't get you to wake up, so we brought you here."

"You and Tate, together?" I asked.

"Technically, the ambulance did."

"That's probably safer," I said.

"Do you know how someone could have given you aspirin?

I shook my head and winced. That was a mistake.

"No, I have no idea. I either ate at home or at my parents' today. It wasn't like I was eating or drinking in a public place."

He frowned.

"And don't go thinking my parents did this."

He sighed. "I know they didn't. There must be something else. Think long and hard over it."

I tried, but my head throbbed.

"You look like you're in pain trying to think about it."

"I do have a massive headache," I admitted.

"Get some rest," Austin said. "I will check in with you tomorrow. I can see your eyes are closing again."

They were. I could barely keep them open. I thought I felt a kiss on my forehead, but I was too tired to know for sure.

When I woke up later, it was dark in the room except for the dim bathroom light. My head wasn't throbbing any longer, and I had a terrible wave of homesickness. I hated being in the hospital, but it would take hours to convince the doctors to discharge me.

I moved my head and saw Tate sitting in the chair by my bed. "Hey," I said.

"Hey." He was bent at the waist and staring at the linoleum floor.

"Are you all right?"

He didn't look up at me. "I'm fine."

I didn't believe him, and I didn't think he expected me to. I hesitated for a moment and then lightly touched his upper arm. We sat there for a moment until he moved his hand and covered mine on his arm.

His hand was warm and comforting. "I'm glad you're all right. When you went down, you went down hard. Is anything broken?"

"I don't think so. The nurse didn't say I had any injuries like that." Now that he mentioned my fall, my body ached. It was as if my sore muscles had been waiting for me to be reminded they were in pain.

"What's going on with you?"

"Being in the hospital, it brings up some bad memories. That's all."

"Of your parents?"

He shook his head. "I never saw them in the hospital. It's Jess. He was my best friend—no, more like my brother—over there in the service, and we were hit. He didn't die right away." He closed his eyes as if he was trying to hide from the memories. "He died in the Army hospital a few days later. It wasn't as a nice as this place, of course. It was a battlefield hospital. When I saw you in the stretcher, it came rushing back."

"I'm so sorry." I squeezed his arm.

"I saw him die. I was in the room when he flat-lined. They pushed me out of the way, but it was too late."

"Is that the reason you left the Army?" My voice was hoarse.

"For the most part, and Jess is why I've been bobbing around the world ever since. He didn't have any family, but he had money. He invented some sort of app he sold for a boatload of money when he was in college."

"And he signed up for the Army after that?"

"He said he wanted to find a place where he belonged, and the Army was that for him. It was the closest thing to family he had. When he died, he had a good amount of cash socked away. He was a simple guy. You wouldn't know he was loaded from looking at him. He left it all to me. I thought I would travel around and enjoy life for the both of us, and I did. Or I thought I did, until the police contacted me and told me about Aunt Samantha." He paused. "It happened again. Someone I'd cared about had died and left me everything." He met my gaze.

"Can I ask you something?" I tried to sit up.

He gently pushed me back down. "Yes, but be careful. You're still woozy."

"Why did you return to Herrington before Samantha died?"

He was quiet for a moment. "I was homesick. My aunt wrote me every month saying I had a job here if I wanted it, and I finally decided to come back. I never thought I would arrive too late to see her. I was going to surprise her. I wish I had gone to the agency instead of her house. Then, maybe, I could have stopped her before she went on that drive."

"You don't know that," I said and realized I had to either accept his answer or go on considering him a suspect in Samantha's murder. There was no way to prove he was telling the truth about any of it. I had to trust him like a partner, as I had trusted Samantha.

"I'm not going to run away this time," Tate said. "I might not have been able to save Jess or my aunt, but I will find out who killed her."

I sat up and held my hand out to him. He stared at

it for a long moment, and for some strange reason, my brain went back to that night when Austin had told me about Samantha's accident, and I'd fallen to the floor. Austin held his hand out to me then, and I was sure I had the same expression on my face Tate that wore now—a mix of suspicion and maybe a little fear about what taking that hand would mean.

But as I had taken Austin's hand, Tate reached over and took mine.

"We are going to do this together," I said.

He squeezed my hand. "Together." He let go of my hand.

My hand tingled until I fell back asleep.

CHAPTER THIRTY-FIVE

I WAS DISCHARGED FROM THE HOSPITAL in the middle of the next day, and Tate somehow convinced my mother that he would be the one to pick me up and take me home. She must really like him to let him do that.

"Careful!" I cried as Tate took a turn down the hospital hall too sharply while pushing me in a wheelchair.

"Sorry," he said with a laugh.

Even though he'd almost run me into the wall, I was glad to hear that his good humor was back. I much preferred carefree Tate to sad Tate.

"I don't know why I need a wheelchair anyway," I complained. "I can walk fine."

"Doctor's orders," he chimed.

I ground my teeth and held my breath until we made it to the exit. He stopped the wheelchair, and I hopped out before he could pop a wheelie or pull another move that would likely have me back in the hospital again.

"Your convertible is waiting," Tate said.

I sighed.

"I really like it. I think I'll buy one when I settle down here."

"You can't be serious. That's not the kind of car someone can drive in the New York winter when there's ten feet of snow on the ground."

He grinned. "I could do it. I'm an excellent driver."

From what I'd learned of Tate over the last week, he thought he was excellent at everything.

"Just take me home," I said.

He opened the car door for me.

When I got home, I went straight up to my apartment to shower and change, and when I came back downstairs, I found Tate, Nat, and Matt Billows sitting in Nat's office.

I looked around the room. "What's going on?" I addressed my next question at Billows. "What are you doing here?"

"My ex-wife told me you came to see her at the resort. I wanted to talk to you." He scowled at me.

I should have known that Portia couldn't keep it a secret that Tate and I had visited Lake Waters.

"We all want the same thing here. We want to know what happened to Samantha," Billows continued.

"Were you dating her?"

Nat gasped. "I don't think I should stay to listen to this. Since I won't be working for the agency any longer."

Billows frowned.

"I got another job," Nat said. "I know it's bad timing

for Darby, but is there ever a good time for this sort of thing?"

"You can stay, Nat. You are still a member of the agency until next week."

She nodded and sat back at her desk.

"Portia said you were dating her."

"That's Portia's jealous talk. I wasn't dating Samantha. I was trying to convince her to come on as head of security at Lake Waters. She was playing very hard to get. I could pay her more than she made here at the agency and she wouldn't have the overhead of running her own business."

"Is that really true when Lake Waters was falling apart?" Tate asked.

Billows' head snapped in Tate's direction. "Where did you hear that?"

"From Portia."

"It seems to me she gave you quite a bit of misinformation."

"I don't think it was misinformation," I said as I sat on the arm of the huge couch. "I saw the state that the resort is in. Paint is peeling off of the buildings, and there are no guests to speak of."

He pressed his lips together. "That is only temporary. The new rejuvenation center will solve that."

"When you were meeting with Samantha, did she ask about her father's murder?"

"She did ask about her father a lot. I remember when he was killed, of course, but I was a teenager at the time. I wasn't paying much attention to the story. She wanted to know if we had anything in the old security office about it, but I said no. His stuff was cleared out years ago. Where the security office was is now part of the spa." He paused. "She seemed to lose interest in accepting my job offer after that."

That made sense to me. If Billows wasn't going to be able to help her find out who killed her father, he wasn't much use to her. It made me feel better that Samantha hadn't seriously been considering leaving Two Girls Detective Agency. I still wished she'd been more honest with me.

"Maybe you should put the money that you want to give Mrs. Berger for her house into the resort," Tate suggested.

It wasn't a bad idea.

"You don't understand how my business works. I can't just fix what I already have. I have to make something new so they will come back and see it. They aren't going to come back for something they had before."

"Well, make something new on the land that you already have instead of bothering Mrs. Berger," I said.

Billows stood up. "We would get it back to where it needs to be if that old bat would sell her land. It makes no sense for her to hold on to it. I am offering her more money than it's worth."

"But," I said quietly, "it's her home, and that's all that matters to Mrs. Berger."

"Maybe you can convince her to sell," Billows said. "I could pay you to help me. I'm desperate for that land."

I shook my head. "I can't do that to her."

"Then I think I have nothing more to discuss with you. Stay away from Lake Waters, and mark my words, I will get that property, sooner rather than later." He stormed out of the house.

"My word," Nat said. "If Mrs. Berger shows up dead, we have a suspect."

I shivered. "We do, but we aren't any closer to finding out who killed Samantha." Or who drugged me.

"Another dead end," Tate said.

I nodded.

"Darby?" Nat asked. "What was all that about Samantha's father?"

Tate lay on the couch. It really was the perfect size for him, which made me miss Samantha even more. How happy would see be to know he was back in Herrington?

"Tate and I believe she was killed because she was getting close to figuring out who killed her father."

"And," Tate added, "it seems my grandfather had another daughter named Penelope, whom he never acknowledged. I have to say, this has been an enlightening week in my family history."

"I didn't know that," Nat said. She opened her desk drawer, peered inside, and then closed it. "What happened to Penelope?"

"Don't know," Tate said. "Piper's mom is on the case at the library, so if anyone finds out what happened to her, it will be Mrs. Piper. She is a fierce librarian."

"She is that," Nat said.

CHAPTER THIRTY-SIX

N IGHT CAME FASTER WITH EACH passing day, and I still wasn't feeling my best. I was thinking about going to bed early and waking up for my run like normal before jumping into the investigation again the next day.

Nat and Tate had gone home. I walked around the lower level of the house before going upstairs. It seemed so empty to me now. Samantha's office was quiet, and now Nat had all but cleared her desk. There was just a pen and blank notepad on the desktop. I walked around the desk and decided to peek in the drawers. I didn't want to infringe on her space, but I wanted to know if she took everything. She still had a few more days with the agency. I opened the top drawer. It was empty, and so was the next drawer. On the floor by the leg of the desk, I found two pennies. I scooped them up and set them on the desk. She would want to add them to her collection.

I opened the last drawer in her desk, and a small bottle of aspirin rolled to the front of the drawer. My stomach dropped. "Everyone has aspirin in their desk," I said, but I couldn't shake the odd feeling I had. I gaped at the pennies on the desk and the bottle and back.

Across the room, the coffee maker was clean and the mugs sparkled. Nat had always made sure the office dishes were washed and put away for the night. She had always made the coffee for Samantha and me.

Pennies. Penny, Penelope, Joshua Porter's unacknowledged daughter.

My breathing picked up as I considered the possibility. "This can't be right," I whispered to myself. I jumped out of the desk and ran into my office. I brought up the database we used to find public records.

I couldn't find a birth certificate for a Natalie Stowe who was in her fifties today. All the Natalie Stowes were either much younger or older. Had she changed her name? Had Nat ever married? I couldn't remember ever saying she'd been married before. Samantha had hired Nat. Had she ever done a background check on her? It seemed like a major oversight, but at the same time, she had known Nat her whole life. Perhaps she thought it wasn't necessary.

I needed to rest. I had a headache left over from my adventure the night before. I wasn't thinking straight. I would sleep on it and revisit this idea in the morning. I looked down at Gumshoe, who was snoozing on the windowsill in my office. "Are you ready to call it a night?"

Gumshoe was always for calling it an early night,

or a nap, or anything that involved sleeping. He was a world-class sleeper, even for a cat.

Gumshoe and I were making our way upstairs when my phone rang. I expected it to be one of my parents checking up on me. It was Mrs. Berger.

I answered the call. "Mrs. Berger. Is everything all right?"

Gumshoe sat at the top of the stairs with his white plume of a tail wrapped around his feet. He watched me with disdain. He was already disappointed that we weren't curled up in bed with a book.

"Darby, Romy has wandered off again. Can you come get him?" Mrs. Berger's scratchy voice was on the other end of the call.

"Are you okay? You sound strange."

"I think I'm catching a cold. It must be from all the upset with that meeting with Matt Billows, the toad. When will he quit? And now Romy has wandered off again. I can't sleep until I know he's all right."

"Is he in the tree?" I asked. Ten to one that cat was up there again.

"I don't know. It's too dark to see. I'm worried about him. It's getting colder out there, and he's sensitive. I won't be able to sleep as long as I know he's out there shivering the night away."

Romy was roughly the size of a baby bear; he could take care of himself in the cold. He had fur between his toes, for goodness sakes. Even so, that didn't mean Mrs. Berger wouldn't lose sleep over her missing cat. She loved him as much as I loved Gumshoe, who was still giving me the evil eye for disrupting his plans.

"Do you want me to come over and help you look for him?" I didn't know why I even bothered to ask. I already knew the answer.

"Would you?"

"I'll be there as soon as I can."

"Thank you." And she ended the call.

I texted Tate about Romy as I walked back down the stairs and grabbed my leather jacket from the coat rack.

His text came back: *I'm not going up in the tree again.*

You might have to, I wrote. *I don't think I should after just getting out of the hospital.*

He gave me a crying emoji, quickly followed by *Meet you there.*

I looked up at my cat, still at the top of the stairs. "Well, Gumshoe, bed will have to wait. I have to rescue another cat who is not nearly as smart as you about staying inside."

He meowed.

At least I had thought to give him a compliment, which I hoped took some of the edge off my going out again.

I texted Tate. *Would you mind swinging by here to get me?*

Ah, I see. You want to take another spin in the convertible. I understand. Don't you worry—I have the top down for you.

Just hurry. I don't want to keep Mrs. Berger waiting.

The convertible pulled up in front of the house two minutes later. "Need a lift?" Tate wiggled his eyebrows.

I climbed in the car. "You might think you're cool now, but you will be sorry in winter."

"Ouch. That hurts, Piper. I do remember what the winters were like around here. Why do you think I was so quick to leave?"

I sat back in the seat. I had to admit the car was very comfortable. I bit my lip, wondering if I should tell Tate what I suspected about Nat. What if I was wrong? I had known Nat for ten years. Tate and I had just met again. Shouldn't my loyalty be to her?

"Are you sure you can't go up in the tree?" he asked, shaking me from my thoughts. "I just stopped bleeding from the scratches, and my tailbone has a permanent bruise."

"We don't even know for sure Romy is in the tree."

"Don't kid yourself. He's up there waiting for some fool to rescue him. When I was in the tree, I saw into his eyes. He knew exactly what he was doing. That cat is smart, scary smart."

"I think you are being a tad dramatic." I held onto my seat belt. "And if you really don't want to go, no one is forcing you. I do need the ride, but you don't have to hang around."

"I'm not going to leave you there alone with a killer on the loose. We should stick together until this case is solved. I was thinking about what Caster said, and I don't agree with him on almost anything, but he is right. By poking our noses in the case, we we're putting a large target on our backs, and you have the biggest target of all. So, who's going up the tree for the cat?"

"I was just in the hospital..."

"I'll spot you when you go up the tree," he said with a grin.

"Are you serious?"

"No," he said with a sigh. "I'll do it. Besides, Mrs. Berger will want me to do it again, even if you were in perfect health. I think she gets a kick out of seeing me squirm. There is no talking that lady out of anything when her mind is made up."

At least he was aware his charms wouldn't work on Mrs. Berger. It seemed to me that Tate Porter was finally realizing what it was like to be back in Herrington. I would be lying if I didn't admit a small part of me wanted him to stay. I feared he wouldn't, though. He was a wanderer, and Herrington was a town where people planted roots. Was Tate ready for that? I could understand if he wasn't, now that I knew what he had gone through, but that didn't change the fact that I wished he would stay. He made a good partner in the agency, and that was my only reason...or so I told myself.

"I don't think it's a good idea for you to be by yourself right now," he repeated.

"Are you trying to protect me, Tate Porter?" I teased.

"I would do more than try. If you would let me."

I looked out the window so that he wouldn't the surprise on my face. I wanted to ask him what he meant by that, but before I could, we arrived at Mrs. Berger's house.

The home was completely dark, so dark it was unnerving.

"You would think she would leave a light on for us," Tate said.

"I don't know." I unbuckled my seat belt. "Something doesn't feel right. Maybe we should call Austin and the police."

He cocked his head at me. "Over a cat stuck in a tree?"

"Okay, we'll check it out first and then call him. I hope Mrs. Berger is all right."

Tate patted my arm and nodded. "I'm sure she's fine. I'm also sure she's worried about her cat, so we'd better get to it."

We got out of the car, and Tate and I crossed the front lawn. The grass crackled under the tread of my boots. It sounded like breaking glass. At the front door, I rang the bell. There was no answer. I raised my eyebrows at Tate.

He knocked on the door. Still no answer. I peeked in the windows, and the house was as dark inside as it was out. I had a very bad feeling about this. I never knew Mrs. Berger not to be home when she said she was. It was too much of a stretch to think she would have gone out this time of night. Other than the town council meeting the other night, her outings consisted of getting her hair done and going to the grocery store, neither of which she would do at after dark.

Maybe she was asleep? Not possible. She'd called me just a little while ago to say Romy was missing. She was mostly likely behind the house, standing vigil under Romy's tree.

We came around the side of the house.

"There's the tree," Tate said.

"But no Mrs. Berger." I clasped my hands together.

Usually, Mrs. Berger would be standing below the tree, propped up by her cane and staring into the branches. That or she would be trying to wave me down from her driveway while I was on my morning run.

Beyond the tree, the lake was an inky black pool, and it looked much more sinister on a cold night than it ever did during the day. I shivered. I wanted to find Mrs. Berger, get the cat, and go home. My big plans for the evening were to jump into bed and watch reality TV while eating the biggest bowl of ice cream on the planet. We all had to escape from reality now and again.

"Mrs. Berger?" I asked as I approached the tree, but again, there was no answer.

I shone my flashlight up the tree and, sure enough, there was Romy on the branch twenty feet up. The cat was nothing if not predictable, and the thing was, Mrs. Berger was predictable too, or at least she always had been before.

"We should find Mrs. Berger before one of us goes up there after Romy," I said.

"You mean before *you* go up there after Romy."

I frowned. "I thought you were going to go up since I was in the hospital."

"The doctors gave you a clean bill of health."

I gave him a look.

"I'm kidding. I said I will get the cat, so I will get the cat. You can't take everything I say so seriously."

"I know that last part is true."

Romy yowled in the tree.

"Someone is getting impatient," Tate said. "He's going to be in a foul mood when I climb up there."

"Let's find Mrs. Berger first, okay?" I could hear the tension in my voice. I was still worrying over Nat.

He frowned at me. "You're acting stranger than usual. Are you still feeling dizzy?"

"I'm worried about Mrs. Berger. And..."

"And what?" Tate studied me.

Above our heads, Romy yowled, which made it even harder to focus. "It's Nat."

"You're upset she's leaving."

"It's not that." I took a breath. "I think she's the one who poisoned me."

"What?" he cried.

"Hear me out." I explained to him my suspicions that Nat was Penelope Wring. I told him about the aspirin and the coffee. "But what really made me look into it was the pennies. All this time, the pennies have been on her desk. All these years. She's been collecting them and waiting."

"We have to go to the police right now."

"What if I'm wrong?" I whispered.

"If you're right, she killed Samantha."

"Not before we find Mrs. Berger. I'm afraid she might have fallen down somewhere and may be hurt."

He frowned. "Fine, but the moment we find her, we are going to the police station."

"Deal," I agreed.

Tate and I split up. I went around one side of the

house, and he went around the other. I had a bad feeling about this and decided to call Austin after all. Even if I was wrong about Nat, at the very least he and some of the other officers could help us find Mrs. Berger.

The call went directly to voicemail.

"It's Darby. I'm at Mrs. Berger's house. She called me to get her cat out of the tree again. But she's not here, and her house is locked and dark. I'm worried about her." I paused. "I don't know if this is an emergency, but—"

I was cut off by a cry of pain on the other side of the house.

CHAPTER THIRTY-SEVEN

I ENDED THE CALL AND RAN around the side of the house. "Tate?" I stopped when I saw his legs sticking out from the bushes. "Tate?"

He groaned.

I grabbed him by the shoulder, but he was too large for me to move. "How did you end up here?"

"Be careful," he whispered. "She's here."

"Who? Mrs. Berger? Did she scare you and make you fall in the bushes?"

"Shhh," Tate said. "Call Austin."

Behind me, I heard movement. I let go of his shoulder and flopped back in the bushes.

"Darby," a voice I recognized said.

A chill ran down my back.

I had been right. I turned around. "Nat? What are you doing here? Where's Mrs. Berger?"

"I haven't seen her." Her voice was very cold, nothing like I was used to back at the office.

I swallowed. I couldn't let her know I knew who she really was.

"Have you see Mrs. Berger? Tate and I came to get Romy out of the tree again." I forced a laugh. "You know how he can be."

"I haven't seen her."

"Then how did Romy get outside?"

She didn't answer.

"Well, we will find her. I think Tate hit his head trying to find the cat. Let me make sure he's okay." I start to bend down to Tate. I planned to call 911 while I did that.

"Don't do that."

"Do what?" I asked.

"Help Tate right now," she said. "Turn around."

I let out a breath and did as she asked. When I came around, I saw she held a gun in her hand. I felt all the blood drain from my face.

She smiled.

"He will be fine. I didn't hit him that hard. By the time we're done here, he will be up and around."

"Done here with what?" I asked, while my eyes scanned the dark yard looking for a means of escape.

She held up a gun. "With you."

"Nat, what are you doing?"

I didn't want her to know I knew. If I played dumb, maybe she would let Tate and me go. "Why are you pointing that at me? We have to call for help for Tate, and I need to find Mrs. Berger." My teeth chattered. "Do you know where she is?"

"Mrs. Berger is away tonight. She has a bridge match once a month."

"But she called me to tell me Romy was in the tree."

"Oh, did she?" Nat laughed. "Did she say this?" Nat cleared her throat and spoke in a scratchy, fake Mrs. Berger voice. "'Darby, Romy has wandered off again. Can you come get him?' Mrs. Berger has one of the last landlines on the planet. All I had to do was call from the inside of her house."

My stomach dropped. It was same voice I had heard on the phone, the one I had taken as Mrs. Berger with a cold without question. What a huge mistake that had been.

"You broke into her house?" I asked.

"I didn't take anything," she said, sounding offended that I would consider her a petty criminal.

"You see, Darby, I know everything about everyone in the village. I pay attention. I follow their movements, including yours, which is why I know you won't let go of Samantha's case even after I poisoned you to warn you off. You are very much like her in that way. You're both like terriers with a bone. You won't let go, even though it's the best thing you could do for yourself."

I closed my eyes for half a second. I *had* been right, and the only person who knew what I knew was Tate, who was lying injured under the bush. She couldn't know that I'd told him. Still, I had to stall. "I don't know what you're talking about."

"Don't lie to me. I went back to the office tonight and saw you find the aspirin bottle. I saw you through the window. Your face told me everything I needed to know. Then you confirmed it by searching for my name in that database."

"I can't believe Samantha didn't do a background check on you when she hired you."

"Why would she? She had known me her whole life. She trusted me. I was like family. She didn't know I was actually family."

"Why?" I asked. "Why did you befriend Samantha then? Why did you work for her? You could have gone far away after you murdered her father."

"Herrington is my town too. I won't be chased out, and I always knew that Samantha would want to know about our father's death. When she opened the agency, I knew she would take it even further than that. I had to work for her, so that I could watch her. I had to watch her to keep her from learning what I had done."

"You mean committing murder, Penelope." I didn't see much point hiding my knowledge now. I had to get her away from Tate and call the police, which was a very tall order, since she was the one with the gun. "You're a murderer."

She glared at me. "Don't call me that."

"You killed Samantha." The yard was spinning. Or was is my head with this news? "Why? She was your friend." Another realization came to me. "She was your sister."

"You know why. I can tell you know. Playing dumb isn't going to help you or Tate, whom I will frame for killing you. I have it all worked out."

"Because she got too close to figuring out who killed her father. Was that you, too?"

"Very good. Like Samantha said, you are very bright. Because of that, I can't risk anyone finding out what you know." She lifted the gun a little higher and pointed it at my chest.

"Samantha put two and two together. She didn't know I killed our father, but she did finally learn my real identity. She was so excited that we were sisters." Nat laughed. "It was ridiculous. She thought we could be family. That would never be possible."

Why hadn't Samantha come to me with this information? I could have helped her. If I'd helped her, she might still be alive. Grief washed over me to think of what a waste her death was. She'd needed to tell someone, and she had. The wrong person.

"She wanted to tell you," Nat went on, as if reading my mind. "I talked her out of it. I told her it would be best to wait until things calmed down between the two of you over Samantha leaving the agency. I made her think you were far more upset about it than you actually were."

"I already called the police when I couldn't find Mrs. Berger," I said. "They are on their way here. You should leave and make your way out of Herrington—out of the state, even. Go to Canada and assume a new identity. You did it before, and you can do it again."

With my heel, I gently pushed Tate's foot out of sight. Maybe Nat would forget about him. I hoped he wasn't seriously hurt.

"Let's go for a walk down to the water, Darby." She nodded in the direction of the lake.

Beyond the backyard, Seneca Lake lay in darkness. There was a small lamppost at the edge of Mrs. Berger's dock, but that was the only light other than the pinprick of lights from the homes and little villages surrounding the large lake.

"Why would I go anywhere with you?" I asked, taking two steps away from her.

She laughed. "Because if you don't, I'll shoot him." She pointed the gun at the bushes.

I held up my shaking hands. "All right. Fine. I'll follow you."

"Nice try, Darby. You first."

I carefully walked down to Mrs. Berger's dock. There had to be a way I could get out of this mess.

"Go to the end," Nat said.

I felt as if I were walking the plank. The weathered boards creaked under my weight. Each step felt like my last. Nat could shoot me in the back at any time. The last sound I would hear would be the creaking of the boards and the crack of her gun.

Nat was six feet away from me, too far away to knock the gun out of her hand, but close enough for her to shoot me dead, which I assumed was the plan.

She lifted the gun and aimed. "You should have let the case go. You're like Samantha in that way. You can't leave well enough alone."

"Samantha was murdered, and you expected me to ignore it? She was my friend and mentor. I was never going to walk away from it."

"I expected you to let the police handle it. You have never had any interest in big-time crime before. I thought you would leave it in Austin's hands."

"How could I when you framed me so well?" I asked.

"Austin would have gotten you off. He loves you, you know."

I stared at her.

She laughed. "You didn't know that, did you? He spoke to Samantha about asking you to marry him before you broke up with him for the fifteenth time."

Her words knocked the wind out of me, and I felt like I had been shot in the heart. "I don't believe you. He didn't want to get married. That's why we broke up." How could I believe anything that came out of her mouth after knowing she had lied to Samantha and me every day for ten years? She had lied to Samantha for even longer than that.

She shrugged. "I can understand that. I'm a very good liar." She raised the gun. "I have to leave, so let's make this quick."

Before I could change my mind, I turned around and jumped off the dock. The cold sucked me under, and it felt like falling into a grave. I wanted to wrap my arms around myself and curl into a ball. But if I did that, I wouldn't survive. I had to move. Move, Piper, move! In my head, I could hear Tate shouting the words. Move, or you die! I kicked my legs and swung my arms until I broke through the surface. I blinked and was grateful for the lamppost at the end of the dock. I could clearly see Nat holding up her gun as she searched the water for me.

There was the crack of a gunshot, but it went wide. She was having trouble seeing me in the water, which is what I wanted. The water wasn't very deep here, just four feet, but I was small and could swim along the bottom.

It was cold, so cold. My body begin to shake. I needed to get out of the water or I was in real risk of hypothermia. I knew the beach of Lake Waters Retreat was to my left.

Another bullet sliced through the water to my right, and I gasped before diving under the waves. I didn't open my eyes under the water. There was nothing to see. I swam. The waves stirred up by the change in the weather fought against me. A branch knocked into my arm.

I swam to the pebbled beach in front of Lake Waters. It was deserted.

I pulled my cell phone from my pocket—dead. I had no choice but to go back. Tate was still there. I couldn't let Nat take another life from the Porter family.

My body shook as I ran along the beach to Mrs. Berger's property. I climbed the low stone wall that separated the resort from her backyard.

In the giant oak tree, Romy yowled for all he was worth. Under the tree there was a shadow. It was Tate. I ran over and crouched next to him. "Are you okay?"

He groaned. "I have a massive headache. Someone hit me on the back of the head."

"It was Nat. Penelope, actually."

He blinked at me. "You were right!"

I glanced around for any sign of Nat.

"Why are you wet?" he asked in a groggy voice.

"I jumped in the lake."

"Why would you do that? I must still be dreaming," he murmured.

There was a snap of a twig behind me. I spun around and saw Nat there, holding her gun, pointed at Tate.

I held up my hands. "Shoot me, not him."

"Gladly," Nat said and took aim.

"Darby!" Tate cried.

A second shadow appeared behind Nat. There was a whomp sound, and Nat—Penelope—crumpled to the ground without a word.

"Darby, what are you doing?" Mrs. Berger asked.

I took a ragged breath. "Mrs. Berger! Is she dead?"

"I'm soaking wet," Tate complained.

Mrs. Berger shook her head. "Just knocked out cold. Mr. Berger was a neuroscientist, you see. And he taught me where to hit someone to knock them out cold. It wasn't the first time I needed this skill." She waved her cane.

I stared at her like she was speaking a different language.

"Oh, child, you're soaking wet. Let's get you into some warm clothes," Mrs. Berger said conversationally, as if she hadn't just saved the day. "After you get cleaned up, would you mind going up the tree after Romy?"

I smiled. "I wouldn't mind at all."

CHAPTER THIRTY-EIGHT

I WAS UP THE TREE COLLECTING Romy when the police came and arrested Nat. When she came to, she had been shocked to find Mrs. Berger holding her at gunpoint. I knew that must have been an unnerving sight. I offered to hold the gun for my elderly friend, but Mrs. Berger insisted that she was the one to do it. I thought it best not to argue with her when she had saved both Tate's and my lives.

Austin clamped handcuffs on Nat's wrists as I came down the tree. Romy was under my arm like a football.

Nat glared at me. "This is your fault. This is your and Samantha's fault."

The red and blue flashing lights from the patrol cars played off her face as Louter took her to the patrol car.

She fought him as she went. "I did it for my mother, for how my worthless father treated her. I'm not ashamed of that."

Tate winced. "She's going to need a whole lot of therapy."

As Mrs. Berger took Romy from my arms, Austin smiled at her. "You're a hero. If you hadn't been here,

I don't know what would have happened to Darby." He choked up.

I stared at Austin. He swallowed hard and pulled at his collar. Had Nat told me the truth? Had he been planning to propose before I'd broken up with him that final time? Did it matter now? I shook my head, trying to clear my confusion. When I looked up again, I found Tate watching me.

"Now I'll have no chance to get your property," a deep voice grumbled.

I turned around. Matt Billows and Lake Waters head of security Cliff Ritter stood a few feet away. Cliff scowled at me.

"We saw the lights and heard the sirens and came down to see if we could offer any help."

"That's awfully neighborly of you," Mrs. Berger said.

"And it seems we will be neighbors for a long time to come," Billows said with a sigh.

She grinned. "That we will, young man."

"You know, I'm not a heartless businessman," he continued. "I have been thinking about the points you made at the town council meeting, and you do deserve to keep your home as long as you live. I will think of another way to save Lake Waters. I might even turn it into a family retreat. There are other ways to make money than catering to celebrities."

My mouth fell open.

"Are you kidding?" Tate asked. "After all you did to try to get Mrs. Berger's land?"

"I tried and lost. A good businessman knows when to regroup and try a new strategy." He nodded to Cliff. "Let's get back to the resort. I'm glad to see you're all right, Mrs. Berger."

Mrs. Berger shook her head. "Miracles never cease."

Austin cleared his throat. "I'm going to need statements from all three of you."

"Start with me." Mrs. Berger hugged Romy to her chest. "I have a story to tell you! I was at bridge club when it all began."

Tate grabbed my hand and pulled me away from Austin and Mrs. Berger. By the look on his face, Austin didn't miss the fact that Tate took my hand. I tried to pull my hand away, but Tate held it fast. Tate let go of me as soon as we were out of earshot of them.

I studied him. "How are you feeling?"

"I have a massive headache, but I'll live."

I frowned. "Maybe you should talk to one of the EMTs."

"Whatever you say, partner." He grinned.

I blinked at him. "Partner? You're staying in Herrington? You want to keep the agency?"

He nodded. "I have a request, though."

"What?" I asked, with a sigh. I could not imagine what his terms would be.

"I'll agree to this new partnership on one condition."

My stomach sank. Maybe his talk about keeping the agency alive had been for nothing. It was too good to be true. I should have never gotten my hopes up. "Okay, okay, spit it out already. You're killing me here."

"I will only do it if we go fifty-fifty in the business. I'll give you another ten percent."

I stared at him. Of all the things he could have said to me at that moment, this was on the very bottom of the list. "Fifty-fifty?"

He nodded solemnly.

"But you would be giving up control of the business. You would give me an extra ten percent in the company? That doesn't make any sense at all."

"It makes perfect sense. I want this agency to flourish, and to do that, we need to be on equal footing. I don't want you to resent the decisions I make because I have veto power. You've been doing this a lot longer than I have. You have the experience, and that should be reflected in how we make decisions as a company. It has to be unanimous."

I could feel the excitement well up inside me, but I kept my face blank. It was a skill I had learned well as a ballerina. Even when you were jumping out of your skin, you had to be graceful, stand tall and elegant. Be ready to move like you were floating in the air. Jitters were not allowed. "If that's what you want."

Tate grinned as if he knew I was calling on my iron composure to remain calm during this conversation. I wished he didn't know so much about me. It would be much easier if my past was as closed to him as his was to me.

He nodded. "It is." He held out his hand.

I stared at the hand.

"Come on, let's shake on it, okay? That's what partners do, right? They shake hands."

I slipped my small hand into his much bigger one and shook. Piper and Porter Detective Agency was born.

Across Mrs. Berger's yard, Romy yowled as if that sealed the deal.

THE END

BERRY TRIFLE

In *Dead-End Detective,* both Darby and Tate want answers about the murder of someone they both loved... but Darby isn't so sure about Tate and his true motives. Darby's mother, on the other hand, isn't a bit suspicious of Tate; she invites him over for a delicious dinner, concluding with a homemade berry trifle, and Darby's whole family gives Tate a warm welcome. Our berry trifle is as impressive-looking as it is delicious, and it'll make any guest feel special.

Prep Time: 10 minutes
Cook Time: N/A
Serves: 12

Ingredients

- 1 prepared pound cake, cubed
- 1 recipe strawberry-orange liqueur cream
- 4 cups strawberries, hulled and quartered
- 1-pint blueberries
- 1/2 cup Strawberry Syrup

Preparation

1. In a large bowl, toss the strawberries and blueberries together with the syrup.
2. In a large trifle dish, arrange half of the pound cake cubes in an even layer. Spoon half of the berry mixture over the pound cake cubes. Spoon half of the strawberry-orange liqueur cream over the berry layer.
3. Repeat layers with remaining pound cake, berries, and cream.
4. Refrigerate one hour to let the cake soak in the flavors. Serve.

Strawberry-Orange Liqueur Cream

Prep Time: 30 minutes
Cook Time: 15 minutes
Serves: 5

Ingredients

- 1/4 cup strawberry-orange liqueur
- 1-pint heavy cream

- 6 egg yolks
- 1/2 cup sugar

Preparation

1. In a double boiler over medium heat, whisk yolk and sugar together until very thick and creamy. Take off heat and whisk in strawberry-orange liqueur. Cover with plastic wrap and let cool.
2. Whip heavy cream until thick and whisk about a cup of it into the egg mixture to lighten it. Spoon the rest of the whipped cream onto the egg mixture and gently fold in until incorporated.